What happens when magic collides with reality?

Donald is a young fisherman, eking out a lonely living on the west coast of Scotland. One night he witnesses something miraculous … and makes a terrible mistake. His action changes lives – not only his own, but those of his family and the entire tightly knit community in which they live. Can he ever atone for the wrong he has done, and can love grow when its foundation is violence?

Based on the legend of the selkies – seals who can transform into people – *Sealskin* is a magical story, evoking the harsh beauty of the landscape, the resilience of its people, both human and animal, and the triumph of hope over fear and prejudice. With exquisite grace, Exeter Novel Prize-winner Su Bristow transports us to a different world, subtly and beautifully exploring what it means to be an outsider, and our innate capacity for forgiveness and acceptance. Rich with myth and magic, *Sealskin* is, nonetheless, a very human story, as relevant to our world as to the timeless place in which it is set. And it is, quite simply, unforgettable.

'*Sealskin* is an accomplished and intelligent novel, a fine piece of craftsmanship and a pleasure to read' Allan Massie

'Bristow has taken a known myth, and created an enthralling, human love story. A profound achievement, and a stunning debut' Richard Bean

'An extraordinary book: original, vivid, tender and atmospheric. Su Bristow's writing is fluid and flawless, and this is a story so deeply immersive that you emerge at the end, gasping for air' Iona Grey

'I love books in which magic takes on a gritty reality, and *Sealskin* is just such a book. Dark and brooding and half-familiar, the tale steals over you until you're half-in, half-out of a dream' Jane Johnson

'An evocative story, told with skill and beauty, that held me spellbound until the very last page' Amanda Jennings

'On the face of it, *Sealskin* is a gentle tale, a lovely reworking of the selkie legend many of us have known and loved since childhood. Do not be fooled, dear reader; beneath this simple re-imagining lies a story as deep as the ocean the selkie comes from. I was captivated from the first page to the poignant last one, by the sympathetically drawn characters and a mesmerising sense of place. In between are moments of tragedy, moments of grace and redemption; the whole wrapped in Su Bristow's charismatic writing. This is a story that catches on the edge of your heart, leaving tiny scars; reminders of a journey into a beloved legend, the human lives caught up in it and the consequences of the choices they make. It is, quite simply, exceptional' Carole Lovekin

'In this achingly beautiful retelling of the classic Scottish folk tale, Su Bristow brings psychological depth and great warmth to the characters, making the ending all the more heart-breaking. It's a story about the tensions of life in a tiny fishing community, about bullying and violence as well as the healing magic of nature. It's written smoothly and skilfully with not a word too many or a word too few. I absolutely loved it and can't recommend it highly enough' Gill Paul

'A beautiful and bewitching read that haunted my thoughts for days. The sense of the sea, of this small community, of guilt is palpable. This is one of those books you place reverentially on your bookcase, and envy those who are yet to dive in' Michael J. Malone

'*Sealskin* is the most exquisite tale of love, forgiveness and magic. Inspired by the legends of the selkies, this gorgeous novel is a dark fairy tale, an ode to traditional storytelling, a tribute to the stories we loved hearing as children. But be warned – this is no happy-ever-after tale. The language is just glorious, poetic and rich but precise. And her characters – oh, they will remain in your heart long after you've closed the last page. Mairhi – especially since she never really "speaks" – is a beautiful mystery, but one who haunted me when I was between chapters. If this is her first, then I can't wait to read whatever Su Bristow bestows upon the literary world next' Louise Beech

'Ms Bristow's skill in weaving a centuries-old tale into a current-day fiction novel and binding the two together is simply superbly done. *Sealskin* is boldly written, brilliantly told and a tale of legendary proportions' JM Hewitt

'*Sealskin* is a magical and moral tale woven with a deft hand' Sara MacDonald

'With its beautiful language and magical storytelling, *Sealskin* is a clear winner for me' Sophie Duffy

'*Sealskin* is exquisitely written with haunting prose and evocative descriptions of the Scottish landscape. It's filled with beauty, surprises and subtle twists and turns. There's a mesmerising love story at its heart. I really didn't want the story to end, and felt bereft when it did, surrounded by boxes of tissues. I'm sure I'll be reading this book several times to feel that magic again and again. It's no surprise that Su Bristow is an Exeter Novel Prize winner. Her writing is beautiful and this book is stunning. *Sealskin* is destined to go far' Off-the-Shelf Books

'*Sealskin* really is one of the most beautifully written books I've ever read … a flowing tale of love, friendship, acceptance and coming of age for the varying characters. Set against the ruggedly beautiful Scottish backdrop, the vivid descriptions draw us in, detail oozing from the pages and giving the reader a chance to feel the coastal winds whipping at their faces, taste the salt in the air, feel the uneven terrain underfoot as they clamber through the heather and over rocks. There's a magic in these pages … poetic and hauntingly beautiful' The Quiet Knitter

'A compelling and beautifully written book. At one level *Sealskin* is a delightful re-working of the selkie myth. But it is also a great deal more than that … The fishing village is a close-knit community wary of incomers, the suspicion with which they greet Maihri is typical of how they behave. Strangers, especially ones who are a little out of the ordinary, are not made entirely welcome. It is a story of how relationships develop and grow. *Sealskin* is a quite delightful and extraordinarily well-written book. Highly recommended' Trip Fiction

'A sensuous and beautifully written retelling of the Selkie legend which captivated me' Margaret James, Creative Writing Matters

'I knew this was special, right from the first paragraph. A beautiful book written with a deceptive simplicity. But Su Bristow does not shy away from asking some very big questions. How can a man atone for violence? Will he ever be forgiven? Will he ever forgive himself? Utterly spellbinding' Cathie Hartigan

Su Bristow is a consultant medical herbalist by day. She's the author of two books on herbal medicine: *The Herbal Medicine Chest* and *The Herb Handbook*; and two on relationship skills: *The Courage to Love* and *Falling in Love, Staying in Love*, co-written with psychotherapist, Malcolm Stern. Her published fiction includes 'Troll Steps' (in the anthology, *Barcelona to Bihar*), and 'Changes', which came second in the 2010 CreativeWritingMatters flash fiction competition. *Sealskin* is Su's debut novel, and it won the Exeter Novel Prize in 2013. Her writing has been described as 'magical realism; Angela Carter meets Eowyn Ivey'.

SEALSKIN

Orenda Books
16 Carson Road
West Dulwich
London SE21 8HU
www.orendabooks.co.uk

First published in the United Kingdom by Orenda Books 2017
Copyright © Su Bristow 2017

ISBN 978-1-910633-60-1

Typeset in Garamond by MacGuru Ltd
Printed and bound by CPI Group (UK) Ltd, Croydon CRO 4YY

SALES & DISTRIBUTION

In the UK and elsewhere in Europe:
Turnaround Publisher Services
Unit 3, Olympia Trading Estate
Coburg Road, Wood Green
London N22 6TZ
www.turnaround-uk.com

In USA/Canada:
Trafalgar Square Publishing
Independent Publishers Group
814 North Franklin Street
Chicago, IL 60610
USA
www.ipgbook.com

In Australia/New Zealand:
Affirm Press
28 Thistlethwaite Street
South Melbourne VIC 3205
Australia
www.affirmpress.com.au

Sealskin

SU BRISTOW

**ORENDA
BOOKS**

For Moraig MacLauchlan,
my mother,
who never found her way back

'You can't trust moonlight.' His mother set the lantern down. She hesitated, and Donald guessed what was coming.

'It'll be a grand night for fishing, with the full moon,' she said, looking away. 'Your Uncle Hugh came by this morning, and he says they'll be out overnight. They could do with your help on the boat.'

'They'll manage.' He moved towards the door, but she stood her ground, looking up at him, and he could not push her aside.

'Callum's not well. They're a man down, Donald.'

That made him pause. Callum Campbell was the worst of them. His uncle said it was only banter, but the sting of it stayed with him, sometimes, longer than cuts and bruises; and there had been enough of those, too, in the schoolyard and in other places where there were no adults to see. Maybe it wouldn't be so bad if Callum wasn't there.

His mother saw the change in him. 'Hugh asked for you specially. You know, none of them thinks the less of you because of your hands. Here, let me see now. Wait while I fetch the salve for you.'

But now she had said too much, pushed him too far. What could she know, anyway? Women never set foot on the seagoing boats; it was bad luck. And nearly as bad luck to take a man whose hands cracked and bled on the ropes, who could barely hold a knife by the end of the night. Much better to make his own way, out of sight of their pity and their scorn.

He pulled his hands away, and shouldered the empty creels, making a barrier between himself and his mother. 'Leave it. They'll be fine. I'm more hindrance than help, and Uncle Hugh knows it.'

'Oh, Donald. A night like this, you shouldn't be out alone. Go with Hugh, just the once?' She was almost pleading with him; but now he only wanted to be off, away.

'I need to see to the crab pots. Anyway, it's too late to go with them now. They'll want to catch the tide.' Armoured with his burdens, he made his way to the door, and after a moment, she came to open it for him.

He went out into the moonlit garden. His mother stayed in the open doorway, watching him out of sight, but he did not look back.

Picking his way down the path to the shore, on his own at last, he began to feel easier. A night like this! Where else would he be but alone? Cooped up on the boat with the others, there'd have been no time to look, to listen, to breathe it all in; but out here, with the vastness of sky and sea all to himself, a man might witness marvels. There was not a whisper of wind tonight, and no sound from the sea at all. As he walked along the strand to where his rowboat was drawn up, the waves were lapping at his boots, just stroking the shoreline, hushing it like a woman soothing her child.

The boat was silvered all over with tiny frost-flowers, sparkling in the moonlight. Donald paused, unwilling to lay hands on it, to spoil its perfection, to mar the utter stillness of the night by dragging it over the shingle and rowing out from the shore. Almost, at times like this, he could love the sea. But there were jobs that had to be done, and the tide was turning. He bent to the task.

Donald heaved again at the sodden, barnacle-crusted rope, hissed at the pain in his cracked hands and hauled the crab pot aboard. Cold water washed over his feet, but along with the sea wrack that somehow always got into the pots along with the crabs, there was movement. Hard to tell how many, in the shifting moonlight. He reached in, feeling past the slimy strands of weed for flat shells, crawling legs, and lifted out the first catch, its claws waving uselessly as he dropped it into a clean creel.

He was right in the moon's path, as clear as a straight road to the Land of Youth on this calm, windless night. Where the souls of the dead go, the fishermen said – not in church, of course, but in the bar on stormy nights when the boats were still out; there to drink mead and take their ease in the gentle fields rich with barley. Donald, flexing his sore and frozen fingers, doubted the truth of it. Drowned fishermen stay down, he thought; his father and all the rest who'd ever put out from this coast and not come home. Crabmeat, and anchorage for limpets and anemones, that's what they became. Pulling again on the rope, he moved on to the next pot.

There were seals on the skerry tonight, no more than fifty yards of black water and hidden rocks away, on the little strand that was only clear when the tide was low. They looked as though they were basking in the moonlight, though it was far too chill for that. As he watched, a couple more dragged themselves up from the sea, heavy and awkward, moving slowly up the sand. They were rolling, heads swaying to and fro, buffeting each other as they moved clumsily forward.

Moonlight silvered everything, casting doubt and shadow. So he scrubbed at his eyes and looked again, but they were still rolling, rising up, standing and stepping out of their heavy skins, helping each other to get free. Six, seven, maybe nine young women, lithe and graceful, holding hands, beginning to sway and dance as though the moon had pulled them up and out of the sea, almost airborne, drunk with the joy of it.

Drifting silently by the rocks, he stared. All of them were up now, leaving their sealskins like wet rocks on the sand, running and leaping, barefoot and naked, gasping with hoarse laughter as they chased each other along the beach. He could not stop staring. Another bar story: the seals who are also people, who come ashore from time to time in places no-one sees. But he was seeing; he was drinking with his eyes, as full of elation as they were. Maybe the Land of Youth was true, too, then; maybe all those wishful, drunken tales were true. But he could not spare a thought for them. Only this was true, and real, and now.

Almost without thinking, he had taken the oars and begun to move nearer, staying behind the rocks though it meant he lost sight of them for a time, and rowing with hardly a splash, the way he'd taught himself on all the long nights out fishing alone. Weaving between boulder and boulder, he found a place to step out and drag the boat ashore. They were still out of sight. Inch by inch, he made his careful way onto the strand, hearing the creak of his boots and the shift of stones under them. But, after all, the beach was empty.

He only realised he was holding his breath when he took in the pile of skins, still lying where they had been shed, and let it all out in one great whoosh. His eyes had not been playing tricks on him; this was real. No sign of life; though now, as he listened through the thudding of his own heart, he could hear laughter some way off. As cautious as a hunter, he crept towards the skins, crouching low, watching for movement. There was none. They lay, mottled and glistening in the moonlight, abandoned.

He put out a hand and touched the nearest. It was warm, as though some of its owner's life still lingered in it. Bolder now, he pulled it towards him, running his hand along the grain of the smooth pelt. You could never get close enough to touch a seal, unless it were dead or caught in a net, but the skins were useful to keep out the cold. And who knew what magic these might hold. Surely, this was a gift, just for him. Glancing around, he lifted it and pushed it between two of the rocks. He could come back for it later; right now, his mind was elsewhere.

They had moved off between the birches and rowans that grew above the tideline, into the places where the thick, unwieldy body of a seal could never go. They were picking rowan berries, eating them and spitting out pips, hanging the bunches over each other's ears, picking leaves and running them over their breasts and thighs. Those heavy pelts must keep out most sensations, he thought. They looked like children fresh from the bath, more naked than naked, like the white inner twigs of fir when the bark is stripped off. He had never seen a girl without her clothes, did not even know if these would pass for human; but his body at least was in no doubt. He stood there, rigid, the blood roaring in his ears, and wanted to weep for the glory of it.

And then one of them saw him.

She gave a sharp cry of alarm, almost a bark, and all their eyes were on him. The next moment they were streaming past, leaping and slipping on the hidden boulders, as he stood there with his arms outstretched, hoping somehow to hold them back. They jostled him as they fled, and he stumbled after them back down to the beach, where they were already melting down into their skins and heaving themselves towards the water, all grace gone. As he reached the water's edge, the last one slid off the rocks and was received into the gentle, swirling waves.

Donald stood there, exultant and desolate all at once. He could see their heads turning to look at him, but he knew they would not return. He watched for a few moments longer, seeing in his mind's eye their glorious, dancing forms. Then a small noise to his right made him glance up, and freeze.

There was one left. She was pacing along the edge of the waves, wringing her hands, uttering little short cries as she yearned towards the dark water. The heads of her sisters gleamed as they waited for her some yards off.

Donald understood in a moment what had happened. He started forward, hands held out, and she backed away, her eyes wide. A few more steps and she would stumble into the rocks where her skin lay hidden. He broke into a run and was upon her almost at once. She seemed weightless, slight as a child, and they fell together on the hard, ribbed sand.

She writhed like an eel under him, but he held on tightly, feeling her breasts crushed against his chest, one leg between her thighs. For a moment her black eyes stared straight into his, and there came a great rush of terror – the fisherman's last grasp at life as the hungry sea swallows him – and the stink of drowned things was in his nostrils. He closed his eyes and hung on. Then her defence was down. She cried out once as he entered her, and after that made no sound at all.

When he came to himself again and looked around, there were no more bobbing heads in the water. She lay still, her head turned away, but as soon as he began to get up she twisted aside and tried to run. Grabbing her wrist, he pulled her up and towed her towards his boat, avoiding the place where he had concealed the skin.

Once in the boat, he rowed hard for the shore. He was afraid at first that she might jump into the water, but it seemed that, although she stared across the gleaming waves and reached out to her sisters, she could not join them.

Soon they came safely to land, and now he took thought and stripped off his shirt. He tried to get her to put her arms into the sleeves, then gave up and wrapped it around her, and so they came stumbling through the darkness, up to the cottage, where his mother had placed a light at the window to guide him home.

He pushed open the door and she was there, seated by the fire, stirring something in the big pot.

At once, he began to talk. 'Look what the sea cast up; there must have been a wreck, I think. I found her like this, down on the shore. She doesn't speak; it'll be the shock, maybe. Have you something to clothe her with?'

His mother looked at them both, and suddenly Donald thought of what she must be seeing: her son holding the wrist of this near-naked girl, wide-eyed in the firelight, with blood on her bare legs. He would not meet his mother's gaze. There was a long moment of silence, and then she was up, putting an arm around the girl and leading her into the bedroom, murmuring something soft and reassuring. Over her shoulder she said, 'Go and get water and put on the kettle. Now!' and then she shut the door upon him.

Donald turned away, letting responsibility slide from his shoulders. She was in charge now, as she had been all his life. She would take care of it all.

He went to and fro, filling buckets from the well, making up the fire and setting the kettle to boil – all the simple things he had been doing every day of his life as far back as he could remember. There was no room for what had just happened, no sense to be made of it, and so he did not try. He thought about the sealskin, bundled where he had left it between the rocks. It was safe enough; it was well above the tideline, and there were no storms due. His mother came through for hot water, and left without speaking to him. There was nothing to do but wait for what came next.

He was staring into the fire when the bedroom door finally opened again. His mother stood in the doorway, so he could not see past her into the bedroom. She put a hand up to the doorframe and rested her weight against it for a moment, as though she were very weary.

He started up, holding out a cup to her. 'Shall I pour one cup, or two? I wasn't sure if…' He faltered to a stop under her straight gaze.

'Donald,' she said, 'what have you done?'

'I found her like that, just by herself there. Will she be all right? Maybe there'll be others from the wreck; I'll go and look, shall I?'

She cut him off with an impatient sweep of her hand. 'For God's sake, boy, there's not a spar or a cask comes ashore but everyone knows about it. There's been no wreck. Now tell me exactly how you found her, and where.'

Resentment rose hot in his throat, mixed with a strange kind of relief. He had never been able to lie to her. 'Mother,' he said, his voice rich with the wonder of it, 'she's a selkie. They were dancing on the skerry, and I saw them.'

She nodded, once, as though she'd already guessed the truth of it, and came slowly forward to drop into the other chair by the fire.

The story came tumbling out of him now, all of it except the thing that he had done to her, the thing he could not bring himself to think about, here at his mother's hearth. When he had run out of words, she looked up at him, and there was something in her expression he had never seen before. Respect, or scorn? Elation, or fear? Or, somehow, all of those things at once. Donald was unnerved. 'What is it? Why are you looking at me like that?'

'Well,' she said. 'Where to start? I never thought I'd see you married at all, Donald Macfarlane, but it seems you've managed it in your own strange way, and we must make the best of it.'

'What? What are you talking about?'

'Use the brains you were born with, boy. That dance was never meant for you. They were maidens, ready for mating. If you hadn't come along, she'd have had a husband of her own kind by the end of the night. But you took her instead. You've made your bed, and now you must lie in it.'

He pushed back his chair, away from her and her senseless words. 'What are you saying? I can't marry that … that creature!'

His mother's eyes hardened. 'It's too late now. You can't undo what you did.'

'I'll take her back there, tonight! I'll give her back her sealskin, and there's an end of it!'

'Oh, Donald. You could have just left her there, let her go back to the sea. But you brought her home. Why?'

'I don't know! I don't know how it all happened; I never meant to…' He faltered to a stop, then tried again. 'It felt as though it was just for me. If you had seen them! I couldn't just leave her. They were so marvellous…'

His mother said nothing. Only watched, and waited.

'Well,' he said at length, 'I was wrong, then. I got it all wrong, like I always do. I'll go now, while the moon's still high.'

'Donald,' his mother said patiently, 'there will be a child.'

'You can't know that!' he shouted at her. 'How could you possibly know that? Even I know it's weeks before you can tell for sure. And anyway, how could you even think of such a thing? What sort of monster would it be, for God's sake? You're out of your senses. I'll take her down there right this minute.' He had risen from his chair and was starting towards the bedroom door, but his mother was there before him, and he could not bring himself to lay hands on her.

'Donald, will you sit down and listen to me? We haven't much time. The whole village will know soon, and we have to think out what we're going to say.'

Again, she'd caught him off balance. The whole village? What had it got to do with anyone else? He turned away and went to the window, to stare out at the moonlit garden. It looked just the same as ever, but he listened, despite himself, as his mother's words unmade his world.

'I don't know for certain, of course, but it's very likely,' she said slowly, as though she were thinking it out as she spoke. 'They would have been maidens, ready to choose their mates. It's the right time of year for that. And you're both young and healthy, so that's the way of it. We'll know for sure before too long. And in the meantime, people will be talking.'

'But there needn't be any meantime! I can just take her down to the skerry now, and no-one will be the wiser!' He had swung round to face her, but his resolve withered again at the look in her eyes. Not many people would cross Bridie Macfarlane when she was determined, and her own son least of all.

'I don't know if she could change back, with your seed inside her. And even if she could, would you condemn your own son or daughter to be born out there on the rocks, when the time comes? You may find it hard to imagine what goes on in other people's minds, Donald, but you're not a cruel man. And in any case, I won't let it happen. This is my grandchild we're talking about, and I will do all I can to give it the best possible chance in the world.'

She saw a change in him, saw that she had won, at least for the time being. She came to sit down again. He said nothing, and after a few moments she went on.

'I was thinking it through while I was tending to her. The best way is to say she's some kin to me, say a cousin's child, back inland, where I grew up. That's fairly safe; no-one travels there much. We can say her parents have died recently, and when we visited last spring, you and she made ... an understanding.'

Donald snorted. 'As if she could understand anything! How will you explain that she's wordless and witless too? And how could she have come here by herself, with nobody noticing?'

Bridie nodded at this. 'It's a problem, that's true. If we can keep her hidden for a few days, we can say you went to see her and brought her back with you. As for the way she is ... maybe we can say she had the fever as a child, and it's altered her mind. But Donald' – and here she looked straight at him – 'you don't really think she's a witless creature, do you?'

'I don't know! No, I suppose not – how can I tell?' He thought of the selkies' playfulness on the skerry, the way they had helped each other. And he thought, too, of the terror she had put into him as she lay under him on the sand. Was that her doing, or was it his own sense of wrong that had given him those nightmare visions? He wrenched his mind away from that place. 'No,' he said again, more slowly. 'It's more like they were children, just doing everything for the first time.'

'That's how it seems to me, too. Her eyes are like a young child's who has it all to learn. And her skin is so soft, so fine; it's like Maggie Kildare's baby's, that was born before its time. But we'll know, soon enough.' Bridie got up again, and her weariness was stronger now.

'We must get some rest. And you must stay out of sight, if you can. The rest we'll have to leave until morning.' Without another word, as though it was all decided, she went through into the bedroom and shut the door upon him.

For the next few days, Donald took himself off before dawn – to beaches and coves that were far away from the village, and inland to hunt rabbits and gather herbs for his mother's medicines. If the weather had been fairer he would have slept out somewhere, for he had no desire to come back to the house at all; but it was too cold for that. He crept back under cover of darkness, to eat a hot meal and fall into bed. Once, when his mother was seeing to the beasts in the barn, he went to the bedroom door and looked inside. She was there, curled in the big bed, dressed in one of his mother's nightgowns. Her long, dark hair spread over the pillow, and slow, silent tears welled from her open eyes. At the sight of him she shrank back against the wall, and he quickly closed the door. I've seen the seals weep like that, he thought; it doesn't mean anything. Even as he thought it, he pushed the idea away in disgust and flung himself out again, into the rain.

On the fifth evening, when he came in, his mother and the girl were sitting at the kitchen table. Bridie was holding a bowl of hot barley broth and spooning it into the girl's mouth as though she were feeding a baby. The girl opened her mouth obediently, waiting for the next spoonful, but she started up when she saw Donald.

Bridie said to him, 'Don't move!' and then, with gentle hands and soothing words, she persuaded the girl to sit down again. 'There, you see, nothing to worry about at all. It's only Donald; he'll do you no harm, I promise you.'

The girl could not have understood the words, but she grew calmer as she listened. Then Bridie said, 'Watch now,' and she put the spoon into the girl's hand. Curling her own hand around it, Bridie guided the spoon again up to the girl's mouth, and then let go. After a moment, she pushed it into her mouth of her own accord, and when Bridie smiled and said, 'Well done, lass! That's the way!' she smiled back.

'You see?' said Bridie to Donald, without turning around. 'She's learning all the time. Maybe she'll even start to speak, one day. What stories she could tell! If she remembers her old life by that time, of course.'

'Why would she forget, if she's so clever?' Donald could not stop himself; they looked so cosy there by the fire.

Bridie gave him a hard look. 'Enough of that. We must give her a name. If she had one before, she can't tell us what it was. What do you think?'

'How should I know?' said Donald, sullenly.

'Well, I think Mairhi would be a good name for her; it's in my family, after all, so no-one will think anything of it.'

Mairhi. The name on the headstone, wearing away now, up in the churchyard under a rowan tree. He could just remember his little sister, stumbling after him down the path, crying when she stung her hand on the nettles, laughing when he tickled her. She had had it all to learn, too, when the fever burned her life away. His mother was looking down at the bowl of broth, so he could not see her face.

'Aye,' he said, more gently, 'it's a good name.'

'Well, then,' she said, and her voice trembled a little, 'that's who you're to be, my lass. Mairhi.' And she reached out to touch the girl's chest. 'And I'm Bridie, and this is Donald.' She beckoned him forward. 'A new start, Donald,' she said in a low voice. 'And better than the last one.'

He felt his face flame, but said nothing. After a moment he came to sit at the table, and nodded awkwardly to Mairhi. His mother brought him some broth. When he picked up his spoon, Mairhi picked hers up as well, mimicking him as he put it in his mouth and swallowed. When he blew on the broth to cool it, she did the same, and pieces of barley and carrot sprayed onto the table. Donald laughed, and then she laughed too; that same hoarse chuckle he'd heard on the skerry. She blew again, harder, and crowed with delight.

Even his mother was smiling, though she put out a hand and said, 'That's enough, now.'

'What's happened to her arm?' he asked sharply. Where the sleeve of the nightgown had fallen back, the skin was red and blistered as though it had been burned. Mairhi cringed back in her chair, and his mother soothed her again, though Donald saw that she avoided touching the sore place.

'It's just her skin, reacting to being clothed, I think. Remember how yours used to itch and burn, when you were a wee lad? You still need my salve on your hands and face when you've to go out in the cold wind. I didn't realise at first, but when I wrapped her in my woollen shawl, it brought her out in great weals all over. It's as though her skin's too new, or too thin. I'm hoping it will get stronger in time. I'll need you to get me some more chickweed and nettle tops tomorrow, if you can find any; I've used up all my stock. But she really is learning, Donald; you can see for yourself.' There was a hint of pleading in her voice, but he gave his attention back to the hot broth, and she said no more.

He remembered, all right; remembered the jeering in the school-yard when they pulled up his shirt to look at the latest crop of blisters. No-one else seemed to have trouble with ordinary things, like wool against flesh; no-one else had hands that cracked and bled so easily when they hauled ropes or mended nets. It was one of the reasons he went out alone so much, staying inshore and working the crab and lobster pots, though it paid poorly. He could not pull his weight, and he knew, in their eyes, it made him less of a man. He still itched and burned on hot nights, but he did not cry for his mother's salves any more. Some things you just had to learn to bear.

The next day, they took her outside for the first time. Both of them together, though neither of them voiced the fear that she might try to run away. But Mairhi only looked around her as though dazed, at the vegetable garden and the hens and the low wall between croft and open hillside, and at the distant seashore. The sound of the waves came to them on the wind, and they watched for some sign that she recognised it; but there was none. Perhaps it was simply that she had never been without it; or perhaps, for her, the world was so changed, she did not recognise the traces of her old life.

She lifted her feet up and down, feeling the weight of Bridie's old boots, which were too big for her, and, staying close to Bridie, watched the hens scratching for food. She shrank away when Donald brought out the cow for milking, but when one of the barn cats came and rubbed itself against her, she laughed, and put out a hand to smooth the soft fur, her arms sore, blistered. Donald knew how that must feel, how the cold wind would be soothing even while it made the soreness worse. Maybe the other children had felt the way he did now: a queasy mixture of pity and revulsion that made them want to hurt him. His mother had tried to help, telling him it was not his fault; but somehow that never quite felt true. And now, of course, it was his fault, and there was no getting out of it.

When the milking was done, they went back to the house. As they rounded the corner of the barn, Bridie nodded towards the nearest house in the village, almost out of sight behind the hill. 'This'll bring them out, sure enough,' she said.

She was right, of course. There had been no sign of anybody all the time they were outside, but while they were at breakfast the next morning, a knock sounded at the door.

Bridie threw Donald a look as she went to open it, a look that said plainly, 'Let me do the talking.' Donald was not about to argue. He always let her speak for him, except when he could not avoid it.

It was not Hector Macdonald, their nearest neighbour, but old Mrs Mackay from the main street of the village, by the harbour. She rarely went far from home these days, but her appetite for gossip, and her status as one of the oldest married women, meant that she had claimed the right to be the first to come calling. It also meant that the whole village knew by now, and there was no more hiding. Faced with a visitor, Donald would normally have muttered some excuse and made his escape, but he knew better than to try that this time.

'Mrs Mackay,' Bridie said brightly. 'What brings you out in this weather? Come in by the fire and take some tea. Donald, would you fill the kettle for me?'

The old lady sank into the fireside chair, taking her time. 'Oh, well now, it's not so bad. But my joints have been aching with all the wet, and I've just about used up the ointment you made for me. I was hoping to catch you in the village, but no-one's seen you about for days, so I thought I'd come and ask you before I run out altogether.' Her eyes were busy as she spoke, flitting like summer flies here and there, but never resting anywhere for long. Most especially, she did not once look directly at Mairhi, who still sat at the table, spoon in hand.

'Goodness me, and I thought I'd given you enough to last for months! I'll see about making some more later on, then I'll bring it down to you myself. I would have been out sooner, but we've had sickness in the house.' Bridie glanced at Mairhi, and back to her guest. 'Oh, we're safe enough now, I should think; it's been almost a week since she came, and no fever for the last few days, though she still has a rash.' And then, as though it had just occurred to her: 'But where are my manners? This is Mairhi McArthur, my cousin James' daughter from Kilbeag, where I grew up. Donald's been away to see them, and he brought her back with him.' Then, lowering her voice, as though Mairhi, sitting not three feet away, might somehow not hear her next words, she said, 'He found them all poorly and stayed to help, but it was too late for her parents, poor lass. She's got no-one else in the world, so he brought her away. And we've stayed indoors until I was sure it was safe, you see.'

'Dear me,' said Mrs Mackay, looking directly at Mairhi for the first time. 'And no family left at all, the poor lassie. That must have been a terrible fever. What were you thinking, Donald, to bring a poor sick girl all this way?'

Donald opened his mouth, though he had no idea what might come out of it. But Bridie intervened: 'Well, you see, they met last summer when we visited, and they have … an understanding.'

'Oh, well now. An understanding, is it? So am I to congratulate you, young Donald?' Mrs Mackay's sharp old eyes fixed him where he sat, blushing and stammering; but that was nothing out of the ordinary, so her gaze moved on to Mairhi, stirring her spoon around and around in her porridge. 'I'm sorry for your loss,' she said formally.

Mairhi looked up, smiling. She picked up her spoon, took a mouthful without spilling a drop, and looked to Bridie for applause. Donald tried to keep a straight face, but the old lady missed nothing. Again, Bridie came to the rescue.

'The thing is, she's a little … touched, you see. Scarlet fever, when she was a child – like Callum Campbell's daughter. She couldn't have managed on her own, and there was no-one who could take her in. And we're hoping there'll be a wedding, in the summer maybe.'

The silence stretched just a little too far this time. Mairhi put down her spoon, looking wary, and Bridie hastened to reassure her. 'It's all right, now, nothing to worry about.' Over her shoulder she added, 'She doesn't understand, you see.'

'I see,' was all Mrs Mackay had to say, but the words were heavy with meaning. Whatever she saw, there was no doubt that, before sunset, the whole village would see it too. With luck, they would see no more than daft Donald finding a poor lass who knew no better than to accept him, and that would be the end of it. That was Bridie's hope; but Donald himself was less certain. The older folk might well decide it was making the best of a bad job, but those nearer his own age – the ones who had made his life a torment in the schoolyard – they would hardly let such a grand joke pass them by. He began, dimly, to understand what he was in for.

It would have been right and proper for them to visit their own family next, but even Bridie's stout optimism quailed at the thought of taking Mairhi into Hugh's noisy household, with dogs and small children and shouting and questions. Bridie had married into one of the more prosperous families in the village. Her husband John had owned his own boat, and after John was lost, his younger brother, Hugh, had taken over the captaincy. In the bigger boats, you could go further out to sea, and stay there for days at a time. When the boats came in laden with riches, those were the festival times. Donald had the right to crew for his uncle, but he only went when Hugh was hard-pressed to make up the numbers, and he knew the rest were as relieved as he was when he made his excuses. He did not much like visiting the shieling, either; all that activity made his head spin, and he had never learned to cope with teasing. In the end, Bridie set out by herself, taking some medicines to give them, and leaving him to watch over Mairhi.

It was the first time they had been alone together since he had found her. She was less afraid of him now, or else she had learned to hide it; but still it felt different with Bridie gone. He went about, doing the everyday tasks, and she watched him solemnly. Then he banked the fire and fetched a heavy woollen shawl to wrap her in. It still made her itch, but there was nothing else to keep out the cold. She stood still, letting him pin the shawl, and then he took her hand and said, 'We're going for a walk now.'

She went along willingly enough as he led her down the path to the shore, the way they had come less than two weeks before. It was bright and windy today, with little waves dashing against the rocks and a knot of gulls quarrelling over something beached on the sand. Donald moved along the high-tide mark, scanning as he always did

for anything useful that might have washed ashore. Up ahead, he saw
part of an old barrel, the staves still attached to a hoop of rusty iron.
He let go Mairhi's hand and went to pull the wood free. 'See here,'
he said over his shoulder. 'We can burn this on the fire.' Then he
turned to the business of prising the staves loose; but all the time he
was aware of her – not moving or even looking around, just standing
there gazing at the sea.

It was a strange business, being with her. Other people came at
him all the time, with their words and their looks and their judgments. He spent his life defending himself, waiting for the next
squall to strike, never understanding what was going on. He did
not understand her, either, but she asked nothing of him. And yet
she needed him to make sense of it all. For the first time he could
remember, here was someone more at a loss than he was. What went
on inside her head? He set the wood down and went to her side,
looking where she looked, out to sea. He had wondered if they might
see seals, but there were none today. Her hands were clenched, and
slow tears welled from her eyes.

What could he possibly say, or do? If he had come across a creature in that much pain – a lamb, say, or a deer – he would have
known how to deal with it. But she was not a creature, not any more.
He knew that, now. His own fists had closed so tight the nails were
cutting into his palms. He made himself uncurl them, stepped away,
busied himself gathering more wood for the fire. When he came back
to her, she had not moved at all.

'Here,' he said, lifting her hand and opening it. Into it he put a
stone, shiny from the water, granite veined with pink and green,
sparkling where the sun caught it. She gazed at it, and he turned the
stone about to make it glitter. 'That's for you,' he said, and closed
her hand around it. She raised her eyes to his. 'You never know what
you'll come across, down here. We'll walk on a bit and gather the
wood on our way back. Come on now.' He started to trudge along
through the shingle. After a moment, he heard the crunch of her feet
on the stones, following him.

They had eaten supper and he had washed up by the time Bridie returned. She emptied her basket onto the table, talking, filling up the silence. 'Here's a good piece of mutton for the pot, and some of Hugh's latest batch of ale. And clothes for Mairhi; I told them we'd had to burn all of hers, and nothing would do but they had to turn out all the chests. There's your cousin Catriona's old shoes, too; they'll fit her better than my boots. I couldn't carry it all, but no matter. They'll all be along soon enough to have a look at her. You're quite the curiosity, my lass! See here,' she went on, shaking out a dress dyed a faded moss green. 'This'll suit you well. We can take it up a bit for you.' She held the dress out to Mairhi, and a smile passed between them. Donald had not seen her smile all day, but she had kept the stone. It lay beside her now on the table, and she held it out to Bridie. Something of her own, perhaps, to trade for all these gifts.

'I gave her that,' said Donald.

Both women looked at him, and he began to blush. He got up, scraping his chair on the flagstones, and went out into the cool darkness to fetch more wood.

It was his cousin Catriona who showed up first, bearing more gifts and a flood of talk.

She came down the path to meet him as he returned from the crab pots. 'So, you've got yourself a sweetheart!' she said, taking his arm as they walked. 'But such a strange one, she is. Tell me how you met, and everything. Typical Donald, to find someone who can't talk back! Is it true love, Donald my dear?' She stopped, so that he had to stop too, and gazed intently up at him.

Catriona was one of those who came at him, touching and guessing and dragging things out into the light, never noticing – or not caring – if she was welcome or not. A year older, and much more worldly-wise, she had been both a bane and a blessing when they were children. Sometimes a protector, but never to be relied on. Sometimes a tormentor, when it suited her. Most of the time Donald thought she was laughing at him; it was safer to assume that, at any rate.

She was laughing now. 'Cat got your tongue? You're as dumb as she is! What times you'll have together, to be sure. There can't have been much talking in this courtship, I'm guessing.' She laughed again as he blushed. 'Oh, Donald, you've got a lot to learn.'

She pushed the door open ahead of him, talking as she went. 'Well, Auntie Bridie, look what the tide washed up! Now, how shall we make this handsome young lad into a bridegroom fit to walk at your side, eh, Mairhi? Come here now,' and she took Mairhi by the shoulders. 'Stand by Donald and let's see how you look. Goodness, you're as small as a fairy's child!' She darted a quick look at Bridie.

His mother was busy laying the table; her hands barely paused as she counted out the knives and forks. But Donald froze, like a wild thing when the shadow of the eagle passes over. Unknowingly, he squeezed Mairhi's hand, and she looked up at him in wonder.

'That would be from the fever when she was a bairn,' said Bridie, as casually as if Catriona had suggested it might rain later. Then she stood beside her niece and inspected the happy couple. 'Donald, you're a taller man than your father. I'll need to let down the trouser hems on his suit. Wait while I fetch the measure, and we'll see if the sleeves need altering, too. We'll sort Mairhi out when you're out of the way.' She and Catriona exchanged a conspiratorial glance, and Donald breathed again. Maybe Catriona had meant nothing; maybe it was just her running on, coming out with whatever entered her head. But he had seen the way she looked at Bridie, and he did not think so.

He took himself off after dinner, leaving them to their pinning and tucking. They were going to bring out Bridie's wedding dress and make Mairhi try it on; and all the time his cousin would be watching – judging, looking for clues. It was not going to work, and he did not know whether to be relieved or sorry.

Burdened with the biggest basket, full of crabs for sale, he made his slow way down to the harbour, stepping across ropes and piles of netting on the cobbled path between the sea wall and the first row of cottages. More than one man had taken an unexpected dive here after dark, stumbling home from the bar, and woe betide him if the tide was low. Donald was careful, but even so he nearly went sprawling over a sudden obstacle. He dropped the basket and grabbed at a rope hanging from the wall of the nearest cottage, where the Bains' scabby mongrel spent most of its miserable existence, cowering from the wind and rain, and the passing feet. There was no dog there today though. Aly Bain, sitting on his doorstep mending nets, had stuck out his leg just as Donald was passing.

He giggled – a high, nasal whickering that took Donald straight back to the schoolroom. Aly's seat had been directly behind Donald's, and he had appointed himself tormentor-in-chief, scenting a victim from the very first day, though he was a runty little weasel of a boy, who, at first glance, looked ripe for picking on himself. His two elder brothers – strapping lads both – certainly thought so, taking their cue from their heavy-handed father; but Aly's weapons were sharper than fists and more deadly. He used words like his blunt wooden netting needle, stabbing in and away before Donald could ever muster a reply. Words, and those other ways of the underdog: the sneer; the whispered joke sent rippling around the schoolyard; the sudden pinch as Donald started to answer a question in class. There was never any point in trying to fight back; the Bains would close ranks and, shoulder to shoulder, take swift and unsubtle revenge. Donald learned to lie low, just like Aly's wretched dog and his sullen, scrawny wife. He bit his lip now, as he scrambled to gather up the crabs that had fallen from the basket.

'Hey, Donald. I heard you've got yourself a halfwit for a wife! Nobody with any brains would have you, eh?'

Nor you, either, mused Donald, thinking of Jessie Bain, who cringed from the kindness of the other women and threw back their attempts at charity, knowing what the price would be. He dropped the last runaway into the basket and straightened up, looking down at Aly for the first time. 'Going out tonight?' he asked, prodding the tangle of netting with his foot. It was a feeble response, but the best he could do.

'What's it to you? You're too scared to go out of sight of land. Maybe the sea monsters will reach over the side and drag you out of the boat, just like your daddy, eh? They're waiting for you, Donald, and they're getting very hungry now.' Aly giggled again. Donald stood like an ox under the lash. He worried about the selkies these days, kept as far from seals as he could, but still imagined them coming up under the boat and rolling it over, dragging him down and battering the life from him. Mairhi's husband should have been one of them – one of the great grey bull seals, longer than a man and twice as broad. Maybe he was out there, biding his time.

'Oi, Macfarlane. You're a halfwit yourself, d'you know that? Well, you might if you weren't so stupid.' Aly sniggered at his own cleverness. 'You'll make a fine pair. When do we get a look at her, then?'

'Go to hell,' said Donald, to his own surprise, and strode off as quickly as he could. He knew what kind of comments Aly would make, the kind of things he might do when he did meet Mairhi, and for one red moment there he had wanted to haul him out of his sheltering doorway and toss him onto the rocks beneath the harbour wall. The picture rose in his mind of his wife-to-be as he had first seen her – dancing lithe and free among her sisters – and sudden tears came to his eyes.

9

The next day, Bridie went to see the priest. She came back full of talk – too much and too fast. 'He wants to see you both, give you the instructions about marriage and so on. I explained about Mairhi, but he said it was still right to do it. If she has any wits at all, he says, she must have some understanding of what it means, and if she doesn't, she can't be married in any case. I don't know if she's ready yet; what do you think?' She turned to Donald, and for the first time he felt that she needed his support. Until now, he and Mairhi had been going along with her plan. Now, she wanted him to be her ally.

'I wouldn't know. She understands quite a lot now, but the way the priest talks will be beyond her, surely.' He did not bother to mention the obvious thing: that the whole business had been against her will from the start. 'Can't it wait a bit? The more time we have, the more … like us … she gets. What's the hurry?' They both looked over at Mairhi throwing grain to the hens, laughing as they scrambled over each other.

'Donald, have you no sense at all? The child will come in just over eight months now. It's fine to marry when you know a girl can have children, but not when she's too far along. The wedding will need to be in the next month or so at most.'

'But you don't even know for sure yet…'

'Oh, I'm fairly sure now. I know the signs, after all; who better?' She looked up at him, squinting against the sun, trying to see his expression. 'You're going to be a father, Donald.'

He could take no more. He turned without a word, and she did not try to hold him back. He strode down to the beach, his thoughts buzzing like wasps around his head. How long had she known? How dare she just assume that it was all fine by him? She had managed this whole ridiculous situation right from the start, and he had let himself be poked and prodded along like the halfwit everyone thought he was. Well, they were right; but no more. It was time to take matters into his own hands.

He flung himself into the boat and sat there, trying to breathe. His arms trembled as he gripped the oars, wanting to pull hard and fast, without thought or direction, out and away. And that's how you go down, he reminded himself. The sea never lets you forget; the rocks are always there, under the surface. One lapse is all it takes. Despite everything, he was not ready for that, not yet. Carefully, he eased the boat into open water.

The wind was veering about, driving the waves every which way, and it took all of his concentration to make his way along the strand and then across to the skerry. No sign of seals today; where did they go when the sea was rough? He hadn't been back since the night he saw them, three weeks ago or more, but still he glanced along the beach where they had been. No trace, not even a footprint. He turned away and went over to the rocks where he had stowed the sealskin.

It was not there.

It seemed then that he split in two: one part searched and searched again, went over every inch of the skerry, scanned the sea for watching seals in case they were out there, mocking him; the other simply stood and waited, thinking of nothing, listening to the endless, meaningless drench and suck of the waves on the shingle. At last, worn out and heartsick, he came back to himself. The skin was gone, taken. Not by the sea, for there had been no great storms lately. Not by a stranger, either; nobody would ever steal another man's salvage. It had to be someone who knew, maybe had even seen. What that might mean, he could not begin to imagine. But Mairhi could not go back. The pattern of her life, and his, was already woven, and there was nothing at all to be done about it.

He dropped to his knees by the clutter of boulders that had marked his hiding place. With both hands, he grasped at the nearest rock, pulling with all his strength. It did not budge. Still holding on, he threw back his head and roared defiance at the sky. Then he went at it again, straining until the veins stood out on his neck and arms, until at last the stone came free, slowly at first and then with a sudden rush and a swirl of foam. He gathered it in his arms, cradling it against his chest, then got to his feet and staggered down the beach into the sea. With another hoarse yell, which was partly a sob, he heaved the stone as far as he could. It fell a few feet away, and the waves swallowed it.

10

'Well now, Donald, so this is your young lady! Welcome, my dear. Come in, come in out of the wind.' The priest pushed the door shut against the squall that had blown them here. 'You're soaked through; come in by the fire now. Would you take some tea?'

In the pulpit, Father Finian spoke with divine authority and with no shadow of a doubt that God was with him, but in his own parlour he seemed less sure of himself. Kirsty, his housekeeper, hovered in the doorway, staring with frank curiosity.

'Sit down, sit down,' said the priest. 'Kirsty, would you fetch us some tea? And how is your mother, Donald? Keeping well, hmm?'

Donald kept his eyes on the carpet. It was only three days since Bridie had been to speak with the priest – if anything had happened to her since then, he would certainly have heard about it. 'She's fine.'

'Good, good. And you, Miss McArthur, you're fully recovered from your fever?'

Donald squeezed her hand, and she nodded. They had worked out the signal beforehand. She had to have enough understanding to seem to consent to the marriage – although, if she did understand what the priest was saying, it surely could make no sense to her at all. Donald cleared his throat. 'She doesn't speak, father.'

'Of course, of course, your mother explained it all to me. Poor child, it's a hard road you've had to travel.'

Unbidden, Mairhi nodded again, and smiled. Without thinking, Donald tightened his grip on her hand, and she nodded a third time, more vigorously.

'And she's a bit ... well, as you see, sir. But she knows what we're saying, if the words are simple, and she picks up how people are feeling, if you take my meaning.' *Which is more than I do*, he thought. He laid his free hand on top of hers. 'Reassure her,' his mother had said. 'Don't let her get frightened. As long as she stays calm, it'll be fine. And be sure to show him that you care for her.'

'Indeed, yes. And has she no family left at all?'

'None except us, sir.'

'Well, well, we must each of us bear our own burdens. So, we must keep it simple, hmm? Tell me, my dear, do you want to be married?'

The direct question took Donald by surprise, and it was a moment or two before he remembered the signal this time.

'Very good. But you must be clear, the both of you. Marriage is not all plain sailing and sunshine. No, indeed. Marriage is a solemn sacrament in the eyes of the Lord. Now, do you understand what your, er, your marital duties will be?'

Donald flamed red. Mairhi, unperturbed, swung her feet and looked about her. There were no ornaments at home, nothing that was not made for use, and used many times. But here there was a glass vase full of dried grasses, a heavy paperweight on the desk, framed texts on the walls, and a whole shelf of books. He could not blame her for staring.

In pride of place on the mantelpiece stood a wooden carving of a herring gull in flight. Mairhi's gaze travelled there and stopped. She made a noise in her throat, a small exclamation of surprise and wonder, and without warning she jumped up, went over and lifted it from its place. Both men watched as she ran one finger along the length of an outstretched wing, and then touched it to the tip of the sharp, curved beak. With a sudden swoop of her arm, she made the bird soar and then dive towards an invisible sea, and from her open mouth came the high, mournful cry of the gull. She stopped, looking astonished, and then laughed aloud. Kirsty, coming in just then with a tray of tea, would have dropped the lot if the priest had not come to her rescue.

'Well, well, that's truly remarkable,' he said, putting down the tea tray and turning again to Mairhi. 'So you like my little carving, do you? Now, wait a moment,' and he hurried out of the room. Left alone, Donald tried to avoid Kirsty's gaze, but there was no holding her back.

'Merciful heavens, Donald, whatever next? She's got no more sense than a child of six! Oh, there, hush now.' For Mairhi had begun to tremble and look wildly about. The older woman went over and took her in her arms. This was a step too far; she was used only to Bridie's touch, and she pulled away. Kirsty folded her arms, looking affronted.

'For goodness' sake, what a fuss to be making!'

'She's not used to strangers,' Donald began, but with a little cry Mairhi ran to him and curled herself against his chest, still clutching the carved gull. He held his breath for a moment, and then put one arm around her shoulders, holding her awkwardly. In all of his life, no-one had ever come to him for protection. It was a new and strange feeling.

Father Finian came back in, and Kirsty, not looking at Donald, began fussing with the tea things. The priest's arms were full of small sculptures. 'Let's see what you make of these, my dear,' he said. 'Just a few of my own humble efforts,' he added to Donald, although he had not asked. 'A little pastime of mine, hmm?' He laid out the birds and beasts on the table.

Most of them were crude and poorly shaped, but Donald recognised a deer, a badger, and some other birds that were less distinctive than the gull. The priest had done better with the curved forms; the fish, the dolphin. The seal. Donald's eyes widened. His first thought was to snatch it up and fling it on the fire, but after a moment, curiosity won out over dread. He picked it up and held it out to Mairhi. 'You know this one, I think,' he said.

Her mouth was a round 'O' of amazement. Certainly, she knew this one. She looked at him as though asking permission, and then, putting the gull carefully down on the table, she reached for the seal. It lay in the palm of her hand, and she looked down at it, quite still.

'And what noise does the seal make, my dear?' asked the priest, as if to a small child.

Slowly, she lifted her head. The silent tears were falling. She held the seal away from her, as though it hurt her hand, but when Father Finian went to take it from her, she snatched it back, crowding against Donald.

'Oh dear me, now, I didn't meant to upset you,' said the priest helplessly. He offered her his handkerchief, which she ignored. 'There now,' he said, 'there's no need for tears. No, no, you can keep it, if you like. Would you like that, my dear?'

'That's very kind,' said Donald, as his mother had taught him. 'She'll be fine, she's just a bit upset. It's all new to her, you see.' He stopped. Should he have said that? But neither Kirsty nor the priest seemed to notice; they were watching Mairhi, now holding the seal against her breast.

'Well, she seems to like that well enough,' said Kirsty, acidly.

'It's just new people,' Donald tried to explain. 'She meant nothing by it.' But he could see that the older woman was hurt by the earlier rejection. What could he do? To Mairhi he said, 'She was only trying to be kind.'

'I think, perhaps,' said Father Finian, 'we should continue the instruction another time, hmm?'

'No, no, it's all right, really,' said Donald, not knowing what to do for the best. He put his own hand over Mairhi's, where the seal was cradled. 'It's yours now, my lass. It's for you.' He slipped his arm around her again. His chin almost rested on the top of her head, and the smell of her hair came about him; salt and sweat, and some other warm, animal scent. He wanted to nuzzle into it.

'Well now, where were we?' asked the priest. But no-one seemed inclined to answer him. 'Keep it simple, that's the way, eh? It's clear enough that you care for each other, hmm?' He glanced at Donald, who was still holding Mairhi against him. 'You know the vows, young Donald? For richer, for poorer, in sickness and in health, and so on? You know what it means, to speak those words in the sight of the Lord?'

'I think I do, Father. It means we must stay together whatever

comes, and look after each other, and … and care for our children.'
Donald spoke slowly, and it seemed to him that in saying the words
out loud, he was making the vows, here and now; that there really
was no going back. Unconsciously, he drew Mairhi a little closer,
and, as though responding to his signal, she looked up and nodded.
Maybe, thought Donald in wonder, *maybe she really does understand.*

'Very good, very good,' said the priest. 'Well, it all seems quite …
er … quite satisfactory, hmm? I think you'll do very well. And from
what your mother told me, there's no reason to delay. No family to
come from inland, no grand preparations to be made, hmm? And
forgive me for speaking plainly, young Donald, but although your
mother is with you, it's not quite the thing to be living under the
same roof, now, is it? No indeed; the sooner you are man and wife,
the better for all.' Behind him, arms still folded, Kirsty was nodding
her head emphatically.

'No, sir, I mean yes, sir. I mean thank you, thank you very much.'

Father Finian waved the thanks away. 'All settled, then. Good!
Shall we say three weeks' time, after the banns are called? Excellent!
Well, I'll see you in due course. And give my regards to your mother.'

11

They came out into a scatter of raindrops, sparkling in sudden sunshine. Donald was still holding Mairhi's hand, and he swung it a little as they walked. The thing was done, settled; for better or for worse. His mind veered away from all the other steps along the way. Right now, the path was clear; he had no choice, and there was a kind of contentment in that thought. He glanced down at Mairhi, meaning to say something reassuring, but she was gazing out beyond the harbour at the white sails, bright against the stormy skies out to sea.

The boats were coming in, three of them. He knew them without thinking about it: the Bains; the Macdonalds; and the family boat, captained by his Uncle Hugh, which could have come to him some day. Still could, if he wanted that. Skeins of gulls swirled about them, their cries coming faintly on the breeze. He grinned at Mairhi and said, 'You did well, lass.' For a brief moment, their eyes met.

They were almost at the harbour now. When they came through before, on their way to the priest's house, it had been deserted, except for a few cats scavenging here and there. Now, though, there was a little group of women and children gathered to watch the boats home. Donald had not reckoned with that. All eyes were on them as they came closer. To Mairhi he said, 'Don't worry, they just want a look at you.' Not so long ago, he would have waited for them to make the approach, but now he had to be her protector, and interpreter, too. He flung up his free hand and called out, 'It's all arranged! He's to read the banns next week.' And then the children were about them, staring at Mairhi, pushing and tumbling among the coiled ropes and baskets.

'Well, and it's good to see you settled, young Donald.' This was his father's aunt Annie, who lived down at the harbour these days.

'Welcome to you, lass. I don't know what you'll make of us and our ways, but you'll learn, I'm sure. Bring her in to take tea with me soon, Donald. When's the wedding to be?'

'In three or four weeks, Auntie. You'll be first to know.'

A few of the other women offered their congratulations. None of them spoke directly to Mairhi; obviously, word had gone around. Jessie Bain, hanging back with her shawl pulled low over her eyes, was trying to watch without being seen. Donald saw that she was expecting again. What he could see of her face looked pinched and sallow, and she was leaning against the sea wall as though standing was an effort for her. Her babies came hard; his mother would have her work cut out, if the Bains would lay aside their pride enough to call for her.

'Is she out of her wits?' That was one of the Bain children, keeping expertly just out of reach of adult hands.

'Hold your tongue!' The boy's mother hardly bothered to raise her voice. He was speaking for everybody, after all.

Donald raised Mairhi's hand high, for all to see. 'This is Mairhi McArthur, my … my intended bride. She's a little shy, and she doesn't always understand things, but she's no more halfwitted than you are, Sam Bain.'

That drew a ripple of laughter. 'And that's you told!' said his aunt firmly. To Mairhi she said, 'You're welcome here, and don't you mind their nonsense.'

Mairhi gazed at Auntie Annie. After a moment, she brought up her free hand, and laid it gently against the older woman's cheek. The strange, tender gesture made a pool of silence around them. Donald had no idea what to do next, but he was saved by a shout from the nearest boat, now within hailing distance. He waved, and his Uncle Hugh waved back. He would have to stay now, to help the boat come in.

Turning to his aunt, he said, 'Look after her for me, would you?' And then was off down to the jetty. He glanced up at the harbour wall once or twice – a man, working among other men – and there was Mairhi, arm in arm with Auntie Annie, safe and sound.

It was quite a while, then, before they could get away, having refused offers of food and drink, but accepting a large basketful of fresh sardines for the pot. His aunt held Mairhi's hand at parting and said, 'Bring her again soon. She eases me.' Donald, in his eagerness to go, did not ask her what she meant. His mother would be anxious now to hear how the meeting had gone, and he had spent more time this afternoon in company than he had in a long while. He would have to bear a good deal more of it in times to come, but for today, it was enough.

12

The next three weeks seemed to pass in a bright blur. There were almost always other people at the house these days, or else they must go visiting, to see and be seen. They went to church, sitting side by side in the family pew; a silent place, but full of the thoughts and speculations of the villagers around them. The Macfarlanes had taken the wedding preparations in hand, and now they took Mairhi in as well, enveloping her in their warm, noisy way. The younger children claimed her in their games, and Catriona tried clothes on her, began to teach her how to sew and weave and cook, and filled up her silences with chatter and laughter.

Despite Bridie's fears, she did not seem to mind the crowds at all, and she had a knack for calming a crying baby or a fractious child that soon won her a place at the hearth. Donald watched the easy way of it with a mixture of wonder, relief and something that was almost jealousy. It had always been beyond him, and so he had turned his back on them all. He'd had no need of anyone; his best times were by himself, out in the hills or combing the shoreline for salvage, and he had believed that was enough. But now, walking home with Mairhi after an evening with his family, he carried the warmth of it in his heart. It seemed that through her, who was more of a stranger than they could possibly know, he was beginning to feel that he belonged.

This new security was a small and fragile thing, however, and it did not last long. Ten days or so before the wedding was due, Catriona came to meet him again as he made his way up from the sea. She took some of the creels from him, and then stopped on the path, barring his way. 'So, Donald,' she said, 'where's she really from?'

'Wh-what d'you mean?'

'You know right well what I mean, Donald Macfarlane. Wherever it was she grew up, it wasn't on a croft, that's for sure.'

'How do you make that out?' He had expected this from the start, but now, just when he had begun to think maybe it would all be fine, it caught him like a sudden squall on a calm sea.

'Well, for a start,' said Catriona, 'she's never seen a sheep before! Or a goose, or … well, all kinds of things. She hadn't the first idea how to hold a needle, or build a fire, or pluck a chicken. But she does now. One day she watches you, and the next day she can do it herself. She's learning all the time, you can see it. She's no more simple than you or I.' She glared up at him, daring him to contradict her, just as she had done when they were children. 'You're a rotten liar, Donald, so don't even try. Where did you find her?'

He set his creels down carefully, playing for time. Stay as close to the truth as you can, his mother had said. How could she have hoped to fool everybody? The anger that had slept in him since he had discovered the loss of the sealskin suddenly woke again, hard and hungry. He took a deep breath.

'Listen now,' he said. 'You're not to speak of this to anybody. Can you promise me that?'

'Of course, Donald. You can trust me. Haven't I always looked out for you since you were a wean?' Her eyes were shining. Catriona had always loved secrets. She'd smell them out and give you no peace until she'd teased them out of you, and then run around the school-yard bursting with the joy of it. She could hold the tension for maybe half an hour at most, if you were lucky, and then suddenly all the girls would be pointing and giggling. It was his mother who had shown him the way out of this one. 'That's easy enough,' she'd said, when he'd stumbled home fighting back tears. 'Just tell her some-thing you really want them to believe.'

'All right, then. You know when we went inland last summer, when my grandfather McArthur died? Well, that was when I first met Mairhi.' He had been weaving this story for himself, giving colour and substance to the bare threads his mother had started. 'Her folks lived away up in the hills, and they hardly saw anyone from one week to the next. But they came down for the funeral. She's kind of like me, in some ways. You know, out on the edge of things. And she's easy to talk to. You've seen that?'

Catriona nodded. 'So you fell for her?' she asked, already distracted from the question she'd started with.

'I suppose I did,' said Donald, amazed at how smoothly the story was coming out. 'And you're right, she's not really simple at all. But her mother had never let her do anything for herself, you see. They lost other children to the fever, and it made them too quick to protect her. That was why they kept themselves to themselves, and why she's got so much to learn. And now you're all teaching her things. She's changing really fast. It was a good day for her when I brought her here.' *And if that wasn't true to begin with*, he thought suddenly, *it's up to me to make it true now.*

'Well, but why should that all be such a secret?' Catriona was already, in her imagination, telling it to all her friends. There had to be something more to it than that.

'It's just that they were so odd. They never went to church, or anything. She didn't even know how to use a knife and fork. Mother was worried people might think ill of her, or try to belittle her, if it was known. They were hardly like regular folk at all.' *Stay close to the truth*, indeed. He thought about seals with knives and forks, and a bubble of laughter rose inside him. 'So you can't tell anyone,' he went on quickly. 'You're really helping her, all of you, and I don't want to set her back now.'

Catriona was staring at him. 'I'll keep your secret, Donald,' she said. 'But I'll tell you something else.' She turned around and carried on up the path, swinging a creel in either hand.

What else could there be? 'What's that, then?'

'She's not the only one that's changing.'

13

It was the dark of the year now; the time of small, drab days and endless freezing nights; the time for sitting by the fire, mending and making and telling the old tales. On the shortest day of all, close upon Christmas, no-one put out to sea. Usually they would stay ashore only for Sundays and holy days, but the older traditions still held sway, and the priest was wise enough to turn a blind eye to it.

But Donald went, with a dark lantern and a basket full of fish, and Bridie watched him go and never said a word. She had a private vigil of her own to keep, for it was at just about this time that John had gone out in bitter winter weather, and the boat had returned with a shocked and silent crew, and one man missing. She would set a light in the window and lay a place at the table, the way folks did on All Hallows' Eve, for the lost and hungry souls to find their way home. Mairhi would be with her this time, of course, but somehow her company was never intrusive.

So Donald made his way alone, down to the shore and over to the skerry in the drifting fog. The night was starless, moonless and utterly still. He set his basket down on the strand, with a sidelong glance at the black, gleaming rocks where the sealskin had been, and now of course was not, and walked along to the little grove of birches and rowans where the selkies had played. It was desolate now, every branch and twig encased in silver. No leaves, no bright berries, no life at all. There was no sign that the seals had ever been here. He stood still a moment and then retraced his steps back to the sand. Squatting by the basket of fish, he closed the lantern, and at once the fog pressed in around him; he could see almost nothing and sensed rather than saw the gentle swell of the water a few feet away. He waited a little while, and then spoke aloud into the vast, whispering dark.

'Seals! I don't know if you're out there, or if you'll understand any of this.' He stopped, feeling foolish, hearing his own voice fall flat and small under the iron weight of the freezing fog. Then he cleared his throat and went on. 'My name is Donald Macfarlane, and I have done you wrong. But I can't undo it, she can't come back to you now, and I … and she's with child, d'you see? She has to stay, at least until the child is born. I promise you, I'll take the best care of her that I can. We're to be wed soon; we'll be man and wife. That's how it's done, with us. And when the child comes, if it … if it belongs to you, I'll…'

He stopped again. His throat seemed to have closed over, and for a while he could not speak. At last he muttered, only half aloud, 'I'll bring it here, to you. But if … but if it's human, I'll do right by it, I'll do right by her, and I'll try to be a good husband and a good father, and' – his voice had risen again; he was shouting now into the void – 'I'll try to make it right, d'you see? I'll do my best! And I'm sorry! And … and these are for you.' He stood up, tipped out the basket in a brief glimmering stream onto the sand, picked up the lantern and stumbled away towards the rocks, almost running in his haste to be gone. He tripped, nearly lost his footing, and only then remembered to open the lantern. It made a little globe of light in the fog, and he could not see the place where he had been.

14

It had been a merry evening, up at the shieling with the family. Bridie had been called away halfway through supper by a wide-eyed little lass who appeared at the door, wrapped in a shawl too big for her, saying that her mother's pains had started and could Bridie come now, right away, no time to waste; but Donald and Mairhi stayed. Catriona and her little sisters wanted to teach them to dance for their wedding. Donald refused, point-blank; not even for his own wedding would he be persuaded to do such a thing. Mairhi went along with it willingly enough, but she persisted in moving to her own sweet rhythms, and never seemed to mind that the others were soon weeping with laughter. Indeed, Donald thought that for her that might have been the point of it all, and maybe she had the right of it. He'd been watching them, smiling, and then became aware of his uncle watching him in his turn.

'It's a grand thing, family,' Hugh said then. 'And now you'll be starting one of your own.'

'Aye, I suppose,' said Donald.

'It changes everything, and no mistake. You're a man now, Donald, and you'll need to be thinking about how to look after them. Your mother's done the best she could on her own, and your crabbing's brought in enough for the two of you, but things are different now.'

Donald knew what was coming next. Hugh had no sons, and although he was still hale enough, the seagoing boats were no place for older men.

'I know, Uncle Hugh. I'll come out with you this winter when you need me.'

'Fair enough. But you'll need to look to the future as well. I'm not getting any younger, and you know the boat should have been yours by rights.'

'I know, Uncle Hugh,' Donald said again. 'I don't forget it, I promise you. But you know Callum Campbell would take it on in a second, if you asked him.'

Hugh made a noise in his throat; if he'd been out on the water, he'd have spat over the side. 'Callum's a good man, but the drink's got to him these days, and you need a steady hand. I can't rely on him. I'd far rather see it stay in the family. But there, we'll say no more about it now. There's time enough, God willing.'

It was long past dark when they left, to pick their way carefully down to the harbour. Most folks were already indoors, but as they were passing the bar, the door opened and a knot of men staggered out in a blast of light, heat and noise that was cut off abruptly as the door shut behind them. No telling who it was on this moonless winter's night, Donald muttered a greeting as they shouldered past; but the next moment one of them had him by the arm.

'Hey, Macfarlane! Where's your manners, man? Are you not going to introduce us?' It was Andrew Bain, eldest of the three Bain brothers. Donald cursed his luck. Euan and Aly had stopped too, now, crowding back into the feeble light that came from the bar window. The reek of smoke and whisky was strong on them. It must have been a good catch that day.

'Well, right enough,' Donald said lamely. 'This is Mairhi McArthur, my … my intended.'

Aly tittered. Euan swept off an imaginary hat and made a sweeping bow that almost sent him into the harbour. 'An honour, Miss McArthur!'

Mairhi merely stared, then took a step back as Aly came close, breathing whisky into her face.

'Let's have a look at you, then. Not much to see, is there? But maybe there's some hidden charms about you, eh? What did you do to land a slippery fish like Donald here?' He took another step forward, pushing her up against the bar wall.

Donald started towards them, but Euan's grip on his arm was suddenly tight as a hawser, and Andrew had closed in, barring his way. Beyond him, Mairhi gave a little cry of protest, and Aly laughed again.

'Oh, so you do have a voice, after all? And here they're saying you're dumb and witless. What else is there to know about you?'

'Let her be!' Donald shouted, but both the elder brothers had their hands on him now.

Mairhi cried out again, and there was the sound of something tearing. Donald struggled to free himself, Euan and Andrew holding him back; but suddenly all three were frozen by the ragged, high-pitched screech that ripped across the thick night air. Donald lunged past his captors, only to stop dead. It was not Mairhi who had screamed, but Aly.

He had fallen to his knees now, making horrible choking, rasping noises, clutching at his throat, while she stood like a stone, still pressed against the wall, just watching. Aly's whole body convulsed; he threw himself backward onto the cobbles, arching his back and jerking like a salmon on the gaff. His face, lit up as the bar door opened and men came crowding out, was a ghastly green. Then he went still, sprawled limp as seaweed across the stones. There was a terrible silence.

Just as the tide of men surged forward once more, he shuddered into life again, drawing in a great, hoarse, tearing breath; everyone recoiled as he curled over and vomited, retching over and over again and gasping or sobbing in between. Donald fought his way through the press to where Mairhi still stood motionless. Cautiously, he put out a hand. She jumped at his touch and then shivered all over.

'Are you all right, lass?' The neck of her dress was torn.

She looked at him, and he braced himself for that dark, drowning gaze. Then she came into his arms. Quietly, while everyone was busied about Aly Bain, he held her; but that could not last for long.

'What the hell did she do to him?' That was Euan, and others too now, while Aly still moaned and shook on the ground.

'He hurt her,' said Donald. 'And he's taken a bit too much drink tonight.' Maybe that was all they would see, just another drunkard coughing his guts up. Or maybe not, as Aly turned the black holes of his eyes towards them, and found his voice at last.

15

'I saw them,' he said, slow and flat as though he were dreaming. 'I fell down in the dark, and I saw them. All tangled in weeds, and the fish going in and out through the bones. They reached their hands up like they were asking for help, and I tried to keep away, but I kept sinking, and then—'

'That's enough, now,' said one of the older men harshly. 'It's the drink talking. See him home, Andrew, for God's sake.'

But the others were looking away, crossing themselves, shrinking back. Donald, looking from one to another, saw the same horror in all their faces, the fear that must never be spoken. For the first time, he knew beyond doubt that, whatever his own imagination could conjure up, it was no worse than the secret thoughts of any of these hard-handed, practical men, and that the only way to deal with those thoughts was to keep them dark, private, unspoken. But it was too late. Aly was still speaking, and it seemed nothing would stop him.

'They reached up, and then they had hold of me, the bones of their fingers round my ankles, in my hair' – he reached up to claw at his own hair as he spoke, faster and higher – 'and I couldn't get free, and I could see the boat above me and I tried to call out, and the water came into my mouth, down into me, and they held fast, they wanted me down there with them, and…' He was choking again, drowning again, clutching at his throat.

The other men watched, helpless, unmanned by their own horror. All but Euan. He sprang at his brother, catching him by the shoulders and shaking him hard, until, despite himself, he took in a great, rasping breath.

'Aly, that's enough!' Euan shouted directly into his face. 'Come back, man, come out of it!'

Abruptly, Aly's eyes focussed. He looked wildly around at the circle of men staring down at him, seeing his own fear, his own shame leaping back at him from every pair of eyes. They flinched away as he saw them, one by one refusing complicity. Only one person could bear to meet his gaze. She gave him back look for look, expressionless.

'She witched me!' He raised a trembling arm and tried to point at Mairhi. 'She put pictures in my mind, she tried to kill me!'

'It's true,' Euan agreed. 'She did something! Something uncanny. We were just talking to her, and then … and then he was like this.' He indicated his brother with a sweep of his arm, but he was looking at Mairhi.

Donald had no idea what to do. Old habits held him hard. Cringe, look down, mumble and play the idiot until they leave you alone; it had never served him very well in the past, but it was the only way he knew. But the thing was, he was not on his own any more. Mairhi clearly had her own ways to defend herself, but he had no way of knowing if she could use them against a whole group of men, or even if they were under her control at all. In any case, she might make matters worse. He stepped in front of her, shielding her with his body. Ignoring all the others, he spoke to Euan, who still crouched at his brother's side.

'You saw what he did. He hurt her, he tore her dress. He'd have done worse, too. And you just watched, the both of you. Now you keep him away from her, you stay away from us, do you hear?' The other men would have to make out the truth of it for themselves. He could take no more. Holding Mairhi by the arm, he steered her through the crowd, and they made way for him. There would be a reckoning, of that he had no doubt, but now he just wanted to go home.

The night was far gone, and it was almost time for milking when Bridie finally came in. Donald had not slept, though Mairhi had gone to bed long since. He woke the fire and made tea, while Bridie sank into her chair and stared at the flames. She looked smaller, somehow, his mother; a little bent, like an old woman, though she was far from that.

'Did it not go well?' he asked, as he handed her the hot tea. She started, as though she had been somewhere else in her thoughts. 'What's that? Oh, well, the birth. No, that was all fine in the end. Another daughter. I've no doubt Rob Wallace was downcast; he already has the three. But when they fetched him home from the bar, he had something else on his mind. He barely thanked me, couldn't wait for me to be out of the house. There was something about the way he looked at me. I don't know. It put me in mind of when I was still new here, and some folks thought I had strange ways about me. Well, some folks still do.' She looked up at Donald. 'So tell me, what's it about?'

He told her. It was so familiar: telling her his day, and she smoothing it out, making sense of it all, while he let it fall away. And yet, it was utterly different. He could tell her, but he could not give it up to her. She listened quietly, not interrupting, until he was done, and then was silent for a while.

'I had an idea there might be something like this,' she said after a while. 'It's come sooner than I'd hoped, though. They might try to stop the wedding.'

'They can't!' Donald spoke more fiercely than he had intended. 'The priest wouldn't give any heed to magic and witchery. He thinks well of you, too.'

'Maybe. But he has to think of all the souls in his care. It depends which way they fall, whether they lean to the Bains or to us. We'll see. And there are some, like the ones who still think I'm a stranger, who might find Mairhi's ways a little hard to swallow.' She smiled, a little rueful. 'We'll just have to wait and see. But you know one thing, Donald?'

'What's that, then?'

'You could have let them do what they liked with her. You could have stood back. But you didn't.'

It had never occurred to him, not for a moment; but he saw now what she meant. Not so long ago, it might have seemed an easy way out. He could hardly make sense of the person he had been then; it seemed like a thousand years ago.

'Of course not,' he said. 'I've to look after all of us, now.'

Bridie smiled again. 'You did well,' she said.

16

Donald was halfway down to the shore when he heard his mother's voice hailing him from the top of the path. He looked up and back, to see her on the skyline above, one arm raised, beckoning. All he wanted was to keep walking, but after a long moment he turned around and trudged back to the house. Bridie and Mairhi were both by the gate, wrapped in shawls and laden with baskets, waiting for him.

'I thought I'd see to the pots along the strand—' he began,

But Bridie cut across him. 'No skulking off today, my lad! We'll need to face this down before the story grows any bigger and folk have time to get together and make their judgments. We're all going to call on Auntie Annie. And if we happen to meet anybody else along the way, so much the better. Most of the men will be out on a day like this, but you'll catch them in the bar later, or maybe tomorrow. And I'll make sure to talk to as many of the women as I can in the next day or so.'

'But I never go to the bar—' Donald began, and once again she cut him off.

'There's a first time for everything! You need to be seen about, and you need to hold your head up. Here's Hector already at his gate.' She raised her voice. 'Good morning to you, Hector! It's a fine day for gardening.'

Hector nodded at them. 'Bridie, Donald.' He waited until they were almost past, and then said, as if to the wind, 'I hear there's been mischief afoot.'

Bridie turned to face him. 'And what kind of mischief would that be, Hector? Has the fox been after your chickens again?'

The old man snorted. 'You know right well what I mean, Bridie McFarlane. I've always thought there was something uncanny about yonder lassie, and from what I hear, I'm not far wrong. Can you look me in the eye and tell me it was natural, what she did?' Bent as he was, he looked up at Bridie from under his shaggy eyebrows. His eyes glittered.

'And what exactly do you imagine she did, Hector?'

'I've heard the tale! The Bain boy almost drowned last night, on dry land with his brothers by him. And this morning he won't leave his bed; they've had to go out without him, and folk are saying he'll maybe never be fit to work the boats again.' His eyes darted sideways at Donald. 'You know what that means, when a man can't pull his weight.'

Donald said nothing. He was used to this kind of talk. But Aly Bain had a wife and children; what would become of them? His mother was speaking again.

'It won't come to that; he'll be right as rain in a day or two. He's never had much of a head for drink, and from what I hear, he's not much loss to the crew either. I wouldn't like to say what he did to our Mairhi, but he went too far and frightened himself, is all that happened to him. Maybe he'll stay away from the bar in future, and keep his hands to himself as well. Now, we must be on our way. Good day to you, Hector.'

She was off down the path before he could muster a reply, with Donald and Mairhi trailing behind her. Donald looked back as they turned the corner, to see the old man still standing at his gate, looking after them. He raised a hand, but Hector did not wave back.

'Silly old fool!' said Bridie as he caught her up, but she was wiping her eyes with the corner of her shawl. 'Twenty years we've been neighbours, and he still thinks there's some dark, foreign secret I'm hiding. But it's not Hector we need to worry about; no-one pays him any mind. Aly Bain's not well liked, but his family will feel bound to stand by him. Ah, now we'll see.'

They were coming down to the harbour, and there were a few children about, playing tag among the boxes and baskets. At sight of them, the younger ones shouted a greeting and began to run towards them. Mairhi went to meet them, smiling; she loved to watch them at play, or even to join in, and never minded if they teased her for being halfwitted. But before they reached her, one of the older boys caught up. 'Come back here!' he yelled, and yanked the nearest one by the hair, so hard that the child fell in a heap and began to bawl. 'You stay away from us!' he shouted at Mairhi.

She had bent to pick up a little girl who had taken a tumble, and was setting her to rights. The boy darted at her and dragged the child away, slapping her for good measure. 'Don't you touch her! You leave us be!'

Mairhi stood up slowly, her smile fading. She was staring at the boy – a puzzled, hurt look that Donald had never seen on her face before. He laid a hand on her arm. 'Come away now,' he began, but the boy set up a screeching as he scrambled away.

'She tried to witch me, she gave me the eye!'

Some of the women had come to their doors now. One or two ran to gather up their children, while others just stood, watching.

'That's enough!' said Bridie, in a voice that carried clear down to the harbour. 'Shame on you, James Macdonald! You're too old to be making such a fuss about nothing. No harm's been done, and none will be, if we all pay less heed to lies and gossip and get on with our business.' She turned around, including all the onlookers, and then swept on down the street. Donald and Mairhi followed in her wake, and silence lay behind them.

17

Auntie Annie's cottage was near the bottom, just above the harbour, and all eyes were on them as Bridie reached the door. Auntie Annie stood there already, holding it ajar. She touched Bridie's arm. 'I've got company inside,' she said in a low voice. 'Bad news travels fast.'

Mrs Mackay was seated by the fire, teacup in hand. She stared at them all as they came in.

'Good morning to you!' said Bridie brightly. 'You're out early today. Have your knees been easier with the new ointment I made you?'

'Bridie Macfarlane, I'm surprised at you,' said the old woman. 'Bringing that creature into the village as though you were proud of what she's done.'

'Now why don't I make some fresh tea,' said Auntie Annie, 'and we can all sit down and let Donald here tell us exactly what did happen. He was there, after all, and we know better than to pay much heed to what men say when they're in their cups, now don't we?' She took down the kettle, and Donald went to fill it for her, but his mother stopped him.

'I'll see to that,' she said. 'You stay by Mairhi.' She filled the kettle and hung it over the fire to boil, and then began to set out fresh cups and cut slices of the cake she had brought in her basket.

Donald sat down and took Mairhi's hand, but she would not look at him. Mrs Mackay simply sat and watched them, saying nothing. The silence grew heavier, until he could not bear it any longer.

'I'll tell you what happened,' he said suddenly, startling everyone. 'Aly Bain grabbed her, and the other two held me back, and I know he's your nephew and all, but he had no business doing what he did. And then ... and then he choked and fell down, and then he was sick, and we came away. And that's about the size of it.'

'Well,' said Auntie Annie, 'you don't surprise me one bit. It's not the first time he's been in trouble for putting his hands where they're not wanted. Drunk or sober, he's old enough to know better, wouldn't you say, Peggy?'

Mrs Mackay had not taken her eyes off Mairhi. 'I'd say you're trying to take me for a fool,' she said. 'There's something not right about her. She doesn't behave as a young lassie should. She doesn't speak, but she knows a lot more than she lets on. Things that shouldn't be known, maybe. She put the mortal terror into Aly Bain. Who knows what else she might do, the next time someone crosses her?'

'Come now, Peggy,' said Aunt Annie mildly. 'She didn't put anything into his head that wasn't there already. It'd be a foolish fisherman that didn't think about going overboard and about the souls that have been lost before. It's just that most men know how to hold their tongues and get on with it.'

'It's true,' said Donald. 'I saw their faces. We all have those thoughts, every one of us.' He spoke from the new certainty that had come to him the night before, and knew that none of them could gainsay him.

'That's as may be,' said Mrs Mackay at length. 'But why would those thoughts come to him just then? I'll grant you, he may have been taking liberties – and you should have known better, Donald Macfarlane, than to take a lass in her condition to the bar—'

'I didn't—' Donald began, but she carried on relentlessly.

'—but even so, she called it out of him, somehow. And that's not right. You'd no business bringing such a creature among us, whatever she may be. You should take her back where you found her.' She leaned forward and thumped her stick on the floor, glaring at Donald.

He dared not glance at his mother or at Mairhi. Was it possible, somehow, that she knew?

'I mind well,' said Bridie, 'how some folks said John should never have brought me here. She'll never take to the life, they said; she should go back to her own kind. But I learned, and I stayed, and maybe I've brought something new to this village. I hope I've done some good, here and there. You can't keep everything the same; and even if you turned away all the strangers, what would you do with someone like James Wallace, who's not been right in the head since his accident, or a child that's slow-witted, or anybody that's got too old or frail to do the work they used to do? You can't turn them away, no-one would think of it. We all look out for each other. That's how things are. And if you can think of a better way to manage, I'd like to hear it.'

'That's well said, Bridie,' said Auntie Annie. 'Oh! The tears I shed when I was newly wed, and people mocked me for not knowing one end of a fishing boat from the other.' She glanced at Mrs Mackay, whose eyes were now firmly fixed on her teacup, and then gave Donald the merest quiver of a wink. 'But I got over it. And so will your nephew. Maybe he'll learn something, you never know.'

Mrs Mackay began to rise from her chair, taking her time to arrange her shawl and her stick. 'Well, Annie, I can see your mind's made up. I'll leave you be. Bridie, Donald, good day to you.' Like Hector, she did not acknowledge Mairhi, or even look at her.

Once Auntie Annie had seen her out of the door, she sank back into her chair. 'Well,' she said, 'you've probably faced the worst of it now, at least from the women. My, but she was a holy terror when we were young; you've no idea. She's got soft in her old age. But here' – and she got up again, went to Mairhi and took both her hands – 'don't you worry, my dear. This storm will blow itself out; they always do. Some folks will always be unkind, but you'll learn how to deal with them without scaring them half out of their wits. Ask Donald here; though I wouldn't always recommend his methods, either. Now then, we'll say no more about it. I hear you'll be out on the boat a bit more, Donald. It's a comfort to your uncle, believe you me. And your father would have been proud of you lately, never doubt it.'

She had kept hold of Mairhi's hands while she talked, giving them a little shake now and then for emphasis. Now, as she moved to go back to her chair, Mairhi stood up and took her in her arms. It was hard to tell who was comforting whom; when they drew apart, both women looked close to tears. Auntie Annie had a little, crooked smile. 'That's the way, lass,' she said softly.

18

They made their way home by a roundabout route. 'I think we've had enough company for one day,' said Bridie, despite what she had said when they set out. Donald was not about to disagree. The tide was low, so they took a path along the strand, keeping an eye out for salvage.

They walked in silence for a while, each thinking their own thoughts, and then Bridie said, 'I never knew that Auntie Annie was a stranger here. She's always been kind to me, but she never mentioned it before. I wonder where she grew up. You don't think, when you're young, about older folk having lives before you came along. And later, I suppose you just take things for granted.'

'I suppose,' said Donald, who had always done exactly that, until now. 'Was it very hard for you here, at first?'

'Oh, well, you know. You get over it, as Auntie Annie said. They didn't dare go too far, not then. John's father was very well respected, and the family stood up for me, mostly. The hardest time was later, after John went. The family was all for moving us in with them. I put my foot down, and a lot of people, like Mrs Mackay for one, thought I should either do as I was bid or go back to Kilbeag with my father. A woman living on her own, that's a tricky thing. Other women don't like it. But the men, now, that's a different story. You'd be amazed how many of them lost their way in the fog that year and ended up at my door.'

'What on earth do you mean? You never … surely you never…' Donald could not bear to go on; such a thing had never occurred to him. Bridie was watching him narrowly.

'Of course I didn't! That'd be a sure way to get myself turned out, and serve me right! No. I loved your father, never doubt it. And I had you to think of. Mind you, some of them offered to make an honest woman of me. Even your Uncle Hugh; he'd lost his wife before John and I were married, and he always had a soft spot for me. Still does,

I think.' She laughed suddenly, a bright, clear, carefree sound, like the sun coming out. 'Donald, your face! You look as though you'd stolen the cream and got the whey instead!'

He tried to mask his outrage, gave it up and grinned at her. 'I suppose I asked for that! Everyone's got secrets, haven't they? Just because they seem fine from outside doesn't mean a thing. And there was me thinking I was the only one.'

His mother took his arm, so that he had to stop and turn to face her. Mairhi stopped too, looking from one to the other. 'You're one of us, Donald, and you always have been. And so is our Mairhi, whatever folks may say.' She reached out and took Mairhi's hand. 'It was a blessing, the day you came to us, lass. Don't you forget it.'

Mairhi smiled, but the solemnity of the moment was too much for her. She whirled around and took off down the beach, as usual forgetting to gather her skirts as she ran. Donald started after her. He heard his mother call, 'Be careful on those stones!' And then the only sounds were the surf breaking on the rocks a few yards away, the cry of gulls on the wind and his own feet crunching on pebbles. He slowed as he got nearer to the water, below the tideline, where the rocks were slimed with weed and studded with limpets. Mairhi was still some way ahead, picking her way around the base of the low cliffs that began here and ran on below their own house and northward for some miles. No hurry, now; he stopped to turn over a rotten piece of driftwood, too sodden to burn, but there were some drier pieces higher up. By the time he straightened up again, she had turned the corner around the first headland and was out of sight. Burdened with the slippery spars, he followed slowly.

He rounded the bluff and could not see her at first, just the empty strand, wider here, and the tumble of boulders at the water's edge. Then there was movement among the boulders, a splash as something slid into the sea. One gone, but there were still two – no, three, there in the lee of the rocks. Grey seals, her own kind. She was squatting not two yards from them; he could see her bent head and her outstretched arm.

19

As quietly as he could, Donald set down his load of wood. He was about to move forward when he felt a hand on his arm. Bridie had caught up with him.

'Leave her be,' she said in a low voice. 'It was bound to come, sooner or later. We can't always be watching her.'

'But they might hurt her!' Though that was not really what he feared.

'I think they'd have done it already. Or, more likely, if we get too close and panic them. Besides, it's none of our business.'

He stared at her, but she would not look at him. 'Is it not? What if she tries to go with them? Or they turn her against us? Or—'

'Hush, Donald. Keep your voice down. If she could go, she'd have gone long since. And they're her family; she's not just going to forget them, now, is she? You'll have to make your peace with that.'

He felt silenced, shamed, in the wrong once again. He had thought – had hoped – that maybe she might just forget, somehow. As ever, his mother had seen straight through him. That had always been a comfort in the past, a net to catch him when he fell. He shook off her hand, moved away a little. Below them, the seals were raising their heads to look at Mairhi. As he watched, she straightened up, smoothing out her dress, and stood still for a long moment. Then she turned and went on her way along the strand, not looking back.

Donald was beginning to move off when Bridie stopped him again. He pulled away, but she hissed, 'Wait!' and something in the intensity of her voice made him pause. As he glanced at her, she made a little upward gesture with her eyes, and put a finger to her lips. There, on the edge of the cliff, maybe thirty yards above them, someone was standing. He could not make out whether it was a man or a woman, and even as he looked, the figure drew back and was gone.

They both stood stock still, as though by not moving, not going on, they could somehow undo the moment. At last Donald said, 'Dear God! How much do you think they saw?'

Bridie shook her head. 'All of it, we'll have to suppose. It's what they think they saw that counts. A simple-minded lass going too close to the seals before we could stop her, or … something else. But there's nothing we can do about it now. I've had enough, Donald. Let's go home.'

By the time they caught up with her, Mairhi had salvage of her own to show them: shells, a piece of sea-glass, an empty crab claw. Her face as she displayed her treasures was as open as ever; hiding nothing, hiding everything. Donald could not bring himself to ask what had passed between her and the seals, and she could not have told him anyway. It was her business, and hers alone.

∵

In the days that followed, Donald was reluctant to let Mairhi or his mother out of his sight, but Bridie made him go about his business as usual, and every day she and Mairhi went off to the village or to the shieling, spending time with the other women.

'Oh, some were a bit fearful at first,' she told him one evening, 'but the younger ones seem inclined to take Mairhi's part. They're not too bothered about Aly Bain; he's needed teaching a lesson since he was a bairn. Jessie hasn't shown her face, though. She sends the older girl out when she needs anything. I'm guessing she'll take the brunt of it, poor woman.'

After the greeting they'd had in the village, Donald guessed that Bridie was making the best of things. Well, that was her way. His way was to steer clear of people as much as he could, going to the village only when he was sure the men would be out at sea. He did not go to the bar, and Bridie did not try to force the issue.

It seemed as time went by that perhaps she was right, and folk would think no more about what had happened to Aly Bain. As for the figure on the clifftop, whoever it was seemed to be keeping their own counsel. Donald began to feel easier – just a little – though his heart still leaped when he saw Bridie and Mairhi coming home along the cliff path. He, who had always fought shy of other people, now wanted only to gather them close and keep them safe. Of his own safety, he never thought at all.

20

The arm that snaked around his throat, crushing it and cutting off his wind, caught him completely by surprise. He dropped the basket he'd just been lifting, ready to climb the cliff path up to the house. His arms went up, and the blow to his stomach drove the breath right out of him and sent him to his knees. He hardly had time to register the dark shapes closing in; he keeled over, gasping for air, almost not feeling the boots connecting with his back, his legs, his unprotected head. Something crunched in his back, and then came a flare of bright agony as someone stamped hard on his left knee. There was shouting, but the voices buffeted him like a storm wind, without meaning.

Even when the breath finally came searing back into his lungs, he stayed curled over, trying to shield his face. Under his cheek, blood mingled with sand and seawater. He tasted grit and hot metal, felt the stones bite as his body was driven into them, and still tried to lie as limp and unresisting as seaweed. Let them think he was unconscious, or too cowardly to fight back. Schoolyard tactics; Donald had learned that it was over all the sooner if he gave them no sport, though the beatings then had never been as bad as this.

But he began now to be able to make out their voices. Three, maybe four. Euan and Andrew Bain, of course, and their friend James Wallace, who always tagged along. The fourth was unfamiliar, the reedy pitch of a very young man, now shrill with excitement, egging on the others from a little distance. Donald risked a glance from between his laced fingers, but could see nothing beyond the legs of those close around him. They were tiring now, or their blood was cooling. They drew back a little, watching to see what he would do.

'Get up, Macfarlane!' That was Andrew, breathing heavily.

'He's not moving. Maybe you've killed him!' The young voice, closer now, bending low. Donald did not move.

'Don't talk daft, Fergus.' That was James Wallace, sounding rattled. Fergus was Campbell Callum's boy; he had crewed with them for the first time last autumn, and Donald remembered his white, scared face as they cleared the harbour and the first real waves hit them. He had thrown up, not once but many times. When they'd unloaded the catch, Hugh, meaning to be kind, had said, 'You'll get used to it soon enough.' But as he turned away Donald had seen the look of miserable hatred in the boy's eyes. He did not know what he himself might have done to earn Fergus's enmity; they had scarcely exchanged more than a word or two.

But now Euan was speaking. 'He's not dead, you fool,' he said. He nudged at Donald with the toe of his boot. 'But maybe that's enough for now. He'll not forget in a hurry.' He leaned down, and his voice came again, close to Donald's ear. 'Mind how you go, Macfarlane. We'll be watching.'

'We'd best move along before someone comes,' said James, already some way off, eager to be gone.

Somewhere near by, Andrew's laugh rang out, and then his voice, slow and deep. 'Lost your pluck, James? He knows who we are, all right. It's a bit late to be hiding yourself now.' They were moving off as they spoke, along the strand towards the village.

Donald began to uncurl, just a little. His moving fingers found blood in his hair, and then he cried out as his hand was ground into the shingle by a heavy boot. Fergus let out a shrill yelp of laughter as he danced back out of range and hurried to join the men.

Donald did not move again until the sound of their boots had been completely swallowed up by the wind and the surf. Even then, he only took stock of what he could see. The dark hulk of his boat, drawn well up and secured for the night; he would have heard if they had damaged it, but he breathed easier knowing that it was safe. Twisting his head a little, he could see the basket, still upright. They must have moved it aside to get at him, but they had not harmed or stolen his catch, either. Good fishermen, first and last. He grinned, despite himself, then gasped aloud as the pain came surging back. It swept him into the dark, and when he came to himself again he could not tell how much time had passed.

Inch by inch, he made his body move. His left hand a mangled mess, part numb and part burning. His back bruised and bloody, his shirt torn and something badly amiss with his left leg. It did not want to straighten, would take no weight. But his head seemed whole apart from two or three lumps, growing bigger even as he explored them with the fingers of his right hand. Ribs bruised, probably cracked, but that was nothing out of the ordinary; every man took injuries of that sort from time to time. They would heal, though not quite as they had been.

He sat up. It took a long time, each movement finding new sources of pain. Awkwardly, one-handed, he eased himself over to the boat, reached over the side and freed one of the oars. It would make a poor crutch, but it would have to do. He had to get up the path somehow, before his body stiffened too much; a night in the open would likely finish him off.

Even with a good catch to carry, he'd have been home within twenty minutes on any other night. Now, the journey loomed over him like the clifftop, unreachable among the distant stars. No good to think that way. The world shrank down to little patches of sand and stones, giving way to rocks and heather, as he moved, step by agonising step, not looking up.

They found him near the top of the path; he had abandoned the useless oar and half crawled, half dragged himself the rest of the way. He must have shouted, seeing the light of the cottage window, though the wind would have thrown his voice away. Bridie told him later that Mairhi, in the act of banking the fire for the night, had looked up suddenly, and had run out into the dark, without shawl or lantern, leaving the door wide.

He knew only that she was there at his side, crooning over him the way he'd heard her with the calf when it was scouring, and laying her hands flat on his body, here, and here, and here. Where she touched, cool water flowed to ease the burning. The wind died to a whisper, and the sea rocked him softly, sweetly, all its many colours sparkling in the sun. He was hardly aware of them both, supporting him for the last few steps, laying him face down on the bed, and easing off his clothes to clean and salve his injuries. Donald floated, far from land and completely without fear, and the waves caressed him and bore him up. He thought, *I never knew it could be like this*, and then that thought too drifted away on the gentle tide.

'So, how is he doing?' Someone was speaking not far away. A slow, deep voice – not one he feared, but one you'd pause before crossing. Donald kept his eyes closed and lay still. Moving was not a pleasant experience just now.

'Oh, he'll live.' That was his mother. 'Some broken ribs and a twisted knee, and a lot of bumps and bruises, but he'll mend, given time.' Her voice sounded muffled.

Donald opened his eyes a crack and saw that he was lying in the big bed; they must have brought him in here when they got him back to the cottage. The door was not quite shut. Bridie and Hugh – of course, the voice that had woken him was his Uncle Hugh's – were standing just beyond it, by the hearth in the main room.

'Does he know who did it?'

'He hasn't said much yet. But it's not hard to guess, is it?'

'Well, now,' said Hugh, 'the Bain boys are cock-a-hoop this morning, and James Wallace has a look to him like a whipped mongrel. But Callum Campbell's boy is sticking to them like a burr, and that's a thing I don't understand. He's even crewed with them in Aly's place, though he'll be no great catch if I know anything about it. I've no idea what his quarrel with Donald might be. Maybe you can tell me?'

Bridie laughed. 'I see where Donald gets it from! Think about it for a minute, Hugh. How long has Callum been in your crew?'

'Thirteen years, on and off, though more off than on lately.' Donald could hear the frown in Hugh's voice. 'And the boy, Fergus; he's been with us a few times, though he's neither use nor ornament. Donald seemed to get on with him all right, as much as he ever does. But, you know, Donald's really put his mind to it lately, no doubt about it. There've been times when I've despaired of him, but he's getting to be a good crewman, after all.'

'And there you have it! You've made no secret of your hopes for him, I'm guessing. Callum thought the boat might come to him, did he not? And if it went to Callum, then in time it would come to Fergus.'

Hugh snorted. 'He'll never make much of a fisherman, let alone a captain.'

'What difference does that make? He'll have had the thought of it, the standing it would give him. No matter if he doesn't take to the fishing. He's just a lad, he wouldn't think of that. And now it looks as though you're minded to pass it on to Donald, after all. Do you not think that might stick in Callum's throat, just a bit? Maybe the whisky helps to wash it down a little. But there's young Fergus, watching. He's got to go to sea whether he likes it or not, unless he leaves here altogether. Do you see, now?'

'Dear God, Bridie, how can I possibly do right by everybody? It's simple on the boat; you just do what you have to do. And Callum's not the man he was. He knows it, too.'

'And so does his son, most likely. But who is he going to take it out on? Not his father, and not you. It's the weaker ones who feel the sharp end of it. I wouldn't be in his mother's shoes right now. And that's why he hates Donald, you can count on it. This chance came along, and he jumped at it.'

There was the sound of a chair scraping as he drew it closer to the fire, and then a deep sigh from Hugh. 'So what am I to do? I wouldn't hand the boat on to Callum now, in any case. And I've always hoped Donald would come to it in the end, even when he seemed dead set against it.'

'You're a patient man, Hugh. I wouldn't have blamed you if you'd given up on him, the way he was. There were plenty of others who did.'

'Now, Bridie. The poor lad was so lost after John died. What else would I do? He's as good as a son to me. And you know, whatever folks may say about Mairhi, I think this marriage will be the making of him.'

Donald, who had been quietly flexing his fingers, working through his body and testing for the pain that waited in ambush, stopped moving and tried to stop breathing altogether as he listened.

Bridie said softly, 'You're right. But what if they stop the wedding? I don't know what he'll do then. She's good for him, you can see that, but she frightens people, even when she means no harm.'

'Not the younger children. Nor the beasts. It's only those whose heads are full of how things ought to be.'

'You've noticed that?'

Hugh laughed. 'I do notice things, Bridie, whatever you may think. And so does Donald, these days. I should have got him a dog when he was younger, something of his own to look after. Remember how he nursed that crow he found, with the broken wing? He should have had something that would look up to him, and not be off and away as soon as it could. And now there's Mairhi, and soon enough there'll be the bairn. It's good for him.'

'I know. John would have been proud to see him now.'

'We're all proud, Bridie. But will you not think again? If you come up to us at the shieling, there'll be protection for you when Donald's away. And Mairhi's strange ways won't stand out so much. I'd be easier in my mind, knowing you were there. She'd have help with the child when it comes, too, in case she doesn't care for it too well.'

'Whyever shouldn't she? You've seen how she is with the little ones. I think she'll be a fine mother, even if she never does learn to darn properly! And I'm grateful to you, Hugh, but no. We'll stay here and weather this storm like all the others. Hiding away would just make them think we have something to be scared about.'

Hugh laughed again, quietly, as though to himself. 'And if he gets his lack of wits from his father's side, then I know where his stubborn streak comes from!'

Donald heard his mother laugh too, then. 'You know I didn't mean it like that!'

'Well. But I wish you'd lay aside your pride for once, and let us look after you. It worries me; you're alone so much.'

'It's not us you should be worrying about. Why do you think they went after Donald? They respect me, most of them, and they're frightened of Mairhi now. It's Donald you should be keeping close to you. Take him up to the shieling when he's fit to walk, and let him stay there until the wedding. You can keep him busy, and they won't touch him under your roof.'

Donald had heard enough. He made to sit up, forgetting for a moment and gasping aloud at the pain. Hugh had begun to speak, but there was the sudden rasp of chairs on the stone hearth, and then they were both beside him, Hugh's strong arm at his back while Bridie held a cup of water for him.

'Where's Mairhi?' he said as soon as he could speak. 'Is she all right?'

'She's with Catriona, learning to wash clothes, or so Catriona would like to think,' said Hugh. 'How are you feeling, lad?'

'I'll mend,' said Donald. He tried to sit up again, coughed, and fire flared in his chest. For a few moments, he could not speak at all. He was aware of Hugh's steadying hand on his shoulder, but he wanted to shake it off, to twist away from all of it: their concern; their guessing or knowledge of his feelings, when he did not even know them himself. He remembered the crow, remembered splinting its wing; the greasy feel of its feathers as he held it close; the black sidelong eye that avoided his gaze. He had tended it, fed it, even slept beside it in the barn when his mother refused to have it in the house. He remembered opening the barn door one morning and starting back as it clattered out and away without a backward look.

Hugh was speaking again. With an effort, Donald made himself hear the words.

'You took quite a beating there. Do you remember what happened?'

'Some. They just meant to warn me, that's all. Did you bring up the catch?'

'Never mind about that now,' said Bridie. 'They could have killed you!' His mother was not really angry with him, he knew that, but her words battered at him. He could not look at her face, at her tears.

'I've taken worse,' he lied. It hurt to breathe, to move at all. He did not remember his thoughts after Mairhi had found him, only the blessed ease of her presence. He wanted her now, wanted them to let him be, to find again that amazing place of safety she had shown him.

'I heard you talking,' he said abruptly. 'And I'll not leave them here alone, Uncle Hugh. I'll come up before the wedding, the way we said, but that's all. Thanks for the offer, but we'll be fine.'

'A lot of good you'll be right now, if there's any trouble. Well, I'll leave one of the dogs with you, at any rate.'

'That would be a comfort, Hugh,' said Bridie, and Donald knew, the way he had begun to know things these days, that the comfort would be more for Hugh than for herself. But he had not known about Fergus Campbell. He laid that aside, to think about later.

'What are they saying, down in the village?' he asked his uncle. 'Do they really mean to stop the wedding?'

Hugh did not reply directly. He was silent a moment, and then he said, 'If I were you, I'd speak to Father Finian before too many others get to him. You need to set his mind at rest. Once the wedding's over, folks will settle down to it, but if he decides it can't go ahead, things could get very difficult.'

'I'll go this afternoon,' said Bridie. 'Donald won't be going anywhere for a while.'

Hugh hesitated, then said, 'Well, I suppose he'll be safe enough now. They've done what they wanted to do.'

'But we can't know that.' Bridie got up from the bed, took a step or two, and stopped. She was wringing her hands; Donald could hardly remember seeing her so agitated. 'Maybe they'll be back to finish the job!'

He tried to sit up further, and pain shot through him again. More irritably than he meant, he said, 'Listen. If they'd wanted to kill me they'd have done it there and then. They left the boat and the catch alone. It was a warning; they said so. And that's about the size of it.'

'Well,' said Hugh again, 'I hope you're right, at that. But a word with the priest wouldn't go amiss in any case. I'll be on my way.' He got up and went through to the main room, then reappeared in the doorway. 'And here I'm forgetting what I set out to bring you in the first place, with all this business. See what I've got for you, Donald.' He laid a bundle on the bed – a parcel wrapped in oiled cloth. 'Take a look,' he said, smiling now, pleased with his gift. 'I traded for them. They're not new, but if you keep them lubricated they'll see you through a winter or two and save your hands on the ropes.' Donald was unwrapping the parcel as Hugh spoke. He lifted away the last layer of cloth. They lay on the counterpane like the paws of some huge, dead beast: gloves, or gauntlets, rather, made from cured sealskin.

22

Donald jerked back, then cried out at the wrenching pain. He stared at the gloves and his gorge rose so that he retched suddenly, though there was nothing in his stomach to bring up. Behind Hugh, Bridie had gone white as milk. Hugh's smile vanished; he looked from one to the other, utterly bewildered. Into the long silence came the clamour of the dogs outside, and Catriona's voice over the top. 'Get down, Tam! Jack! We're wet enough as it is. Go on with you!'

'Oh God, the girls are coming in!' Bridie snatched up the gloves, bundling them back into their wrapping. She looked around wildly for somewhere to hide them, but there was nowhere, just the chest where they all kept their spare clothes, and Hugh stood solidly in the way.

'Uncle Hugh,' said Donald urgently, 'could you keep them at the boat for me? That's where I'll be needing them, and ... well, it's better Mairhi doesn't see them. She has a ... a fondness for the seals, and it might upset her. Would you mind? It's a good gift, really, I'll be glad of them.' He was talking too much; but no-one else seemed to be able to say anything.

After a long moment, Hugh nodded. 'I've seen her with that toy of hers. She sings to it sometimes.' He sounded as though he were talking to himself, telling a story that grew as it went on. 'She's had enough upsets for a while; so have we all. I'll put them by for you.' He went to take the bundle from Bridie, but she still clutched it to her chest. 'Give it here, now, I'll take them away.'

'Where did you get them?' Bridie stared at him, wild-eyed. She looked half mad.

'I told you, I traded for them. A fellow I met at market, from down the coast. They had a seal drowned in a net. He cured the hide himself; he's done a good job. Bridie, you'll have to let go if you want me to take them.'

Bridie thrust the bundle at him as though it had stung her. Empty-handed, she sank onto the bed. 'Oh, Hugh. I'm sorry. What you must think? They gave me a start, that's all. You're right, we've all had enough upsets for one day.'

Hugh might have replied, but just then Catriona came in with Mairhi in tow. 'Look at the state of us, we're wet through! We might as well have got in the water and be done with it; but there's most of the blood out of those sheets, Auntie Bridie, though I think Donald's shirt is past saving. Heavens, Donald, you'd think you were back in the schoolyard, only you didn't have me to come to your rescue this time. You wait till I see Andrew Bain, I'll give him a tongue-lashing he won't forget in a hurry! Boys never grow up, Mairhi, that's one thing you'll learn soon enough. Now, you'll have to change your dress before you catch your death of cold, but first we'd better spread out the washing on the bushes, or it won't dry before the rain comes.' She was half out of the door again, still talking, and Mairhi followed like a lamb after its mother. 'I'd better go with them,' muttered Bridie, and was gone before the silence could flow back.

'She's had a scare,' said Donald. 'She's not herself.' That was what you were supposed to say, wasn't it? He was not himself either, or not the self he was used to. There was his strong, resourceful mother lost for words, and he, Donald, the tongue-tied, slow-witted, graceless boy, coming up with a quick excuse to save the situation. At least, he hoped he had.

'Now your mother's out of the way, you can tell me straight, Donald,' said Hugh. 'Do you really think they only meant to give you a scare, or were you just saying that for her ears?'

'It's what they said,' said Donald, though he could not really remember now. 'They were paying me back for what happened to Aly.'

Hugh frowned. 'And that's another thing I've never got to the bottom of. What did happen, exactly?'

'Do you want to know the truth, Uncle Hugh? I don't know. One minute he was pestering her, and the next he was coughing his guts up and babbling about drowning. Then he pointed the finger at her, and that was about it. It looked to me like he'd taken too much drink, gone too far and then his own bad conscience did the rest.' *Listen to yourself*, he thought in wonder. *Who'd have thought you had it in you?*

'Knowing Aly Bain, I'd say you weren't too wide of the mark. But Donald, listen. I stand by my family. If you tell me that there's nothing uncanny about your lass, then I'll believe you. Can you do that?'

Donald took a deep breath, or as deep as he could manage. 'I can't say that for sure. But I don't believe she'd set out to harm anybody unless they hurt her first, and that's the truth.'

Hugh was looking at him intently. 'Well, I suppose that'll have to do,' he said. 'There's plenty of folk I couldn't say that about, though they might be canny enough. And Donald…' He paused, choosing his words. 'You do want this marriage, don't you? You're not being pushed into it by your mother? I know how she can be. If this is the right thing for you, then I'm with you all the way. I haven't always looked out for you as well as I might, but things will be different now, I promise. I've seen the way you are with Mairhi, and the way she is with you, and I still can't make it out, Donald. What's brought the two of you together? But if you can tell me this is what you really want, then I'll hold my peace and give you my blessing. Can you do that?'

Donald glanced up at him, still holding that terrible bundle, and could not meet his eye. 'It's what I want, Uncle Hugh,' he said hoarsely. 'I'll be a father soon, and I've sworn to care for her and for the child.'

Hugh looked down at the bundle in his hands, as though he had forgotten it was there. 'Well, there are worse reasons for being wed,' he said. 'And now, lad, you look all in. Get some rest; I'll come over again tomorrow.'

23

Left alone, Donald could barely summon up the will to ease himself back down onto the wide bed. His head ached, and he could not even remember what he was supposed to be worrying about. Half sitting, half lying, he fell into an uneasy sleep. When he woke, the shadows had shifted in the room, and Mairhi was sitting on the edge of the bed, watching him. For a long moment, they simply looked at each other. It seemed she might go on that way forever, but Donald could not bear it.

'Would you get me a drink of water, lass?' While she was gone he shifted about, trying to get comfortable, trying to clear the fog in his head. She gave him the cup, watched while he drank.

'What is it, Mairhi? Where's mother?'

She lifted her shoulders a little – a gesture learned from Catriona, though his cousin's shrugs were much more emphatic.

'Maybe she's gone to see Father Finian already. How long have I slept?' It was easy to talk on when he was with her; not that he expected an answer – his words falling like stones into the bottomless well of her silence. 'Mairhi' – he caught at her hand, and then lost his train of thought. 'Look at your skin now. It's getting stronger, isn't it? No new blisters here on your arm. Looks better than mine!' He laid his own forearm against hers, turned it over to show the thickened parts, like old lichen, where it had inflamed and settled again and again over the years. 'I don't think mine will ever heal properly, but maybe yours will, if you don't scratch at it. See here, you can rub it with the backs of your nails to soothe the itch.' He almost said, *I could do with stepping out of my skin the way you did*, but the image of the sealhide gloves, lying just where her hands were resting now, stopped him in time. There were so many thoughts that could not be spoken, after all. 'You helped me, lass,' he said instead. 'I'll be up and about again soon, and next time someone tries to hurt you, you come to me before you do anything back to them. Can you do that?'

He was still holding her hand, and perhaps he squeezed it as he spoke, for she nodded as though she were agreeing. How could he tell? He looked up, then grinned and said, 'And between you and me, it was a grand thing you did what you did! Worth a few cuts and bruises, any time. But don't tell mother I said so!' It was strange. When he was younger and Bridie had tried to fight his battles for him, he had wanted to die of shame, though he would not stand up for himself. Now, although he knew Mairhi had been fighting her own battle, he felt that he had gained an ally; that in some strange way, the beating he had just endured was a kind of victory. 'Just go easy next time,' he said. 'Don't waste it on small fry like Aly Bain.'

He did not really care whether she understood or not, in the end. Seeing Aly like that, hearing him pour out his terrors onto the wet cobbles for everyone to see, had changed something in him. It hadn't settled yet, it was still new and uncertain, but the prospect of facing the village in his bruised and battered state did not make him want to slink away into the hills as once it would have. Almost, he looked forward to it, though he was not inclined to wonder why that might be. Instead, he said, 'Help me up, would you? I need to see if I can walk at all now.' He knew well enough that it would be hopeless, that his injured leg would buckle as soon as he tried to put weight on it, but he wanted Mairhi close to him; there was something marvellous, just out of reach of his questing mind, that she had given him when she came to his rescue, and he hungered for it. Now, though, there was none of that, just her warm and solid presence at his side.

He kept his arm around her after he had collapsed back onto the bed, and she did not pull away. They were sitting like that, leaning companionably against each other, when Bridie came in.

'It's too early in the year yet for some of the things I need,' she said, 'but I've got some birch bark and some juniper to help the healing.'

Donald made a face. Mairhi, watching them both, looked startled and then laughed aloud. He smiled back, then stuck out his tongue and screwed up his eyes, pretending to gag, and she copied him, giggling like a little girl.

Bridie said, 'You'll be glad of them once you've got past the taste.' And then, not quite looking at the place where the gloves had lain, 'Hugh took them away with him?'

'He'll keep them on the boat,' said Donald. 'It's there I'll be needing them, anyway.'

'Good,' said Bridie, and she shuddered. 'I thought for a moment…'

'I know,' said Donald. 'But it can't be, can it? Uncle Hugh said so. Put it out of your mind, now,' and he drew Mairhi closer again.

Bridie gave him a strange look, almost beseeching, and then she left the room to tend to the fire next door. Once again, she had followed his lead, although why he should know better was beyond him. It might be that whoever had taken the precious sealskin was simply waiting for the right moment to bring it out and denounce them all; or it might already be beyond saving, turned into gloves and boots for men to wear. That was what had so horrified Bridie, he thought. For himself, it was his own guilt that had confronted him. And that would happen again and again, every time he put on the gloves in the sight of his uncle and all the crew, as he would have to do. For the first time, he understood that there would be no end to it, no matter what kind of a life he gave her, this woman who was to be his wife…

The sound of the sea was in his ears – a great, slow heartbeat surging through him as he lay on the hot sand, held between sky and water; and the blessed sunshine laid gentle hands on his wounded body…

He drew away, looked down at the top of her bent head. 'I don't deserve it,' he said. 'On you go now, and let me rest.'

24

Father Finian arrived the next day, attended by a straggle of children who hung about just beyond the garden wall. 'At least their parents had more shame than to come too, though no doubt they'd have liked to,' said Bridie, hurrying to secure the barn door before they could get up to any mischief. They had settled Donald by the fire this morning, where he was trying, one-handed, to sort out some fishing tackle.

'What did you say to him?' he asked.

Half out of the door, she called back, 'He's come of his own accord. I never got there yesterday, I'd other things to do.' So that was that.

Donald tried to rise as the priest came in, but the effort was beyond him, and in any case, Father Finian was having none of it. 'Sit down, sit down, for goodness' sake! I'm glad to see you're in one piece at least, but you won't be taking the boat out for a while, hmm?'

'A few days, maybe. There's nothing that won't mend, Father.'

'Indeed. I'm very glad to hear it, but I'm afraid it's not just about broken bones, is it, now? There are a lot of stories flying around, and I need to know what this is all about. You seem to have stirred up quite a bit of ill feeling, young lady.' He shot a glance at Mairhi, who was sitting at the table arranging pebbles. Her collection was growing day by day, and she liked to set them out in changing patterns, which meant nothing to anybody except, presumably, herself. The priest leaned over the table, watched for a few seconds, and said, 'But that one should go there, surely? Like with like, hmm?' He picked up one of the stones and set it down in a different place, stood back and said, 'There, that's better, do you see?'

Donald held his breath. Mairhi stared down at the stones, and then suddenly she swept them all into a heap and began again to lay them out, one by one. She did not look at the priest at all.

'I'm sorry,' said Donald quickly. 'She's got her own ideas. I can't make head nor tail of it either, Father.'

'Ah, well, there we go,' said Father Finian. He seemed lost now, standing there in the middle of the room, rocking from heel to toe and back again. Donald remembered him doing the same thing in the classroom, when some ignorant boy had asked a question too far. *He doesn't know what to do for the best,* he thought. *Do I have to save the situation yet again?*

But this time it was not up to him. Bridie came in, saying, 'They were after chasing the hens in the yard. We'll have to keep an eye out. Mairhi, love, what are you thinking? Draw up a chair for Father Finian and put the kettle on, would you?'

The priest stopped his rocking movement, watching as Mairhi did as she was told. 'That part's true then, at least,' he said. 'She's come on a great deal lately.'

'Part of what?' Bridie faced him squarely. 'I'm sorry, Father, but we've had a lot to bear these last few days.'

'I know, I know, Bridie. I meant nothing by it. Part of what they tell me, is all.'

'And what's the other part?'

'Ah, well now. Tales have a habit of growing in the telling, hmm? Why don't you tell me your side of things? I know you to be a woman of good judgment, and that's more than I can say for some of those whose tongues are wagging. Come and sit down now, Bridie, and let's have this out once and for all.' Father Finian drew the chair that Mairhi had fetched up to the table, and sat down. Absent-mindedly, he picked up one of the stones that lay there, then threw a quick glance at Mairhi and put it down again.

Despite himself, Donald grinned, and was startled when the priest smiled back at him. Before Bridie could say anything, he spoke up. 'She won't hurt you, Father, if that's what you're thinking.'

'Donald, for goodness' sake—' began Bridie, but the priest held up his hand.

'Peace now, peace. It's fine; he saw what went through my mind there, just for a second. And that's why I need you to set me straight. I am not inclined to give weight to stories of witchery and magic, but it's what people believe that leads them to think or do one thing rather than the other, and not what really happened. I cannot have the souls in my care at odds with one another like this. So tell me: not what poor Mairhi may or may not have done, but why folks should be so quick to believe ill of her.'

Donald was impressed. He had not thought Father Finian capable of such insight; but then, before Mairhi, he had not thought much about him at all, other than to keep out of his way as much as he could. So they told him, leaving out only the things that could not be told. Donald glanced at Mairhi from time to time, but she had gone back to her stones, as though she were a child and had no part in it all. He could not tell whether she was listening or not, except that after a while he noticed that from time to time she would grow still, as though waiting for some signal, and then she would move another stone here, or there. Perhaps, he thought, she was telling the story too, in her own way. But he could not spare much attention for that; his mother had come to the end of telling how they had found Donald on the path, and Father Finian was speaking again.

'Thank you, Bridie, and you too, Donald. Your story is a great deal less fantastic than most of the other accounts I've been given, and so of course I am much more inclined to believe it. And I also know, though this is something I would not speak about to anyone whose discretion I could not rely upon, that there are things in this world that do not quite fit. Some people are drawn to them, and sometimes great good can come of it.'

He paused, looking up at the ceiling, just as he did in the pulpit on a Sunday, as though waiting for God to tell him what to say next. 'That is why I have always respected you and your profession, Bridie, and turned a blind eye to the … hmm … the finer details of your craft. And there are other people who are frightened by them, or try to denounce them, or feel a need to take some kind of stand. I am bound to say that, in my opinion, this tends to lead to trouble rather than to anything good.'

Again, the silent appeal to heaven. 'So that leaves a third category of people, among whom I count myself, and they are those who choose to leave well alone. As the appointed shepherd of this little flock, I find myself obliged to turn a blind eye to a great many things, or we would simply not get by. Unlike sheep, people do not always go in the same direction, much as one might wish it. God has given us free will for a reason, after all.'

Donald had not understood a good deal of what had been said, but he saw now that the priest was beginning to get tangled up in his own words; he stopped, took a deep breath, and his ears went bright pink.

Bridie said, 'That's very kind of you, Father,' and got up to pour the tea. She turned her face away, and Donald saw that she was hiding a smile. He thought of the women in the village, dipping their heads respectfully as the priest went by and smirking behind his back; of himself as a small boy among others, daring each other to place a dead mouse on his chair in the church, or knocking on his door and hiding in the bushes. He thought of the men, working on the boats, harvesting the oats or the barley, telling stories in the bar. Father Finian was never among them, though sometimes he was standing at a little distance, watching. Up until about half an hour ago, Donald would have said that, of course, the priest was at the centre of the community. Now he realised that he was looking at a man who was perhaps even more isolated than himself.

'You do a good job, Father.' Where had those words come from? The priest looked away, and his ears grew even pinker. Behind him, Donald heard Bridie cough, scraping the kettle on the hearthstones to cover the noise. Then Mairhi got up and went to stand in front of the priest. When he did not look up, she placed a hand on his bent shoulder and into his lap she put one of her stones. Donald craned to look. It was a large one, a piece of granite shot through with streaks of mica, glittering as Father Finian held it up and turned it about.

'Goodness me! Well, thank you very much, my dear. I wonder what it signifies. Of course you can't tell me, but I shall treasure it none the less. And do you still have your little seal, hmm?'

'She keeps it always by her,' said Bridie, as Mairhi's hand went to her pocket, and she drew back, wide-eyed.

'No, no, I don't want it back! It's yours to keep. Fair exchange, hmm?' And Father Finian held up the stone again. 'And now, let's see. If there is any harm in you, young Mairhi, it is not apparent to me, but perhaps that is because I have not threatened you in any way. No, no, you need not say anything' – Bridie had made as if to speak – 'I know my parishioners very well, including those who do not come to church as often as they might. I know what is, and is not, likely to have happened between Aly Bain and yourself. So what I would like from you, Miss McArthur, and I feel fairly sure that you understand me well enough, is a promise. Can you swear to me that you will do your very best not to let such a thing happen again?'

Donald sat quite still as Mairhi and the priest held each other's gaze. Then, keeping hold of the seal in her pocket, she nodded. Whether she really understood, or whether she simply remembered that a nod was the right response to his questions, Donald could not tell and did not care. Father Finian smiled at her.

'Good girl! Then we can trust one another, just like myself and your mother-in-law-to-be. Isn't that right, Bridie?'

She could not look away this time, in the act of bringing him his cup of tea. She blushed like a girl, and her voice trembled as she said, 'That's right, Father.'

'Well then, that's settled. Now the wedding is in six days' time, is it not? Do you think you'll be on your feet by then, Donald, or shall we have to carry you to the altar?'

After one appalled moment, Donald realised that this was supposed to be a joke. He said, 'Oh, I'll be walking, Father, don't worry.'

The priest's eyes twinkled. 'But not dancing, perhaps?'

This time Donald did laugh, and so did his mother. Some things could not be kept secret. 'No, Father, I'll not be dancing.'

'Ah, well. And you, young lady, do you dance?'

Mairhi nodded eagerly. She got up to show them, holding up her skirts as the girls had taught her, jigging from one foot to the other and then laughing, open-mouthed, as they had done only a few nights ago. Most likely, she thought that was all part of the dance, and she was not far wrong.

'Splendid! We shall all look forward to it. And let us hope that, once you are man and wife and there is no question of anything else, things will settle down. It may even turn out that some people's behaviour might be improved in the future, hmm? You never know. And now, Bridie, what do you think we can do for old Hamish McDiarmid? I'm inclined to think that at this stage, the whisky he's so fond of is the best medicine for his pain. What would you say?'

25

Over the next few days, time seemed to Donald to slow right down, almost to stop, the way it did sometimes out on the water, when the wind held its breath and the sea turned to glass. It wasn't just that he couldn't take the boat out, or go looking for salvage or even work in the garden. A one-handed man who could barely drag himself across the kitchen couldn't find much at all to do, beyond getting in the way of the women as they went about their daily work.

But it wasn't simply idleness that made the time drag. It was the waiting. He knew now that from the first day Mairhi had spent in the house, he had been waiting for something to happen that would put an end to all their planning. Down on the beach in the dark, when the first blow had landed, he had thought, *This is it, then*, and there had been a kind of relief in that. But, after all, it seemed that it was not. The preparations for the wedding went on; the priest was on their side, at least for now; and every day brought more visitors, to lend a hand or offer food, or merely to gossip.

It was hard to tell what folks really made of it all. The Bains and their friends did not come calling, of course; but for the rest, as Bridie said, 'What people say to your face and what they'll tell each other can be a long way apart. And as for what they feel in their hearts – that can be another thing entirely.' Donald could not even begin to fathom it all out, except to suppose that, like him, most of them would simply wait and see. Meanwhile, day by day, his wounds were healing and he could walk a little further. As he had promised Father Finian, he would walk to his wedding on his own two feet, though still limping. Beyond that, he could not imagine.

So he looked on as his mother and his wife-to-be cared for the animals and tended the garden, cleaned and cooked and mended. He saw how Bridie dealt with people who came wanting help with their ailments or just to tell their stories, knowing that, from this one hearth, at least, they would spread no further. And he saw how Mairhi watched too, and listened and learned. It came to him that the way she watched was different from his own. He dealt with people warily, looking out for blows or pitfalls, always glad when the ordeal was over. Nor was she like the priest, watching in order to manage his flock rather than to be like them. She seemed to have no sense of separation, no self-consciousness, and yet she was set further apart than any of them. Perhaps, he thought, that was part of the strangeness folks felt about her. It was no good guessing. How could he tell what other folks might be thinking or feeling, when he did not know his own heart?

He was in the barn, laying down fresh bedding for the cow, when he heard Hugh's voice hailing him from the yard. It was two days before the wedding, and he had promised that he would spend his last nights as a bachelor up at the shieling, as was right and proper; but he did not want to go. It was true, he'd be no use to the women if anyone tried to harm them, but common sense had no part to play here. He just wanted to keep them close, where he could see and hear and touch them, as if that alone, that constant reassurance that all was well, could somehow keep them safe. And aside from that, there was the slow, halting journey through the village to be faced, where every eye would be on him and he would have nowhere to hide. He knew why Aly Bain had gone to ground after his encounter with Mairhi. To be seen like that, unmanned by your own fear and weakness, that was a hard thing to get past. Maybe it was different for women. That was another thing he could never know.

'Donald, are you there?' Hugh's voice again.

Bridie and Mairhi were down on the strand; Donald would have to come out. But as he came to the door of the byre, narrowing his eyes against the sunlight, he saw that Hugh was not alone. There were James Findlay and James Rennie – two of his crewmen – hanging back by the gate. James Findlay saw him and looked away at once.

The other James – always called Rennie to avoid confusion – seemed to have found something intensely interesting about the hill behind the house. Leaning on his staff, Donald went out into the yard.

26

'What's this, an honour guard?' he said. To his surprise, James looked
up at that. Behind Hugh's back, he grimaced at Donald. Rennie still
appeared to be gazing at the horizon, but he was grinning.

'It'll do no harm,' said Hugh. 'If anyone wants trouble, they can
go looking for it elsewhere. And besides, it's an honourable thing
you're doing.' All of them were grinning now, and Donald saw that
this was a pathway they'd trodden before. This was what men did
when one of their number tied the knot. He'd looked on, but he'd
never been part of it until now, let alone been the man at the centre
of it all. *And I don't know,* he thought, *if the thing I'm doing is honourable or terrible, but it seems it's all right by them.* He came forward
to stand with them. 'I'll just need to get my things,' he said.

While Donald was fumbling through his clothes, the women
arrived back, and tea had to be taken. Another strange thing: an
hour beforehand, he would have said he only wanted to stay where
he was, yet now a part of him was already away with the men. James
and Rennie were just crewmates; no more. But it seemed there was
more to be had if he wanted it. They had been in the bar the other
night, he thought suddenly; they had seen what happened. And yet
they were here, and he knew they would never speak of it unless
that was his choice. The warmth of it was like firelight on his skin.
He felt his mother's gaze upon him and knew that she saw it too,
and that it made her both glad and sad. It seemed he was getting
used to the idea that a person could feel more than one thing at a
time.

Hugh set down his cup and stood up, and the younger men fol-
lowed with a great clatter of chairs. They had sat silent, except when
Bridie asked after their families, but as they were taking their leave,
Rennie spoke up suddenly, glancing at Bridie and quickly away. 'My

father says he'll be happy to give her away, seeing as she's no family of her own,' he said.

'That's very kind,' said Bridie before Donald could react. 'I hoped he'd agree; it's right and proper that an elder of the church should do it. Be sure to give him my thanks.' It had not even occurred to Donald that someone would have to do this job, but, as usual, his mother had it all in hand.

Rennie looked at Mairhi. 'We'll make sure your man doesn't run off, don't you worry,' he said, and smiled at her. Once again, Donald was taken by surprise. He barely spoke to the other crewmen except about matters at hand, and supposed that they despised him for not pulling his weight. Bullying he understood, but teasing was another thing entirely.

Mairhi was looking blank. 'It's all right, lass,' he said. 'I'm going with Hugh now, but I'll see you the day after tomorrow. You stay here with mother.' To Rennie he said, 'I'll not be running anywhere for a bit!' and gestured with his stick towards the door. It wasn't much of a reply, but he felt as pleased as though he'd just helped land a good catch of herring. It seemed, though, that there was more to be done; the men were still standing around, grinning and looking from Donald to Mairhi and back. Belatedly, he understood, made his awkward way around the table and gave his wife-to-be a one-armed hug. 'Stay safe, lass,' he whispered into her hair.

Honour was satisfied. The men moved off, keeping to Donald's pace, and the children tagged along at a respectful distance, no doubt reckoning them to be less dangerous than the women. Maybe they were hoping for a fight; if so they were disappointed. Progress through the village was slow, almost as though they were inviting some reaction, but those who did come out either wished them well or simply watched as they went by.

The last of the village children dropped away as they took the path up to the shieling, but now here came Catriona with the two little ones, chattering and getting underfoot. Donald was tiring now and glad to let James come alongside and take some of the weight off his injured leg. He saw the look that passed between James and Catriona, and another piece of the pattern fell into place; but still, he thought, even if the men had not come forward just for his sake, it was something. It sustained him for the last half-mile, through increasing pain and weariness, until they reached the house. He had no appetite then for talk, or food, or anything other than a clean, warm bed, almost sleeping even as they eased him out of his boots and clothes. The last thing he was aware of was the cool touch of Mairhi's hand on his forehead. He thought, 'That can't be right,' but he could not remember why, and then all thoughts floated away into the dark.

27

'So, d'you think I've got a chance?'

'What?' Donald was half dozing, drunk with the heat of the great hearth. They had put him on the settle in the inglenook, to be out of harm's way as the children tumbled about, racing each other round the long table while Catriona tried to get supper ready. She'd picked up little Jeannie twice: once to comfort her when she knocked her head on the table leg, and once to slap her for pulling her sister's hair. She'd re-tied Ailsa's braids, got them to practise their dance for the wedding for maybe the twentieth time, and now she was running out of patience.

'For the Lord's sake, would you get out from under my feet? You'll have the kettle over in a minute, and then you'll have something to cry about!'

James reached out as Jeannie whirled past, scooped her up and slung her over his shoulder. 'Now, what shall I do with this sack of potatoes?' he asked of no-one in particular. 'I think it needs to go out in the barn with the beasts. What d'you reckon, Donald?'

Jeannie shrieked and beat him on the back with her fists as he made for the door, but before he reached it, Hugh came in with a gust of wind and a flurry of snow. James set her down, and both girls ran to their father.

'Leave off, now, I'm wet through.' Hugh was struggling out of his coat, his hands numb and clumsy with cold. 'All shut up tight,' he said to Catriona. 'It's a wild night, to be sure.'

'You should have let me help,' said James. 'It's not right, me indoors in the warm while you're out there.'

Catriona threw him a bright glance. 'You've been a help to me,' she said. Her cheeks were red from the fire, and her hair had come down a little. She tried to brush it out of her way with her arm and left a smear of flour on one cheek. 'The weather's not the only thing that's wild tonight. These two will never get to sleep at this rate, but James has been doing his best, telling them stories and playing games. I never knew you were such a family man, James Findlay.'

James' cheeks were red now, too. 'Well, I've younger brothers myself,' he mumbled. 'Anyway, Donald needs his supper if he's to keep his strength up for tomorrow.' He looked down. 'Will I give you a hand now?' As he helped Donald to his feet, he said again, 'D'you think I've a chance, at all?'

Donald tried to clear his head. He had a vague memory of James, just as they reached the shieling last night and Rennie went to unlatch the gate, saying, 'Could we have a word; tomorrow, maybe?' But he had no idea what the word might be about. Yet, as James supported him to the table and drew out a chair, he felt Catriona's gaze upon them, watching with such tenderness that he thought perhaps he might have some understanding, after all. While they ate, he saw how James' eyes followed her as she moved between the table and the fire, and grew more certain. But what would Hugh make of it? Catriona had mothered her two little sisters ever since their own mother's death four years before. How could he manage without her?

'Uncle Donald!' That was four-year-old Jeannie, banging her spoon on the table to get his attention. 'You're not listening!'

'Jeannie, for shame!' Catriona snatched the spoon away. 'Donald, you were woolgathering again. You'll have to do better than that when you're married – not that Mairhi has a lot to say. You could take some lessons from her, Jeannie Macfarlane.'

So could you, thought Donald, but was wise enough to keep it to himself. He gave Jeannie his attention. 'Sorry, Jeannie. What were you wanting?'

'I *said*,' declared Jeannie with great emphasis, 'after you're married, will you still be my Uncle Donald?'

'Of course he will,' said Catriona. 'And Mairhi will be your Auntie Mairhi; she'll be Mairhi Macfarlane, same as us, d'you see?'

'And when the baby comes, it will be our cousin,' said Ailsa suddenly. 'And it will be a Macfarlane, too.'

There was a little silence around the table, broken by several voices at once. Hugh said, a little too heartily, 'Right enough!' at the same moment as Catriona said, 'Finish up now, you two, I've plenty more to do before tomorrow!'

Donald had begun to speak too, but with no idea what he might say, and he gave it up with relief. With James' help, he retreated to the settle again. The man still needed an answer, but his concerns seemed simple compared with Donald's own. They had only ever talked about fishing. Why should his opinion matter – about Catriona, or indeed about anything? But he was not left in the dark for long.

Tea was brewed, and James brought him a cup. As he sat down, Donald surprised himself by speaking first. 'I think she likes you well enough,' he said. He watched as a series of expressions passed across James' face: surprise, rue, relief and then a great smile of joy. He huffed out a long breath, and sat down.

'Well, then,' he said a little shakily. 'Well. I did think so, but – how can you be sure?'

'I wouldn't be the best man to ask,' said Donald, and James laughed aloud.

'True enough!' he said. 'But she is your cousin, after all. I was thinking … if you could see your way to having a word with her, I'd be easier in my mind. Just to make sure, you know?'

'I know.' Donald spoke with feeling; he would go a long way to avoid risking Catriona's scorn. 'Not that she pays me any mind. But I will if you want.'

'Good man!' James clapped him on the shoulder, almost as though they were two friends sharing yarns, and then had to apologise as Donald gasped at the pain. When he was able to talk again, James went on. 'I haven't spoken to Hugh yet. How do you think he'll take it?'

'That's a hard one. I know he thinks well of you as a crewman, but you'd be taking Catriona away from him. What about the little ones?'

James looked shocked. 'I wouldn't dream of taking her away! I'd come and live here – with Hugh's blessing, of course. Wouldn't that be a help to him, rather than a hindrance? I've talked it through with my own folks, and they're agreed that would be the best way. What do you think?'

Donald considered this. He was used to taking new ideas away with him, to be turned over and tasted in peaceful solitude, but here was James watching him expectantly. 'I suppose...' he began, but James pushed on.

'Oh, I'm not after taking your place on the boat, if that's what you're thinking. You'll be captain after Hugh, we all know that – if you want it, that is. And I hope you do. You've a right to it. My first time out, I went with your dad, you know. It's right you should take it on.' He looked away as he spoke, remembering, and Donald was grateful for the respite. Tears pricked at his eyes.

'I never thought of it,' he said, and cleared his throat. 'You're used to the farming, too.'

'Right enough. But me and Catriona; do you think we're suited?'

Fresh from that strange and intimate moment, Donald tried a small joke. 'You wouldn't have to do much of the talking,' he said.

James laughed again. 'But that's just it!' he said. 'I like a woman who knows her own mind and isn't afraid to speak it. Oh – not that your Mairhi isn't a grand lass, I don't mean that at all. But you never know where you are with some women, and I can't be doing with it. Now, with Catriona, you know exactly what you're getting.'

'So you do.' Donald could not think of anything worse than living with Catriona, but he saw that it would do no good to say so. James did not want his opinion, only his blessing. 'Well, I'll speak to Hugh; see what he says.'

'I'll do that! But not until after you're wed, eh? This is your time, now. How d'you think you'll take to married life?' When Donald did not answer at once, he went on. 'There's men that can't wait to be out of their wives' company, you know, but I can't see it myself. This house, now, it's always full of talk and laughter; there's tea in the pot and a welcome at the hearth, and that's all her doing. When you think how Rennie lives, for one – he and his dad alone in that cottage since his mother passed away; it's no life for a man. You'd think he'd be after courting some likely lass, but he's a bit too fond of the bar, that one.'

'He's just shy, maybe. Catriona says young Annie MacDonald thinks a lot of him.'

'Does she, now? I'll have to have words with our Rennie. There'll be dancing tomorrow, that's for sure.' His eyes had drifted back to Catriona, as she washed the dishes and handed them to Ailsa to dry. 'Not for you, though; you've managed a good excuse, even though it's your own wedding, eh?'

28

On his own two feet, Donald walked to his wedding. There had not been a moment to be peaceful, no time to think at all. He had submitted to the teasing and tweaking of Catriona and her little sisters, as they dressed him and themselves too. Then, after breakfast, James and Rennie had arrived, and while the four men made their slow way down to the village, Catriona and the girls hurried off to be with Bridie and Mairhi.

They left a great quiet behind them, and no-one seemed inclined to talk much, watching where they put their feet in their newly polished boots. Where the path rounded the hill and the harbour came into view, Hugh stopped, gazing out to sea.

He cleared his throat. Donald was expecting some last-minute words of advice or wisdom, but, 'It's a fair day for fishing,' was all that Hugh said.

'There's no-one out today,' said Rennie. 'Folks have other things on their minds.'

He nudged Donald. 'Still time to take to the heather!'

'Get away with you, man,' said James. 'You could do worse than go courting yourself.' He winked at Donald.

'Aye, see where that leaves you. In the family way before you know it, and no peace to be had unless it's out on the water!' He dodged as James aimed a mock blow at him. 'Nothing but trouble, women, eh?'

Hugh turned, then, and looked at them, or beyond them at another horizon. 'Trouble's what life's all about,' he said. 'It's a poor thing, to be a man alone, without family. And Donald's made his choice, now.'

'Aye, and he won't be much good to his new bride if we stand around in this wind much longer! We'd best be moving.' James took Donald's arm. 'Wait now, I'll give you a hand over the steep bit here.'

At least, this morning, they did not have to make their way through the village again. In any case, anyone who could walk would be inside the church by now, except for a few children keeping watch in the yard. Everyone was here but Mairhi's own family, thought Donald. Where would they be today? Wherever he went, unless it was far enough inland, he was always looking out for them these days. There were a few now, down on the bit of beach below the headland where the church stood; but they paid no attention as the men went by on the path above. It seemed there would be no last-minute rescue; another thought to be laid aside.

He had not been able to see beyond this day, had thought it would somehow change everything; but here they were, making their way now through the churchyard and around to the door, and each step of the way seemed plain and simple. This is the way of it, and this, and this. How else could it be? Children darted and swooped around them, some waving green branches that their elders had cut for them. The trees were barely in leaf so early in the year, but they had done what they could. And here in the porch was Auntie Annie, waiting to greet them. She reached up to kiss him and into his buttonhole she tucked a small posy of flowers. 'Sweet violets,' she whispered into his ear. 'I've some for Mairhi, too. I know where to find them!'

'Thanks, Auntie,' he whispered back.

'You do right by that lass, Donald,' she said suddenly, fiercely. Her eyes glittered with tears. 'Don't you mind that lot in there. You make your promises, and you keep them!'

Donald stood very still. Almost, it seemed that she could hear what he was thinking. He looked straight back at her. 'I'll do my best,' he said.

She nodded, once, and let go of his arm. He was aware again of Hugh at his shoulder and of the doorway in front of them. Inside, most of the people he knew in the world were waiting. He straightened up and stepped forward.

29

He had never, of his own free will, walked into such a great crowd of people. Even going to school, when there was no getting out of it, he would lurk by the wall of the yard and try to slip in behind some others. But now he was the reason they were all gathered here. It seemed that all eyes were on him; some smiling and nodding as he and Hugh made their way to the front, and others simply watching. Not all eyes, though. Andrew Bain stood square-shouldered by the nave and never moved as Donald passed by. Beyond him, Euan looked round, lifted an eyebrow and smiled a little. Aly, hunched at the far end, reached out to haul one of the children back as he slid off the seat, and kept his eyes down. There was no time to notice more. Donald was at the front now, facing the altar, and he could feel their stares like a swarm of ants on his back.

Hugh laid a steadying hand on his arm, and together they stood, listening to the whispering and rustling behind them; and beyond that, the everlasting sigh and crash of the sea on the rocks below, the blows of the wind against the church walls, and the light patter of rain on the windows. It seemed they might stand that way forever, but at last the doors creaked open again, the people fell silent, and sunshine streamed in. Donald took a deep breath and turned to meet his bride.

He could hardly see her at first against the sun, veiled as she was, and so small – small as a fairy's child, indeed. As she came up the aisle on the arm of John Rennie, Donald fixed his eyes upon her hand, warm and human where it rested on John's sleeve. Then she was at his side. Her head scarcely came up to his shoulder as they stood there, side by side, and made their vows before God. No-one spoke, no-one made any objection, no sudden thunderclap sounded to stop the ceremony. There was no sound at all, and the only movement was made by Mairhi herself, as she dipped her head to indicate, *Yes, I do.*

When the moment came, his hands shook as he went to lift the veil. Her dark eyes looked straight into his, just as they had done on that other night not so long ago, and it came to him that this was the first time since then that he had met her gaze fully. But this time there was no terror, no nightmare visions of drowned hope; just a steady look that they held for a minute, and then her hand in his as they turned to face the waiting crowd.

And that was that. The rest of the day unfolded with feasting and dancing and speeches, and everyone to be greeted and all the things that must be done. Donald went through it all as though he were at sea, in the sudden windless calm that had fallen upon him when their eyes met. Nothing was changed, and yet nothing could be the same.

The stillness lasted until they were at home at last, putting off their fine clothes and getting ready for bed. Donald now would sleep with Mairhi, in the bed where he had been conceived and born. Bridie would take her place in the bed by the hearth, which had been his since he was a child. When he came into the bedroom, Mairhi looked at him in surprise. He went to her and took her hands, and spoke out of the shining stillness within him.

'We sleep together now, lass. That's what it means, to be man and wife. Well, part of what it means, anyway. But I promise you I'll never touch you against your will. I did you wrong, and I'm sorry for it. I'll try to make it up to you and be a good husband, as best I can. Do you understand me at all?' He could not look at her now, or only at her bare feet on the floor. Her toes were red and pinched together from wearing shoes that did not fit well. The stillness wavered, and wretchedness rose inside him. Then he felt the soft touch of her hand against his cheek. 'She eases me,' his aunt had said, and now he knew what she had meant. He could not speak. They stood there for a moment, and then Mairhi stepped away and bent to blow out the candle.

30

'And see here, this is the wing feather of an eagle. Likely he lost it scrapping over that dead lamb we saw just now; there's been foxes there too. I'll show you one of their homes in a while.'

They were making their way up the rising ground, away from the sea, along a sheep's path that meandered across the slope between the heather and tussocks of marsh grass. Sheep with live lambs scrambled out of their way. Donald wanted Mairhi to see the pine and birch woods that grew under the lea of the crags. He wanted her to see everything, to come to know the land as intimately as he did himself. Catriona was right, he thought; it seemed he could not stop talking these days, the words welling up out of him, trying to catch up with all the years of silence. And there was so much to tell, so much to show, so much he had never shared with anyone.

There was another thing – something he had never put into words, even to himself. Here in the woods, or up in the hills, away from people with their questions and their judgments, he was at ease – no, more than that. He was happy, alive in a way that no-one, except maybe his mother now and again, had ever seen; and now he found that he could share that happiness with Mairhi. She did not judge – or not that he knew – and she seemed as full of wonder as himself, following the tracks of deer or marten, seeing the many colours of the land birds, the landscape, the smells and sounds and solid ground beneath their feet. And there was the core of it, the secret thing. His deepest solace lay here, out of the sight and sound of the sea.

There was nothing to be done about it, of course. Donald sometimes thought that he hated the sea. He feared it, that was for sure; Aly Bain was right about that. It had taken his father and many another good man, and its gifts were capricious – never to be relied on, often too little and then suddenly far too much. There was no tenderness in the life of a fisherman; it was all wrenching and heaving and the sharp work with blood and knives, and then being spat out at the end of a voyage, cold and wet, bruised and stinking. Once, watching his mother tend to a newborn calf, cleaning its muzzle and helping it to suck, he had asked her, 'Why did you stay here?' She had glanced at him, busy about her work, and when the task was done she faced him and said, 'You asked me that once before, when you were nine years old, after your father died. Do you remember?'

He'd shifted, looked away. 'Maybe.'

'Well, you did. And I gave you a child's answer; that our family was here, that John would have wanted us to carry on the croft, for you to learn the fishing, all that. But I'll tell you the true reason now, if you like.'

He'd felt like a child then, not wanting another answer, but it was too late to turn back. 'Well, what is it?'

'Pride.' She'd laughed, then. 'I was a proud young woman, Donald, and I would not turn tail and go back to my folks inland. They told me it would come to grief, that even if John prospered, it would always be waiting and fearing, and him away and gone more often than not, and me managing alone. And they were right, of course. After John was lost, my father came to fetch me home. You were old enough to work on the farm, he said, and they wouldn't see us go hungry. But I wouldn't go, to face their pity and their always knowing better. I wouldn't go and live with your Uncle Hugh's family either, though they offered, bless them.

'So we stayed here, you and I, and I made myself useful with my medicines and so on, and I made them accept me, after a fashion. And the thing is, Donald, I'll never know if it was the best way or not, do you see? You choose your path, and then you have to walk it, all the way. We all do.'

She'd turned away then, still proud, and Donald had taken himself off, not knowing what to do with what she'd just given him. He still didn't know.

Mairhi was tugging at his arm. They were approaching a tall pine, and there was movement on the ground at its feet, a ripple of bright colour as the squirrels flowed up the trunk to safety. She ran to the tree, pressing her hands to the bark and peering up into its branches, as though she might follow them aloft. One of them fled, leaping across to the next tree with scarcely a pause, but the other stayed to scold at her. Mairhi listened, and then gave him back his own words, churring and rattling, accompanied by a shake of the finger that she'd learned from the little girls at the shieling.

Donald stood back and watched. She did that a lot, these days. Ever since the gull-call in the priest's parlour, she would try out the sound of every creature she came across. Donald had tried to teach her not to do it in front of other people, but Kirsty had wasted no time in spreading the story, and now whenever they went to the village the children would be after them, with all the animal noises they could think of, screeching and yammering.

They kept their distance, though. Once, one of the smaller ones had fallen as he tried to scramble away. He'd hurt his knee and set up a downright human bawl, but when Mairhi went to him and tried to set him to rights, he'd fought her off and fled in terror. These days, they avoided the village when they could. Days like today were a pure gift, just for the two of them. Donald took a deep breath and came back again to the present.

'Squirrels,' he said, coming up to her. 'They come out for a bit in the mild weather, to see what they can find. See here.' He hunted about under the scrubby hazels and alders near by, and held out a handful of last year's nuts. 'Here's a good one.' Just a shell, blackened by frost and wet, with a neat round hole, and all the meat gone. 'They've sharp, strong teeth, to get through the shell like that.' She gave a little nod, putting the thought away somewhere in her collection of treasures, to be taken out and examined again later.

'Mairhi, why won't you speak? You understand me well, you can make any sound you like. You'll nod and shake your head and use your hands to talk, but you won't speak. I wish you'd talk to me.' He had not meant to say any of that, but the yearning in him was so close, so constant, it would well up without warning. He took her hand now, and she did not pull away, only looked at him steadily. 'I think you could, if you chose. I'm sorry, I won't say any more. It's your choice, and I'll abide by it.'

For a moment longer, neither of them moved. She opened her mouth, seemed almost about to say something, and then her eye was caught by a flash of movement overhead, and she turned away to follow the small birds as they flew out over the heather. Then back to him, eyebrows raised. And the knowledge came to him in sudden wonder: *She's teaching me. She's teaching me to read people. And if she did use words, I'd miss it, like I always did before.* He had no idea if that was her intention, but this time he would not ask. Aloud he said, 'Sand martins. They're early, too. Maybe it means a good year.' But she was off and away, running through the heather, dipping and weaving like the martins above her, arms held wide. Sometimes the lithe grace of her struck him speechless; even now, with the child growing daily, visibly, she moved like water. And another thought came to him: *I have given her this. She'd have had a few hours at most, and then it would be back into the thick, heavy skin that seals must wear to live as they do. These clever hands, this lovely voice, this body that can jump and dance and feel; maybe they make up, just a little, for what she's lost.* And then she was down suddenly, disappearing into the bracken with a cry of surprise.

He made his way over to her, still a little slow, to find her flat on her back, laughing at the sky, arms and legs spread wide. The yearning swept through him; to fling himself down beside her, take her in his arms, give way to that brief, fierce pleasure. He stood quite still, a little turned away, mastering himself, and then stooped to give her his hand, saying in a voice that was almost steady, 'See what happens when you forget to hold up your skirts? You can't have both wings and hands; now that's just greedy. Should have been a bird instead, maybe.' But then, for all he knew, they could be birds at times, or whatever they chose. What if it was only his action that had trapped her in this one form?

Shame welled up in him. And yet, on this bright spring day, surely she was happy to be here, walking the land at his side? He dared not ask her, for fear of the wrong answer; but even as he thought it she swung his hand and let go, spinning around and around, the way the little girls did, until she tumbled down again – on purpose this time. *And that's all the answer you're getting,* he told himself, *so take it and be grateful.*

31

That was one of a string of stolen days, taken here and there from the pile of ordinary stones and made into a shining, secret necklace. Donald imagined Mairhi wearing it against her heart, known to no-one but himself, like the growing hoard of special stones and other curious objects that he found for her on their rambles. She kept them on a windowsill in the cottage; all but the carved seal given to her by the priest. That she had always by her, in a pocket, and often she would take it out, to stroke or simply to hold, while her attention was seemingly elsewhere. Once, coming in unexpectedly, Donald had heard her singing to it, a strange, crooning, wordless song that drifted like the wind. She'd stopped when she saw him, but he'd simply nodded to her and carried on about his business.

All of it was precious to him: these days; her strangeness; her ordinariness; the way she teased him sometimes; the way she nestled against him in the cold of the night. And then, day by day, the way the growing child came between them. 'It'll be born around midsummer; nine months, like any other child,' Bridie had said. 'She won't wait until autumn, the way the seals do. That's a good sign, Donald.' He thought she spoke to convince herself as much as him, though neither of them could bear to speak directly of what they dreaded. But in any case, for Donald, midsummer was much too soon. He tried to put it out of mind, to make the most of the time they had.

It was little enough. As the days lengthened, he was out on the boat more and more with his Uncle Hugh, sometimes for two or three days at a stretch.

Bridie took Mairhi about with her on her daily rounds, doing the things that women did. 'If they see her every day,' she said, 'they can't help seeing there's no harm in her. And believe you me, Donald, it's the women who'll have the last say. Besides, she's a real help to me now. She's learning the medicines, and she knows how to be with someone who's ailing.' It was true; Donald had seen her with little Jeannie when she took the fever. He knew, though, that, while Mairhi would sit for hours by a sickbed, she would not sew or weave with the other women for more than a few minutes. 'She'll come to it, in time,' Bridie said, but how much more time would there be?

Around May, when there were still no fresh spring greens to be had, Jessie Bain was taken ill. Her belly was huge by then, and the rest of her shrunken and yellow like the last of the winter apples, as though the child was taking all the life from her. The older children hung about until other families took pity on them, and Aly spent all his time in the bar when he was ashore. Bridie did not expect to be called, of course, but one afternoon when Donald was in the kailyard, turning in manure for the new year's vegetables, Euan's wife Shona came past him, ignoring his greeting, and going straight into the house without stopping to knock. He drove his fork into the earth and followed her. Bridie and Mairhi, sorting turnips dug from the clamp, looked up in surprise.

'Jessie's started,' Shona said without preamble. 'She's in a bad way. The baby's stuck, somehow. It's been nearly a whole day now, and she hasn't the strength for it.' She dropped into a chair suddenly, as though telling her tale had taken all her strength, too. 'We don't know what to do.'

Bridie was already on her feet, rubbing the soil off her hands and looking about for her basket. 'Mairhi, could you fetch some clean cloths, while I sort out the medicines we'll need. And bring your shawl; it could be a long time.'

'She can't come,' said Shona bluntly. 'They don't know I've come for you, even. But she's not welcome in that house.'

Bridie gave her a long look. 'You've more sense than the rest of them, Shona Bain. I'll do whatever I can. But where I go, Mairhi goes too. It's time this foolish business was laid by.'

Shona shrugged. 'I thought you'd say that. On your own head, then. You know we can't manage without you.'

Bridie nodded. 'You'd best get back. We'll be along in a bit. I'll say I came of my own accord, if you like.'

'I can look after myself. I'm not like poor Jessie.'

'Well, then. Away you go.' Bridie stood still for a moment, looking after her, not seeming to see Donald at all.

'Are you sure this is wise?' he asked, and realised as he did so that he had never questioned his mother's judgment before.

'We can't go on hiding and avoiding for ever. Best to face it down now.'

'But what if ... well, what if it doesn't go well? Won't they blame you, and her too?'

'Maybe. But I can't help that. That girl will die if I don't go; I've seen that look before, on women near their time. I have to do what I can, Donald.'

He went out then, back to his work, and never paused as they came by him with their burdens, hurrying down the path. *This must be how the wives feel, watching when we go out to sea*, he thought. *We don't say goodbye, we don't wave – in case it breaks the thread. Only come back safe, and I'll never let you out of my sight again. Except I have to, over and over. Only come back.* He worked on until it was too dark to see any longer.

32

After all, he was not at home when they came back, late the next morning. Coming up the path laden with creels, he saw the door standing open to the fresh air and dropped them all, breaking into a stumbling run for the last few yards. Bridie looked up from the fire, shading her eyes against the light. She looked exhausted. Fear clutched at him.

'Where is she? For God's sake, what have they done to her?'

Bridie put a finger to her lips. 'She's sleeping, Donald. Don't wake her. We're not long back.' She poured him some tea, and they took it outside in the gentle sunshine.

'So what happened? What about Jessie and the babe? Are they all right?'

'I don't know, yet. But they're both alive, God be praised. It's been a hard night.'

He took her arm as she swayed, helped her to a seat. 'Tell me, then.'

'Well. I didn't even know if they'd let us across the threshold, but they couldn't manage, and women will lay aside their pride when it's about life and death. But I tell you, Donald, I thought it was beyond me, too.' She shuddered, looking inward. 'That poor lass hasn't much hold on life at the best of times, and she'd about given up. It was all turned around wrong, and she'd lost a lot of blood.

'You've seen me working with the calves, Donald. If it gets stuck you have to push it back so it can come the right way, but she wouldn't let anyone near her, and they were frightened to try. She was screaming and throwing herself about like a beast in a trap. Well, Mairhi just went straight to her, never mind all the mess, and she knelt there and got Jessie to look her in the eye, and then…'

Donald could hardly speak. 'So then, what?'

'So then,' Bridie went on, 'Jessie went quiet. Everyone was watching, to see if she'd go the way Aly did, but no-one quite dared to get between them. But she didn't. Mairhi held her arms and never looked away, and let Jessie down onto the bed, and she just kept looking. And after a while I went over, and she let me do what needed to be done.

'It took a long time, and I thought it had gone too far, but she stayed quiet, and in the end, I got the child out.' She took a deep, ragged breath. 'It was the hardest birthing I've ever done. The child wouldn't breathe for a while, and I don't know if it'll live or not. But all that time, Jessie never let go of Mairhi's arms. Mairhi held her and rocked her like a baby; and then they showed her the child. And then she just went to sleep. And we came home.' Bridie ran out of words and fell silent, hunched over, cradling the hot tea.

Donald looked down at her for a moment, and then he put his arm around her. 'Let's get you to bed,' he said.

∴

The next few days were warm and windless, and the humming of summer bees only seemed to deepen the silence. With no wind to fill the sails, the boats stayed ashore, and the men with them. There was plenty else for Donald to be getting on with in the garden, and he was glad of the excuse to stay close to home. Bridie was all for going to see Jessie the next day, and Mairhi with her, but as they set off down the path, there was Shona coming up to meet them, and Jessie's elder daughter tagging along; a sullen child with an indoor look to her, like the sprouts on carrots kept too long in the cupboard. She hung back when she saw them, but Shona marched straight up.

'Best not go down,' she said bluntly. 'Aly's home, and he's always out of temper when other folks get to see the state of their housekeeping. He'll only take it out on Jessie when she's up and about again.'

'How is she? And the bairn?' Bridie was rummaging in her basket for the eggs she'd brought to give them, but Shona shook her head.

'They're alive; and that's your doing. Whether they'll thrive or not is another matter. You keep your eggs; it's we who should be thanking you, Lord knows.' She lowered her voice. 'Aly knows what happened. I don't know who told him, but we couldn't have kept it from him for long, anyway. He's taken it as a personal insult, of course. You'd think he'd rather his wife died, and the child with her, than take help when it's needed.' She sniffed. 'And someone needs to tell him that's the end of making babies, too. Another time like that would be the death of her for sure.'

'I told him.' The child spoke up, startling them all. Donald could not remember ever hearing her speak before. 'I fetched him home from the bar, and he asked me straight out, because you said we'd have to have the midwife in, and he said no way was that woman crossing our threshold, not if he had anything to do with it.' She stopped abruptly, looking astonished, as though she'd never heard her own voice either. Shona reached out to rest a hand on her head, but she flinched away.

'Don't you worry. I'll deal with your father. You come home with me tonight, and the little ones too.' Shona's face softened as she looked down at the girl. 'We'll make a big fish pie and some biscuits too, how's that?'

The child shook her head. 'Ma needs me.'

Bridie had been watching them both, and now she said, 'Nancy, isn't it? Well now, just you listen to me. We're all looking after your ma now, and we'll do our very best for her. But she can't be doing with the little ones underfoot for a while; she needs to rest and get her strength back. And I'm guessing it'll be you who's cared for them while your ma's not been well; am I right? So you need to go with your Auntie Shona and the others, and then Jessie can rest easy and not worry about them.'

Nancy stood her ground. 'Ma needs me,' she said again. A look passed between Shona and Bridie that Donald could not interpret, but he shivered, as though a cloud had crossed the sun.

'Nancy,' said Shona, 'you can't...' but she did not seem able to bring out the words.

The child spoke suddenly to Mairhi. 'He'd pay heed to you,' she said. 'And you helped her. You could come. He won't raise a hand to you.'

For a long moment, no-one said anything. And then Mairhi began to walk, past Shona and down the path to the village. Nancy stared for a moment, and then ran to catch up with her. Donald left his cabbage seedlings and followed.

Behind him he heard Shona say, 'Well! She's got a mind of her own, that one.'

33

And so they went, in a little straggling procession, down the narrow path. As soon as the track widened near the village, Nancy ran alongside Mairhi and took her hand. Mairhi was watching her step, heavy-footed in the last weeks of pregnancy, but she smiled at the little girl and, when Nancy began to skip, she joined in, laughing at her own clumsiness. Bridie caught up with Donald. 'She's missed the children,' she said.

'I suppose.'

'You'd best stay back now. She'll come to no harm with the rest of us there, but if he sees you he'll have to take a stand.'

'I'm not leaving you!'

'Donald, will you listen to me?' They were at the harbour now, and there were plenty of people about today: men working on nets and baskets, children getting underfoot, women putting out washing to dry in the hot sun, and all of them pausing to watch as they went by. 'You can't go in there in any case, so just take yourself off out of sight, and we'll find you later. Here, take these eggs to Auntie Annie.' And she thrust the basket at him.

There was the row of cottages, their doors open to let in the fresh air. But she was right, of course; he was no kin to Jessie Bain, and childbirth was none of men's business. He stood and watched as they all went in, wanting some sign from Mairhi that she knew he wanted to protect her, but she never looked back. Right now, she had no need of him at all.

∴

Donald took the eggs down to his aunt, but he did not stay there. Why would you seek out company when you could be on your own? He thought of his half-planted seedlings, but they would keep. Instead, he went inland, leaving village and path behind, scrambling among rocks as the way got steeper. He had not been this way since before Mairhi's coming, and the going was hard, hampered as he still was by his injuries. The bones were almost healed, but his ankle was stiff, and he was out of breath by the time he reached the place. Not the top of the hill, but a little corrie just below it; out of the wind – though there was not a breath today – and crowded with trees, like sheep huddling together against the weather.

Up here, if you lay down in the fine grass under the birches, you could neither see nor hear the sea. The world shrank down to the spinning business of insects, the secret rustlings of mice among the dry leaves, and the fine thread of birdsong. He had used to come here when he was avoiding school or other children. In the summer after his father's death, he had stayed for a full week, making a bed of heather against the rock and a small fire between the stones, and keeping vigil through the endless summer nights, when the sun hardly slept. People had shouted at him when he went home at last, told him he was selfish and wicked to worry his mother so; but she had simply put hot food in front of him and asked no questions. At the time he had just accepted it, but thinking of it now, he saw that most likely she had known where he was all along, the way she seemed to know most things. The thought made him smile.

A robin had found him, perching above his head and watching with one bright eye.

'I've nothing for you,' he said softly. If Mairhi had been with him, she would have sung to the bird, and he would have been pointing out to her where the mice had tunnelled through the long grass, where a badger had rubbed itself against a tree, and where the spiders had woven their silken traps. She could not manage the climb up here, not now; and not later when she would have a babe in arms. He missed her at his side; and all at once he was anxious, wanting to be home, waiting for them.

Here and there in the grass were the clear-yellow flowers of tormentil. His mother could use the roots in her medicines, but there was no time for that now, and nothing to dig them with. Carefully, he picked a few of the flowers, and stowed them in his top pocket to show to Mairhi later. Then he got to his feet and began the long descent.

34

He had almost run the last half-mile, risking new injuries; and after all, there was no sign of them when he reached home. Only his seedlings, drooping in the sun, and the ever-hopeful hens clamouring for food.

First of all, he found a cup for his wilting flowers and placed them in the centre of the table, and then he set to work. He had planted out the last of the cabbages, made up the fire and was thinking of starting the milking when he spied them coming up the path. Mairhi paused when she saw him, put her fists to the small of her back and stretched. She looked weary, but no worse than that.

'Here, let's get you indoors, take the weight off your feet. The kettle's on already,' said Donald. He went to help her the last few steps to the door. 'Was there any … trouble?'

She glanced up at him, a questioning look, and shook her head. Why would there be? Behind him, Bridie laughed.

'Seems Aly Bain is learning respect, these days! There was no trouble at all. He never showed his face; he'd taken himself off with Andrew, to make some repairs to the boat, or so they said. There was only Jessie, still too weak to get up, and the other children pestering her for food and the Lord knows what else. Shona cleared them all out and left us to it; she's got her head screwed on at any rate. And when Jessie saw Mairhi—'

'What? She didn't push her away, did she?'

Bridie gave him a long look. 'If you'd only been there, Donald. She held out her arms and smiled like I've never seen her smile before. And that wee Nancy – she wouldn't go with Shona for all our persuading – she was beside herself, tearing around and shouting like a mad thing. So while Mairhi sat with Jessie, I went about and set the house to rights. They'd no food in the cupboard nor fire in the grate, and she's not been able to clean the place while she's been ill.' Bridie paused to take a sip of tea and looked tactfully away, into the fire. Clearly, Jessie's housekeeping had never been up to much at the best of times.

'So then, what?'

'So then, nothing. We made Jessie comfortable and saw to the baby, and she wouldn't let go of Mairhi's hand the whole time. Mairhi fed her some of the broth I took with me, and she took it like a baby herself. I think she'll be all right in time, or as right as she ever is.' Bridie sighed. 'About the child, we'll just have to wait and see. It's a scrawny little thing, never mind the trouble it had getting started, and I don't suppose she'll be up to feeding it. But we've done the best we can.'

'So you never saw Aly?'

'Not at all! He stayed clear until we were well away, if he ever came home. I had to prise Jessie's hands off Mairhi so we could leave.'

Donald frowned. 'It's too much for her now. She needs to rest.'

But Mairhi was already busying herself with the onions and carrots for the night's meal. She brought out the chopping board, and moved aside the cup with the flowers of tormentil floating in it. She looked up, met Donald's eye and smiled. In truth, she looked somehow stronger, more sure of herself. It was Bridie who looked tired.

'She's young and healthy, Donald. And it doesn't seem to take it out of her, helping people the way she does – though I don't know what it is she does, exactly.'

Mairhi looked up at that, and leaned over to lay her hand on Bridie's. Then she went back to her chopping. Again, Donald saw that she needed no looking after; not for now, at least. He got up. 'I'll see to the beasts,' he said.

35

There were still maybe two or three weeks to go before the child would be born, Bridie reckoned; a hot time of year to be carrying a baby. But Mairhi made light work of it, though she sometimes took a rest now in the afternoons. She and Bridie visited Jessie Bain daily over the next two weeks, and Aly managed to be elsewhere whenever they arrived, though possibly it was not entirely on their account.

Bridie found another woman, whose own baby was a few months old, to wet-nurse the child, and Shona looked after the others; all but Nancy, who would not be parted from her mother. 'She's turning into a good little nurse,' Bridie reported. 'Though the poor creature could do with some mothering herself, goodness knows. You never see her playing or asking for anything, the way most children do. It's as though she's always looked after the rest. Still, she let Mairhi wash her hair and braid it, and we took her an old frock of Ailsa's that she's outgrown. Ailsa's younger than she is, but you'd never guess it to look at her, poor thing. And she follows Mairhi around like a little dog.'

Donald had not tried to escort them since that first time, and had almost stopped worrying about it. What could he do, in any case? After the first fortnight, they began to go every other day. It was about a week later when Donald, spreading muck in a newly dug patch of the garden, began to feel that he was being watched; and not just by the ever-present robin, this time. There was no-one to be seen, however, so he carried on pitching. Then, as he reached for the rake, he caught a flicker of movement beyond the wall at the front of the yard. Someone was there; someone who had bobbed down out of sight as he turned.

Moving as stealthily as he could, he went to the gate. At first glance he could see nothing, but there was a quick intake of breath as he unlatched the gate to come outside. It must be a very small person, huddled under the lee of the wall. He looked in the other direction and said, as though to the wind, 'Can I give a message to my mother for you?'

It was not unusual for children to be sent to fetch Bridie, but in the normal way of things they could not wait to spill out their errand. Whatever it might be, it was always urgent, always important, and the only trouble would be to get them to stop talking. Now, though, there was no response.

Donald said, 'She's away over the hill just now, but I'll tell her you came by. Is there anything I can do for you?'

'Not you. Her!' The fierce reply took Donald by surprise, and he looked directly at the speaker. Nancy Bain, still crouched against the wall, glared up at him.

'Oh, well. Is it your ma now? Has she been taken poorly?'

'My dad's back. We need her now!' And Donald realised that it was not Bridie she was after. He guessed well enough what might be happening, but no-one ever interfered directly in another family's affairs. It was not the way, and especially not with this family, not now. He crouched down to face her, and she looked away at once, swiping her sleeve across her face.

'Can you not get Shona to come?' He felt uneasy, even offering this small advice; it was none of his business.

'She won't.' And he saw that Nancy, too, was desperate. She knew the way of things better than most, growing up in that household.

'Well, see here. Mairhi's not far from having her own baby now, and she needs to save her strength. And she can't be fighting other people's battles for them. Your ma's got to—'

'She can do magic!' Nancy interrupted him. 'She can make people drown if she wants to. Uncle Euan said so!' Tears streaked her face.

'Listen now. It's not magic, never you mind what people say. And that only happened because…' But here he ran out of words. The child might know only too well what her father was capable of, but it was not for him to say it, straight out. 'What she did, she was just looking out for herself,' he finished lamely. The child simply stared at him. 'I don't think she can do it for other people, anyway,' he said, and that was no good either. He had no idea, really, what she could or could not do.

In any case, this was a child who expected to be lied to. She stared at him a moment longer, and then was up and away, darting around him and in through the gate. By the time he was on his feet and following, she had run right in through the open front door, and he could hear her calling for Mairhi. Maybe she had even gone into the bedroom. *These people have no decency*, he thought in sudden fury. *Nothing's safe from them, ever.* In the doorway he was brought up short by the sight of Mairhi, emerging from the bedroom with her hair down, still half asleep, and Nancy tugging at her arm.

'Will you not be told? She can't go with you!' he began, but Mairhi stopped then, came right up to him and took hold of him by both arms, so that he had to look her in the face. What he read there was plain enough. 'Then I'm coming too,' he said.

36

It took only a few minutes to be ready, and then they set out, all three of them. Nancy ignored him, pulling at Mairhi to make her hurry, while he tried to help her whenever the width of the path allowed. They must have made a strange sight, Donald thought, though there were not many to see them on this sleepy afternoon. All the cottage doors stood open, like their own, and washing was spread over every available bush.

The Bains' dog came up to them, wagging its tail and cringing at the same time, as they approached the house. Nancy pushed it aside and ran in, calling for her mother, and Mairhi, who also cared nothing for privacy, followed straight after her. Donald stopped on the threshold, still unsure, but as he hesitated he heard a man's voice raised in anger. That was enough. He took a deep breath and went in.

He had never set foot inside the house before. Why would he? But the harbour cottages were all laid out in the same way. The front door opened into the living room, and there would be a bedroom at the back, with another under the eaves, where the children would sleep. His aunt's home was like it, but although the shape was the same, it could not have been more different. The room was unswept, the hearth piled high with ash, and unwashed crockery lay on the table. There was nothing bright or soft anywhere, no curtains or rugs or children's toys.

As he stood there, he heard the child's voice in the room beyond. 'You leave her be!' she screamed, and then a sharp sound that stopped his heart. He was at the doorway in three paces.

Jessie was on her feet by the bed, though she looked as though a breath would be enough to topple her. She was rubbing her arm, looking down, and behind her Nancy lay on the floor. Aly had turned to face her as she ran in, but he was staring now at Mairhi. Donald could not see her face, but he saw Jessie look up, and her whole body changed; she stood up straight and smiled, as Bridie had said, in a way that made her look, for a moment, like a different woman. Mairhi walked past Aly as though he were a chair that stood in the way, and took Jessie into her arms. Tenderly, she lowered her down onto the bed. Nancy scrambled to her side and clutched at her skirt with both hands.

Aly's hands were bunched into fists, but he made no move towards the women. He stood, breathing heavily. 'You get out of my house. Now!' he said, and then he saw Donald in the doorway. For once, words seemed to fail him entirely.

'I think,' said Donald, and cleared his throat, 'I think it's you that's not welcome here just now. You'd best come outside and let the women see to their business.'

Aly stared at him. Donald had no idea what had made him throw the man a lifeline. In truth, he'd have been glad to see him drown. Only there was a desperate, cornered look to him, like a wounded stag brought to bay by the dogs; such creatures can do great harm. He stood aside and, after a moment, Aly came out of the bedroom. He went straight to the front door and out into the sunlight, and there was a sudden yelp from the dog a few seconds later. Donald let him go.

'Are you all right, there?' he said to the women, and was rewarded with a quick flash of a smile from Mairhi. That was enough.

He went back through into the main room, and busied himself about clearing out the ash and building a fire. Aly did not return, and Donald neither knew nor cared where he might be. Something had changed, something so deep in him that he could not even look at it directly, not yet, but he was glad to be alone with simple tasks in hand: laying the fire, filling the kettle, doing the everyday things that hold a life together. He was kneeling by the hearth, coaxing the peat into flame, when a voice spoke behind him, startling him as though he had just woken from sleep.

'I think she's starting,' it said. Jessie Bain was leaning in the bedroom doorway. He could not remember the last time he had heard her speak; back in the schoolyard, maybe, whispering and laughing with the other girls as he went by.

'What?'

'It's her time,' she said.

Donald stared at her, and she gave him a crooked smile. 'It'll be hours yet,' she said. 'I should know. But you'd best get her home.'

Donald started to his feet. 'It's too soon, it shouldn't be for a week or two yet!'

'They choose their own time.'

But he was already into the bedroom and at Mairhi's side. She was sitting on the bed, one hand on her stomach. Nancy had tight hold of the other, staring at her with huge eyes. Donald went to help her up, and Nancy began to cry noisily, tears and snot running down her face. 'She can't die! It's not fair! Why can't she do magic for herself?'

'Hush your noise, Nancy. She'll be right as rain. She's not like me.' Jessie made her slow way across the bedroom and sank down next to Mairhi. 'You're fine, do you hear me? It's just the baby getting ready to come. Donald will take you home now. Nancy, would you fetch Shona for me?'

'I'm not leaving you on your own!'

'Nancy,' said Donald, 'your dad's gone. He won't be back for a while.'

Nancy stared a moment longer, and then she leaped up and scurried out of the room. Mairhi began to get up, and then cried out, more in surprise than pain, and clutched at her stomach again. Donald was at her side. 'Come on now, lass, let's get you home.'

'You've got to wait when the pains come,' said Jessie, and for a moment Donald glimpsed the girl she had been, ordering the others about in the schoolyard, before life had worn her down. 'Don't you know anything, Donald Macfarlane?'

'Not about this,' said Donald. 'I don't know when Ma will be back. It could be a while.'

'I'll send Nancy for Catriona when she comes back. There's no hurry. But you should get her home now,' she said again. Jessie looked white now, as though she might faint. 'Go on, away with you!'

37

And so they went, step by halting step, pausing every now and then as a new wave of pain swept through Mairhi's body. Donald learned to tell when they were building; he could feel the change in her, and had just time to take her hands and face her, and she clung to him as it grew, and broke, and died away again. Not drowning, but riding the waves. Fishermen do not learn to swim – if they fall from the boat, they are lost, and it is best to drown quickly – but seals do. He saw it in her eyes – that she had forgotten nothing; and he was glad for her.

It was a long, slow journey back to the house, and Bridie was still not home when they got there. Donald had a vague idea that labouring women should be in bed, but Mairhi was having none of it. She walked up and down, sometimes holding on to the back of a chair, and sometimes gripping his hands as the pain grew. In between whiles, he rubbed her back or her shoulders, wherever she indicated. The day wore on, and although he feared what might lie ahead, Donald cherished this precious intimacy; just the two of them, and Mairhi needing something that he could give, some small recompense for the fact that he had started this, and at least he could help her to bear it.

Still, he was glad when at last Bridie came hurrying up the track, Catriona and some of the other women with her. Behind them came James and Rennie, waiting sheepishly outside until the women evicted him and they could take him down to the bar, which was the proper place for a father-to-be. He did not even have the chance to say goodbye to Mairhi, surrounded as she was now by women who knew exactly what to do, and who shooed him out of the house with an authority they would not have dared to show at any other time.

It was late evening now; doors were shut and beasts put to bed, though the sun still skimmed the horizon in a net of crimson cloud; it would barely set tonight, midsummer was so close. The sea lay almost still; there was just a distant gentle sighing from the waves breaking below, and then that was suddenly lost in the roar of voices and the hot reek from the bar, as Rennie pulled open the door. Men turned to look, and there was a surge of greetings and raising of glasses. Donald found himself in a seat near the hearth, and the first drink was set in front of him. They would all know why he was here, and they would keep him company for as long as it took.

Some of them would, anyway. Busy with the welcomes and toasts from all around him, Donald was aware of movement near the door, and looked round in time to see Andrew Bain shouldering his way through the crowd, and James Wallace close behind him. Of Aly and Euan there was no sign; perhaps they had been the first to leave. Donald took a deep breath, and some of the tension singing through his body began to ebb away. He lifted his glass, raised it and drained it in one go. There was a roar of approval, and another appeared in front of him at once. He shuddered as the whisky burned its way through him, and James and Rennie, sitting either side of him, laughed and knocked back their drinks too. A long night lay ahead.

38

Much, much later – he had no idea how many hours had passed – someone was pulling at his elbow as he sat, still holding a half-empty glass, trying to follow an endless, rambling story told by old Hector on the other side of the hearth, but with so many interruptions and embellishments by his audience that Donald had long ago lost the thread of it, if indeed there had ever been one. He turned, trying to focus through the fog of smoke and drink.

A small someone, shawled against the cool night air. A woman? He could see her mouth move, but no words reached him. He shook his head, trying to clear it, but that only made everything swim and blur around him.

Then James had hold of his other arm and was pulling him to his feet. 'Away with you now,' he said into Donald's ear. 'Here's Kirsty MacDonald come to fetch you.'

Between them, James and Rennie disentangled him from chair and table and got him to the door, where they were washed out on a wave of goodwill from the other men, and came to a swaying halt in the utter stillness outside. Fresh air poured over them like cold water.

'On you go,' said Rennie, and shoved him towards Kirsty. 'Mind you don't lose him over the harbour wall!' he said to her, as she grabbed at Donald's arm and staggered under the sudden weight. After a dangerous moment he got his balance, and turned to wave to the others, but they were already making their precarious way down to the harbour, and behind him other men were leaving the bar, going home at last, now that the night's work was done.

Kirsty pulled him out of the way and began to steer him up the path. 'They've not got the brains they were born with!' she was grumbling. 'Everyone knows you've no head for drink, Donald Mac-farlane. Watch now, here's three steps up.'

'Wha's? Is she…?' The words slid away as he tried to get hold of them.

'You'll see soon enough. I've enough to do to get you there.' And indeed, he had enough to do to put one foot in front of the other, to keep moving forward, watching his step in the half-light. He stopped. Wasn't there something really important he had to know?

'Kirsty,' he began, but she only dragged at him impatiently.

'Get along with you! It's been a long night, and we all need our beds. Though you'll be sleeping on the floor tonight; not that it'll bother you, the state you're in.' And he plodded after her, obedient and bewildered, trying to feel his way to the thing that mattered. Mairhi, Mairhi and the baby.

The baby. He stopped again, stubborn now. 'Are they all right?'

'For goodness' sake! If you don't keep stopping you'll see for yourself. It's not my place to tell you, as you well know. Come on now!'

He almost turned tail then; dread rose in him and his legs would carry him no further. But here came two more women down the path, making their way homeward.

'Here's the new father!' one of them called, and Kirsty threw him a sour look. 'If I ever get him there!' she said, and gave him a hefty shove that set the other women laughing. 'Too late to change your mind now!' they said, and went on their way, while Donald once more set himself to the task of putting one foot in front of the other.

More women passed them. It seemed half the village had an interest in seeing Mairhi's baby into the world. Whatever kind of creature it might be, they all knew by now, except for him. He plodded on, trying to find again the clear resolve he had felt when he made his promise to the seals at midwinter, half a year and a new lifetime ago, but the straight path was lost now, in the pearly mists of a midsummer dawn.

'Wait there a minute,' said Kirsty, and Donald raised his eyes to find himself in his own garden, and the birds already singing.

He stood, swaying a little, as though he were out at sea. The thought made him smile; a bitter joke. For the first time in his life, he wished it were true.

'Merciful heavens, Donald, look at the state of you!' Here came Catriona with Kirsty and yet another woman, but Donald had eyes for nothing but the small bundle she carried. 'Well, she's just fine now, and sleeping like a baby herself. You can see her in a while, and in the meantime…' and she put the bundle into his arms. And for once, she fell silent, waiting to see what he would say.

Donald looked down at what he held. It was well swaddled, so that nothing but its face could be seen. At least, he supposed it must be a face, though the eyes, if it had any, were lost in the creases either side of a little flat nose. In the half-light, it was the colour of bell heather. As he watched, trying to make some sense of it, it twisted a little in his arms, opened a triangular mouth and gave a strange, wavering cry, like a night bird. Misery rose up in him. He had never seen any creature like this, whether human or otherwise.

39

Better do it now, and have done with it. He turned, gathering himself for the slow trudge down to the strand, where the rowboat waited. Behind him, the little group of women stirred into life.

'Donald, what do you think you're about now?' Catriona was at his elbow, trying to take the child. 'Come inside, he'll take cold out here. I told them to go easy with the whisky,' she said to the other women. 'But you know what men are like when they get going. For the Lord's sake, Donald, there's no need for tears now! You've a fine, healthy boy, and all's well.'

He stopped. Catriona pushed at him, but he stood firm, looking down again at the bundle in his arms. And yes, it did have eyes; eyes like his own, the clean-washed blue of the early-morning sky, which gazed up at him now with an ancient, measuring look.

'What d'you say? A boy, is it?'

'Of course, a boy! And a big, strong one; no wonder he was in such a hurry to be born. What's he to be called, Donald?'

'I haven't thought.' That set the women laughing, but it was true; he had been steeling himself for the worst that could happen, and never let himself imagine how else it might be. A boy. *This is my son*, he thought. And then; *my father must have stood just so, looking down at me in his arms.* With that, the answer was clear.

'His name is John,' he said.

∷

He woke after far too little sleep, lying uncomfortably on the floor by the hearth, when his mother pulled open the front door to let the fresh air in. Sunlight poured over him, hot and thick, and he groaned. Bridie was clattering crockery onto the table.

'Just as well you don't do that too often,' she said, looking down at him. 'And just as well it's not a seagoing day today.'

Donald groaned again. 'How's Mairhi?' he said, squinting against the cruel sunlight. 'How was it?'

Bridie smiled, a smile that took him straight back to childhood. His little sister chanting on their father's shoulders, and himself holding his father's strong, work-calloused hand as they came up the last slope before their own house, and their mother running to meet them, joy shining out of her. Donald shuddered, drawing in a great, ragged breath, and drew his arm across his face.

His mother was watching him. 'I know,' she said softly. 'All this time – but all's well, Donald. Just as it should be. And no-one can be in any doubt; we must have had half the village women here, one way and another! I'm sure some of them were hoping to see something magical or monstrous; but if they did, they've gone home disappointed.' She was about to say more, but then there came from the bedroom that strange new sound. Bridie came to him and took his arm. 'Come now,' she said. 'Come and greet your wife and son.'

At the bedroom door, she stood back and let him go in alone. Mairhi lay in the bed with her hair spread loose on the pillow, and at sight of him she smiled; but as he moved towards her she shrank back a little, holding the baby close. Donald stopped. He lifted his hands and let them fall back, helpless. What could he do? Behind him, he heard his mother take a sharp breath, and then she hurried to Mairhi's side.

'It's all right, it's all right, my dear. Nothing to fear. He'll not hurt you or the babe. It's not like ... well, see now, there's nothing to worry about.' She took Donald's hand and drew him forward. 'We're both so proud of you, aren't we, Donald? Talk to her,' she said. 'Let her see you mean no harm.'

'Mairhi,' he began, and had to clear his throat before he could go on. 'Oh, love, how could you think I'd hurt you? I'm here to protect you and our child, now and always, I swear it.' The baby was crying more strongly now, turning its head from side to side against her breast, and he was weeping too, the tears falling unchecked. The thought came to him of what he had been prepared to do last night, and he shuddered again. He went to the bedside and fell to his knees, sobbing outright. 'I'll never hurt you again. I'll look after you both. I'll go to sea and provide for us all! Please, love, please don't shut me out!'

The raw sound of his own despair appalled him, and he buried his face in the bedcover, shaking as he tried to hold back the tide of grief. After a moment, he felt the light touch of her hand on his hair. Behind him, he heard his mother say something like, 'It's not you, my dear, she knows; she knows you wouldn't...' But her words were lost in the gentle warmth that spread through him from Mairhi's fingers, like clean water washing away pain and guilt, soothing away the false fire of the whisky still in his blood, pouring balm on his wounds. He yearned to give in to it, to be borne out on the sweet, healing tide, but it would not do, not today of all days. He stopped her stroking hand, kissed her palm and then held it still.

'Not now, love, not for me. Save your strength. You've done so well!'

Cautiously, watching her face all the while, he reached out to touch the baby's cheek with one finger. It stopped fussing and turned towards the touch, seeking milk. After a moment, finding nothing to its liking, it let out an impatient wail. Donald laughed. 'It's his mother he needs now! I'll let you be.'

He got to his feet, watched for a moment as the child – John, his son John – found his mother's breast at last and began to suck. He took a deep breath, and let it all out, let it all fall away. 'I'd best go and get washed,' he said.

40

That was the start of a strange new time. John was a strong baby, hungry for life, and right away he became the centre of the household. After the first night, he slept in a cradle next to the big bed; but as soon as he roused, Mairhi would bring him into bed with her, and fall asleep with the child at her breast. She had laid aside her misgivings about letting Donald near him, and Donald learned to sleep lightly, always aware of the child's small stirrings, the rise and fall of his breath. Leaving the bed to go out into the world seemed like a kind of birth, every new morning. His skin felt tender, as though it were not quite healed, every sensation more intense; the touch of the breeze, the sting of blown spray.

It was not that he wanted to stay with them all the time; more that everything he did was charged with new meaning because they were there at his hearth. His hearth: he was the head of a family now. Of course, he would go to sea whenever he could, though he still saw to the crab pots as well. The first day out with the crew, he walked down to the harbour as usual, but somehow his stride was longer; he stood taller when folk stopped him to give their congratulations and ask after the baby. He felt, for the first time, as though he had the right to be there.

And so the summer wore on, and the child grew and thrived. Mairhi was up and about within a few days, and she too seemed to grow more beautiful, so that sometimes he could hardly bear to look at her. Everything seemed clearer and sharper, charged with a secret fire that was fiercer and more pure than anything a man could get from a bottle of whisky; and he went about his business drunk with the joy of it. James laughed at him – 'You'd think you were the first man ever to father a child!' – but Hugh watched quietly, and gave him more work on the boat when he could. Only Rennie seemed to draw back a little, making excuses to be off home as soon as the day's catch was dealt with. When Donald remarked on it, James only laughed. 'He's not ready to settle yet, and his father's after him all the time to find a wife to keep house for them both. It used to be he'd get away from all that at sea, but now you're bringing it with you!'

Donald was puzzled. 'Do I say too much, then?'

'You don't need to! It's there in the look of you, in the way you're coiling that rope as though it were a precious thing. Och, man, don't worry yourself about it. He'll come to it in time, same as you did. From where I'm standing, it looks just fine.'

After a minute or two, Donald worked this out. 'Catriona will come to it as well, I'm sure of it. She likes you well enough.'

James turned away, busy with nets and baskets. 'I think you're right at that. It's Hugh I'm bothered about. It's not that he'll be against it; I don't think so. But to have a younger man come into your household, to give place to him and his children, if we're blessed that way; well, that can be hard. Your mother, now, she seems to be fine with it, but it's different for women, maybe.'

To this, there was nothing to say. Did his mother find it hard to step aside as head of the household? She had schemed and plotted; dealt with reluctance from Donald himself and suspicion or outright hostility from everyone else; and buried her own misgivings, in order to bring this situation about. What it cost her, he had no idea, and he would never ask. Brimful with his own precarious happiness, he drew back from walking that path, unwilling to spill even one drop. But Hugh was another matter; that seemed safe enough.

'I'll have a word with him,' he said.

41

Not so long ago, he would have gone out of his way to avoid having words with anybody about anything. The thought came to him, fleetingly, as he walked up to the shieling with Hugh after the day's fishing, laden with nets for mending, and it made him smile. Not so long ago had become ancient history, as misty and unreal as any of the old stories. Surely, now, it was the same for Mairhi? He hoped so, and dared not ask her in case it broke the spell. But here, at least, was one question he need not shrink from.

'You know, you've set Catriona off, starting a family. The baby's all she talks about these days.' Hugh's words startled him; had his uncle guessed what he was thinking?

'Ailsa and Jeannie too. He'll be spoiled with all the attention.'

Hugh laughed. 'He will not! It's what makes them grow, and thrive. Catriona's done her best with the little ones, and tried to make it up to them for losing their mother, but I know they still miss her at times.'

'So do you, surely.' The old Donald would never have said such a thing to his uncle. Hugh glanced aside at him. 'So I do. You can understand that now.'

Donald said nothing, and they negotiated a narrow stretch of the path in silence, going single file. Then, 'Did you never think of marrying again?'

Hugh smiled. 'Who'd have me?' He became more serious. 'Of course, many a time. But it's a hard thing, to lose two wives. It almost seems you'd be inviting another woman to the same fate, if you married again. And besides, I don't think Catriona would take kindly to giving over her place to anyone else; do you?'

Donald had never heard that becoming a father made a man take risks he would not have dreamed of taking before, but it seemed that for him, it was so, at least where words were concerned. 'You'd have had my mother and me to live here, if she'd had a mind that way.'

Hugh stopped, so that Donald had to stop too, and looked him full in the face. 'And I still would. When I first asked your mother, Catriona still needed mothering herself, and goodness knows you needed a father, though it wasn't me you were yearning for.' Hugh's eyes held his, and Donald realised how rare it was that he ever looked directly at anyone in that way. Except for Mairhi. It made him hot and uncomfortable. He shifted the load of netting, glanced up at the sky. 'There's a squall coming.'

Hugh laughed. 'Best get on home, then.' He walked on a few paces, and then stopped again. 'There aren't many like your mother,' he said. 'John was a lucky man.' And he moved on, not waiting for an answer. Donald had had enough of risk-taking, and so they finished their journey in silence. It was not until much later, when he was on his way home with a share of the catch and some of Jeannie's old nightgowns for the baby, that he realised he had not mentioned James at all.

∷

He had been right, though, about the weather. A summer storm came in overnight, whirling away the bright stillness into which John had been born. Time moved on again. He would go down to the boat, now, and put on his sealskin gloves in sight of the other men, and be glad of them. They made it possible to do what he could not otherwise have done. Whenever he could do it without being seen, he left offerings for the seals on the rocks where they liked to lie. It became a ritual for him, one of the many things fishermen do to bring about a safe voyage or a good catch. He was always aware of the seals, these days; and at the same time, he hoped that Mairhi might begin to forget. Surely the baby would bind her into the life that was now hers, in a way that nothing else could?

'She's a good mother,' Bridie said to him one day, as they watched

Mairhi playing with the baby. He was smiling now, and beginning to reach for things that were held out to him. 'And he's growing just as he should. Not like that poor child of Jessie Bain's.'

'Jessie doesn't seem to miss it, though.'

Once she was up and about again, Jessie had begun to turn up at their door from time to time. At first, she'd made the excuse that she had 'come to fetch Nancy home', and it was true enough that Nancy hung around Mairhi whenever she could; but, as Bridie said, 'she could have sent one of the other bairns after her.' After the first time or two, she seemed to feel there was no need for an excuse at all, and they learned to expect her, usually with a child or two in tow, whenever Aly was at home. She would watch Mairhi feeding little John, see the children fussing over him, and never mention her own baby at all, unless Bridie asked her directly. Her milk had never come in, and the child was still with a wet nurse who lived up in the hills. Bridie herself had seen it there, and said it was a sickly thing.

Jessie had been there the day before, when Ailsa and Jeannie burst in, shouting that Catriona was on her way up the path, and there were scones and fresh crowdie 'and we made them all ourselves!' They fell quiet when they saw Jessie. Bridie busied herself making tea for everyone, but by the time she came to pour it, Jessie had slipped away.

'Did you not see her on the path?' Bridie asked Catriona.

Catriona sniffed. 'She's a strange one! Hiding in the heather, I shouldn't wonder, rather than give me the time of day. I'm surprised you'll have her in the house.'

'I've no quarrel with Jessie Bain,' said Bridie, with a sideways glance to where Nancy sat in the corner, watching Jeannie and Ailsa handing out scones, and doing her best to be invisible. They, too, acted as though there was nobody there. Jeannie was carrying a plate carefully across to Mairhi, who sat by the hearth with the baby in her arms; but when the plate was offered to her, Mairhi took Jeannie by the shoulder, turned her around and pointed at Nancy.

Jeannie stood still. 'Catriona says we mustn't talk to them,' she said, and her clear, small voice fell like a stone into the sudden silence.

'That's all right, my dear,' said Bridie before Catriona could gather her wits. 'Nancy's been helping me and Mairhi gather some medicines, haven't you, Nancy?'

Nancy said nothing. Only stared like a trapped animal, from Bridie to Jeannie to Mairhi, and back again.

'We can help you do that,' said Ailsa. Like a little copy of her big sister Catriona, sitting up straight and trying to take charge.

'Of course you can. This time of year, all help is welcome! So here's a scone for you, Nancy, and some jam to go on the top. And then all you children can go and look for eggs while Mairhi settles the baby to sleep.' Bridie gave Catriona a long look. From Donald, or even from her father, it would have had no effect, but for Bridie she held back the tide of words, if not for long.

Donald got up abruptly, leaving his tea half drunk. 'Better check that Sam Bain's not been in the barn again and left the door wide open.' He was out of the door before Jeannie and Ailsa could jump up, clamouring to come with him. There were too many people, these days; too many unspoken words battering about the room like panicked birds, never mind the ones that were actually said. Home had always been a quiet refuge for him, just himself and his mother and a deep, peaceful understanding between them. Mairhi's coming had stirred up the waters, to be sure, but she brought with her a special kind of peace, and he had learned to cherish it. Now, it seemed the whole world had an interest in her and the baby, and his quiet haven was no more.

A part of him wanted to be off and away, up into the hills or along the shoreline, finding sanctuary in his old way. But he had made a promise to see this through, to stand by his new family whatever it took – though he had never reckoned with having to play host to all and sundry. And it was more than that, more than just a duty. He missed Mairhi at his side, watching and learning and teaching him in her turn. He went only as far as the barn, where he climbed up on top of this year's fresh hay bales, to lie for a while, listening to the patter of rain on the roof and the scratch of mice in the rafters.

A couple of the barn cats came to sniff at him, hoping for food, and then they let him be. When the children came in with a basket for eggs, he lay quiet.

'The speckled hen has a nest under the wall outside. Auntie Mairhi showed me.' That was Jeannie, full of importance. 'But we mustn't take her eggs because she's brooding.'

'The fox will get them for sure. Catriona says it's foolish to let her sit there.' Ailsa, eight years old and armed with certainty. Donald heard the rustle of hay as one of them found a nest. Then, 'You leave those eggs alone!'

Donald raised his head a little. Ailsa stood, hands on hips, and Jeannie was over by the door. Then came another voice, close under the haystack where he was lying. 'She said I could!' Nancy Bain, tremulous but determined.

'Well, *she's* not here, and I say you can't!'

'You can't tell me what to do.' Donald had never heard Nancy so bold.

'Those eggs belong to my family, and you've no right!' Ailsa came a step nearer. 'And that's my dress you're wearing,' she added for good measure.

'It's mine now. She gave it to me.'

Ailsa made a small, scornful noise. 'She doesn't understand about things like that. That dress should have gone to Jeannie when she's big enough. Catriona says so.'

Nancy was silent. This was a defence Donald understood. Give them no handhold, and they'll tire of the sport in the end. He had used it himself many times, with Nancy's own father for one. But he understood something else now, too; how it looked from the other side, how stubbornness became insolence, and how insolence invited punishment. Even as he began to move, Ailsa darted forward, and Nancy gave a sharp cry.

Jeannie saw him first. 'She started it, Uncle Donald!' she called as he clambered down from the haystack. By the time he reached the floor, Ailsa had grabbed the basket and retreated. Nancy crouched against the wall of the barn. One of her braids had come loose, and she looked up at him like a wild beast at bay. There were tears in her eyes. And no defence against him, the looming adult. She simply huddled there, waiting for the blow.

'It's all right, Nancy. You did nothing wrong.'

Behind him, Ailsa and Jeannie had crowded close, anticipating justice. Nancy saw her chance. The look she gave him as she fled for the door contained both gratitude and scorn, but there was no mistaking what his two cousins felt about it.

'She was taking the eggs, Uncle Donald!'

'She was doing as she was told. You leave her be.'

'She's got no right! That whole family is nothing but trouble, Catriona says.'

Despite himself, Donald smiled. It was so exactly what Catriona would say, and in exactly that way. He crouched to pick up the basket, and looked up at Ailsa. 'You're old enough to think for yourself,' he said. 'What trouble has she brought to you, now?'

Ailsa huffed. 'Her daddy hurt Mairhi!'

'True enough. But how is Nancy to blame for that?'

'They're all the same. Give them an inch and they'll take an ell, Ca—'

'Catriona says a lot of things. Too many things, sometimes.' Donald knew he would pay for that later, but at least he had their attention. 'Nancy's daddy hasn't been working much lately, and that means we're all doing what we can. You wouldn't have them go hungry, now, would you?'

Ailsa considered this. She opened her mouth, no doubt ready with another of Catriona's pronouncements, but then gave him a sideways glance, and shut it again. He smiled at her, and after a moment she smiled back.

'I know where there are some more nests,' he said. 'This time of year, the hens can't seem to stop laying, and we've more eggs than we know what to do with. What say you and Jeannie pick a few out to send home with Nancy when she goes?'

'She can't have the brown ones!' Jeannie piped up from her place by the door.

'Well, fair enough. You run and get another basket, and we'll see how many we can find.'

She was off before he'd finished speaking, and Donald turned back to Ailsa. 'Those children are half starved,' he said. 'We're lucky to have all this. Folks would do no less for us, if your father or I couldn't work. Jeannie's too little to understand, but you know better, don't you?'

Ailsa nodded solemnly. 'I'll explain it to her,' she said. 'But Sam Bain was taking the eggs without asking; I saw him. He was stealing!'

'Aye, well. Some people don't know right from wrong. But I think Nancy does, if you give her a chance. Can you try to be kind to her, for Mairhi's sake?'

Ailsa considered this. 'She can't be my best friend,' she said. 'But she can have my old shoes if she likes. They're too big for Jeannie still.' And that was enough for now, Donald felt.

He knew no more than Sam Bain, or his wretched father, about right and wrong, but he knew that hungry children must be fed. He picked up the basket. 'There's a nest under the raspberry bushes outside, I think.'

42

These days, Donald understood how a family man might go to sea for a bit of peace and quiet. There, in the undemanding company of other men, things became simple. Sometimes they hardly spoke, moving around each other and doing the things that had to be done, and there was a kind of solace in that. He even went to the bar from time to time, when the catch had been good, and learned what it was to celebrate with the crew. They trusted each other with their lives, these men, every time they put out to sea. Now that he was no longer holding himself apart, he began to understand the bonds between them, woven of shared danger and hard-won gains, and the fierce joy that found outlet in drinking. But always, before the night was too old and the money spent, he would take his leave and make his way homeward. Other men might take their wives and children for granted; for Donald, that would never be possible.

He was out on his own less often now, and weeks might go by between his visits to the skerry, but at the full moon in late September, he made time to take the rowboat to see to the crab pots. The seals were coming ashore, to give birth and to mate. Like any prudent fisherman, Donald knew and usually avoided the places where they went at this time, but he could not stop himself from rowing over to the skerry. It was a wild night, with a stinging rain blowing every which way, so he had to work hard to get there safely; and after all, of course, it was deserted. What had he expected?

He pulled the boat up high out of the water and plodded home, bent against the weather. It had always been a joy to him, to see the warm light in the window and know that the day's work was almost done, but now it was doubly so. A year, almost to the day, since he'd stumbled up this path with Mairhi at his side, and now? – his life was changed almost beyond recognising. The sweetness of it welled up in him, and he came to a standstill, undone by tenderness. The light blurred and swam; he blinked away tears, and then the door was open and she was there, waiting for him, and his feet were moving again of their own accord.

Inside, the fire was bright and the table laid ready, and little John put up his arms and crowed at the sight of him. Bridie asked after the catch and gave him news of how John had rolled over on his blanket, and how the storm had spoiled the last of the blackberries. Mairhi told him her day too, not in words but with glances and gestures. A different kind of weaving than what went on between the men, but just as precious. It seemed to Donald that in the past year he had been showered with gifts, and all of it began with her.

He watched her, moving to and fro in the firelight, and tried to bring to mind the way she had been a year ago. Not his first sight of her – that he would never forget – but those early days, bundled into clothes and shoes, utterly adrift in a strange world. Now, he saw how her skirt swirled out as she turned, how she tucked back a stray lock of hair, how she rocked the baby against her shoulder, and how she did all these things without thinking, at ease in her humanity. More than that. Feeling his gaze upon her, she gave him a quick sidelong glance, and the rocking became dancing; not a wild reel like the ones she'd learned for their wedding, nor the playful catch-as-catch-can he'd seen her at with her sisters, but a gentle sway of hip and thigh, like the wash of waves on a summer's day. Her skirt brushed against him as she went by, and his skin tingled. *She's soothing the baby, but she's dancing for me.*

He looked away. Sometimes it took every scrap of determination he had – to hold to his resolution. Some nights it was a torment to lie beside her, and more than once he'd pulled on shirt and trousers and stolen away out of the house, to walk the hills or comb the shoreline in the long summer twilight. Now, though, it was full dark outside, and building to a gale besides. There, that was the answer for now. 'I'd better see to the barn doors in this wind,' he said.

43

He stayed in the barn, mending nets by lantern-light, until he was sure they would all be in bed. The wind gusted in with him when he came in at last, blowing up ash from the hearth and making the peats glow, but his mother's breathing, as she lay in bed behind the curtain, never faltered. If she did hear him come in, she let him be. In the bedroom, too, the baby lay in his crib with his mouth open and arms akimbo, sleeping hard. Well, then. As quietly as he could, Donald eased himself out of his clothes and lay down next to Mairhi, taking care not to touch her. He turned away onto his side, closed his eyes and waited for sleep to come.

In the darkness behind him she sighed and shifted, and in the next instant his eyes opened wide again as her arm came around him, and he felt her breath on his neck. She did this sometimes on cold nights, but tonight was not cold. Donald stopped breathing altogether, as she curled against him, nuzzling into his neck, the way she did with the baby. Her hand found its way between the buttons of his night-shirt, and began to stray lower.

'Mairhi—?' He caught at her hand, held it against his heart. He tried to say something more, but words seemed to have deserted him. She answered only with that almost-silent laughter, and took his ear between her teeth, and nibbled it.

'Mairhi?' He tried again, turned over to face her and took both her hands. 'What is it, my dear? What … are you sure? Is this what you want?' In the dark, he could see only the gleam of her eyes, and her shape in the dark as she sat up, and then her hair was all about his face and he could see nothing, feel nothing except the scent of her, her smooth, perfect skin against his own, her sweet breath waking fire where it touched. He lay still, though it took all of his willpower; never again, he had sworn it, right here in this room, on their wedding day. Never again; unless it was her own wish.

'Is this what you want?' he asked again, though his mouth was so dry he could hardly form the words. And she laid a finger on his lips, shushing him. No words, now. He lay back, surrendering.

'Show me, then. You show me what to do.'

And she showed him. How could she know? In all the times when he had imagined, despite himself, how it might be, he had never thought of this. When men talked about women, in the bar or out at sea, it was all about taking, about overcoming. They spoke like brave hunters after their prey; but this was as far from that as could be. He did what she wanted, and when his own pleasure overcame him, she showed him other ways.

Perhaps, he thought – when he could think at all – *perhaps the men who did not talk were the ones who really knew.* For this, at least, words were not the way. And in giving freely where he had taken by force, there was such sweetness! She licked the salt tears from his face, and he caught at her hands and kissed them, each clever, perfect finger. When she finally slept – much, much later – she curled against him, wanting even in sleep that deep comfort of skin against skin, and he lay, holding her close and breathing in the scent of her, open-eyed in the dark.

44

'I'll come out with you tomorrow.' Donald was with Hugh down at the harbour, stowing nets and boxes aboard. 'Where are the others just now?'

Hugh straightened up, easing the ache in his back. 'Rennie's away down the coast, chasing a lassie who's taken his eye. Callum's fallen ill again; I don't know if he'll be out with us this winter.'

'Mother said. Here, let me take that.' Donald gathered up an armful of ropes, heavy with tar and salt water, and swung them into the hold. 'What about James?'

'Aye, well. Right now, he'd be helping Catriona with the garden, or maybe repairing the barn. I wouldn't know.'

'Is he not coming out, then?'

Hugh laughed. 'It's not come to that, yet. But even you must have noticed which way the wind's blowing.'

'Oh, I've noticed, right enough.' Reminded of his promise to James, Donald stood up, balancing on the moving deck, looking down at his uncle. 'He asked me to speak for him.'

'Did he, now? And what do you have to say?' Hugh shaded his eyes, squinting into the sun. 'As if I couldn't guess!'

'Well. Catriona must have said it all, many times over, by now.'

Hugh folded his arms. 'Catriona says everything that comes into her head, and twice over for good measure. But on the subject of James, she has said nothing at all.' He waited.

'I can't speak for her. But James would come to live at the shieling; he wouldn't take her from you and the bairns. He'd help with the farm and the fishing, but he says...' Donald hesitated, cleared his throat and tried again. 'He says the boat should come to me, by rights.' He could not meet his uncle's gaze.

'Leave those nets, now. They'll keep. Here.' And Hugh reached out a hand. When Donald stepped down onto the jetty, he did not let go.

'I never wanted to captain the boat,' he said. 'Did you know that? Your father, now, he couldn't abide the slow work on the farm; he'd always rather be out at sea. But with him gone, what choice did I have? I did what I had to do. That's what it comes down to, in the end.' He stopped, looking past Donald to the houses at the harbour's edge, and to the hills beyond.

'When they're wed,' he said, 'I'll step down, and you'll take the boat. You're a better fisherman than your father, Donald. He took risks; he always wanted to go out further, stay out longer. We should have been safe in harbour, that day.'

With all of his strength, Donald held still. He seemed to be striving for balance on board in a high wind, not standing safe on dry land with his uncle's hand firm on his arm.

'It's a young man's work, fishing. You and James will make a good job of it between you; I've seen how you work together. You'll need another man or two. Oh, now, don't look like that! I'll help out now and then. And you'll get your turn on land, in time. I know what's in your heart, lad, and it will come to you, believe me.' At last, he took his hand away. And somehow Donald remained standing.

He cleared his throat. 'You'll give your blessing, then?'

Hugh smiled. 'I'd say it was me that's blessed.'

45

That year, the autumn storms brought huge shoals of cod up from the warmer southern waters, driving them close in to the shore so that the boats barely had to leave harbour. Such abundance was both a blessing and a burden. All the fish had to be salted, or smoked, or dried before it spoiled, and all who were able lent their hands to the task, working long into the night. Even Father Finian worked alongside the other men, and Donald could see the gladness in him – to be part of things for once. He stood straighter, laughed louder; but then, maybe Donald was only seeing his own happiness. Everything seemed brighter and better these days. Standing on deck, handing over yet more laden baskets to the willing hands ashore, buffeted by the gusting wind and the squall of seabirds, his whole body tingled with aliveness.

Along the harbour ranged other boats, big and small, and others coming in all the time with new bounty. Almost his whole world was here: the women ashore, gutting and sorting the fish, singing some of their waulking songs to speed the task; children, helping if they could, and rushing about senseless with excitement if they could not; men, working together to a common end. Peggy Mackay had come out, and was giving orders to the other women, sitting like a queen in her high-backed chair. Even Aly Bain, though he had not gone out to sea, was helping unload the catch.

And always Donald was aware of Mairhi, who would never sit to one task for long, but moved here and there, like a bright needle stitching it all together. Now she went to retrieve a runaway child, and now she stopped to bind a cut hand, and now she raised her arms to the gulls and skuas clamouring overhead, as though she might take flight and join them. Mairhi, his wife, who it seemed had forgiven him.

He was not the only one watching. Nancy Bain followed her like a second shadow, and Jessie, though she sat with the women and her hands were always at work, followed with her eyes. Donald saw Peggy Mackay marking all of it, and no doubt making her own judgments. She had not spoken out against Mairhi since John was born, but Donald knew that she missed nothing. He glanced along the seawall to where the Bains' boat was unloading, and saw that Aly Bain, too, had paused to watch. Euan shouted, 'Hoi! No time for woolgathering!' Aly turned again to the task in hand, but Donald had seen the brooding look in his eye. It could not be helped.

'Donald!' He turned to see Catriona, hands on hips, looking up at him from among the baskets piled ashore. 'The smokehouses are full and we're almost out of boxes for salting. You'd better make this the last load for today.'

He stood straight again, gazing out beyond the harbour where the fish thronged. One boat was still out there, dancing among the feasting dolphins and porpoises. He saw the brief gleam of a fish as someone tossed it high, catching the westering sun for an instant before it was snatched out of the air and dragged apart by the birds.

'Aye. We've done enough for now. James!'

James, at the stern, raising a bucket of seawater to sluice the deck, waved a hand in reply.

'We won't go out again tonight. They'll still be there in the morning.' He looked around for Hugh, but his uncle had already gone ashore with the last basket of fish, and it seemed the decision was his to make. Little more than a year ago, he'd have been out on the hills, as far away as he could get, and now here he was at the centre of it all. His eyes returned to Mairhi, now nursing the baby, and for a moment she lifted her head and gazed at him. Or was she looking past him, to the open sea and the new bank of rainclouds sweeping in? It was too far to make out.

::

There was a grand feast that night, all of them bringing food down to the sheds where fish were sorted and stored for sale, and boats were brought in for winter repairs. There were no boats now, and in the empty space there was a bonfire. James brought out his fiddle, and Euan his pipes, and there was dancing. Later – after the women and children and the older men had gone their ways home – there might be fighting too, but for now old scores were laid aside. Mairhi sat with Jessie and the younger women, and the children tumbled around them or slept, curled like puppies. Donald's own son was there some-where, and even Jessie's baby, returned to its mother at last, though it was usually Nancy who tended to it. The women were swaying in time to the music, raising their voices in song. From where he sat with his crew, Donald could see that Mairhi sang too, though not the words.

'*Ceud soiridh soiridh bhuam na e ho hao oho…*'

'A hundred greetings to the shores of home
And to the hillside with the lovely birches.
Peas will grow there, beans will grow there,
Corn will grow there, oats and barley,
Sweet is the cuckoo's call, sweet is the thrush's song,
Sweet is the voice of the herdsman, herding the cattle,
Sweet is the voice of the milkmaid, tending the young calves.
I can see the boat making good speed,
Going around the headland.
It is he, my sweetheart, at the helm.'

Their faces glowed red in the firelight, and their eyes shone: exhausted, dirty and beautiful after the hard labour of the day. When the song ended, there was a moment of spellbound silence, and then, from the men, a deep roar of applause. Some of the women began to leave, gathering up children and belongings, while others started on a new song. Donald looked away as Shona Bain leaned over to refill his mug with ale, and so he missed the start of it, hearing only the raised voices and the sudden cry of a child. Then Shona said, 'Oh, dear God,' under her breath and straightened up, leaving his view clear.

46

Mairhi and Jessie still sat together among the children, but in front of them stood Aly Bain. He had hold of his wife's arm and was trying to drag her upright, but he swayed as he stood, and from the rising shrieks of the children, he had stepped on more than one on his drunken journey across the room.

'Let her be, Aly!' That was Andrew, standing up now and beginning to push his way between the men.

Aly ignored him. 'Get up, woman. We're going home. Now!' Jessie leaned back against Mairhi, and Donald saw Mairhi's arm go around her.

'I won't come.' The words were almost inaudible but the meaning was clear. Jessie was shaking her head, pulling away.

'You'll come when I say!'

'Leave me be!' The shout took them all by surprise, and even the crying children fell silent. Jessie Bain, who never fought back, had found her voice.

Aly raised his free hand and slapped her, open-handed. Around Donald, men looked away. It was not their business. But even then, Jessie did not give in.

'I won't come with you! Another child would kill me – she told you that to your face!' Jessie looked around for Bridie, seated with the older women. 'You said so!'

Bridie got up then, leaning on the women next to her for support, but when she spoke her voice was as clear and strong as ever. 'I did say so. Shona, you were there, and Mairhi too.' She looked around, and both of them nodded. 'It won't do, Aly.' She spoke directly to him, just as she had done after the birth of the child; but she did not shame him by reminding him of that now. Even so, he had gone too

far to back down. Jessie screamed as he dragged at her arm again, and
then Mairhi was on her feet and facing him.

It might have been only a trick of the firelight, but she seemed
to be smiling. She reached out a hand towards him, and he let go
of Jessie and stumbled backwards as though he had been burned.
Children scrambled out from underfoot, and men made way for
him. None tried to hold him back. A wild gust of wind blew in as
he threw open the door, scattering smoke and sparks from the fire,
and then he was gone.

Children began to wail again, but no-one else spoke. Most people
looked away, but Jessie was on her feet now, not hiding her face
among the women. She had hold of Mairhi's hand. She said into the
silence, 'I won't go back with him. I'm not going back, ever.'

'Well said, Jessie!' That was Shona, standing among the men and
wielding the ale-jug like a weapon, daring any of them to challenge
her.

Bridie said, more quietly, 'Not before time,' and then sank down
again as though the effort had taken all her strength.

Somewhere among the women, a new song began, a rowing song
with a strong beat. The sound swelled as others took it up, growing
deeper and louder as, one by one, the men joined in. At Donald's
side, Shona sang out, facing Andrew Bain across the table. Andrew
shook his head, but Euan, her husband, raised his ale-mug to her.
And over by the fire, Mairhi took Jessie by both hands and began to
dance, slowly at first as Jessie hung back, laughing and crying all at
once, and then whirling into a wild jig. Donald watched, enthralled,
as others joined in. There was James dancing with Catriona, and
Euan with Shona, and all the children capering around them.

It seemed she could do anything, this woman, and where she led,
they would follow. Donald waited until the dance began to slow, and
when he caught her eye, like Euan, he raised his ale-mug and drank
to her. Then the dance whirled her away, and he took up the rhythm
with the others around him, beating time on the table and shouting
encouragement. Euan joined in with his pipes again, a skirling reel

that seemed to lift the dancers off their feet and set them flying. Even the old ones were clapping and swaying in time; and then suddenly there was a little island of quiet around him, as Mairhi came to a standstill right in front of him, and held out her hand.

He started to shake his head. He never danced, everyone knew it – not since he was a child and everyone had laughed when someone tripped him up. But at the same time he was standing up, reaching out to take her hand, and other people moved out of the way. As soon as they were clear of the table she took both his hands, just as she had done with Jessie, and he held her gaze and let himself be swept into the reel. At the edge of his awareness, people were cheering and shouting encouragement, but for Donald there was only Mairhi, leading him surefooted through the throng, turning around and around, shining-eyed and laughing for joy.

47

'Well, what are we going to do? *We* can't keep them.' Donald faced Bridie across the table, keeping his voice low. Shona had taken the children home with her, but Jessie refused to be parted from Mairhi, and they were asleep now in the bedroom. Donald had slept on the floor.

'I don't know, Donald.' In the morning light, Bridie looked drawn. 'But she can't go back, and she can't stay in their cottage without him. None of the children is old enough to work. She's got no other family. I haven't an answer.'

He stood up. 'How did it come to this? Why can't the Bains look after their own?'

She had no answer to that either, only looked down at her hands, clasped around a mug of tea. He said, 'I have to get down to the boat. We can't miss this tide, and Rennie's still not back.'

'I doubt we'll be seeing him for a while, now,' said Bridie. 'The word is, he's courting a lassie down the coast.'

'I know what the word is. But he'll never settle to it. You know Rennie. And Hugh can't work so long just now, with his back the way it is. It's just me and James with Hugh, today.'

She smiled, then. 'On you go, now. We'll be down later.'

Out in the freshening wind, he felt taller, bigger. Even burdened down with newly mended nets, facing a long, hard day, that tingling aliveness had not left him. She was magnificent! In his mind's eye, he saw again the wild dance, the way she had looked at Aly. For all the problems it might bring, he would not choose to undo one second of it.

The boat, though – that was another matter. He and James worked well together, that was true. They'd be hard pushed today, but he realised that he was looking forward to it, and smiled. So this was what she'd brought him to! He slowed a little as he passed by the Bains' cottage, but there was no sign of life. Now the harbour was in sight, and there was James, already aboard.

'Is Hugh not with you?'

James grimaced. 'He could barely move this morning. Catriona sent me packing. We'll just have to manage somehow.'

'Is there no-one else we can call on? I won't go out with just the two of us, a day like this. It's too big a risk.'

'Then we don't go at all. Every man and boy who can stand will be out today. Most of them are out already.' James glanced along the almost empty harbour. 'We could take the rowboat, maybe.'

Donald shook his head. 'Might as well save our strength; we'd never catch enough to be worth the effort.' He paused. 'Listen. There is one who might come, but I don't think you'll like it.'

James frowned. 'Who would that be, then?'

'If you say no, that'll be the end of it. There's no room on the boat for that sort of trouble.' Donald cleared his throat. 'It's Aly Bain.'

48

'But you can't abide the man!' James put down the rope he was holding and stared at Donald. 'And he's never had a good word to say for you, even before ... He'd never come! Not with us. Not with you, anyhow. He won't even set foot on a boat since ... well...' He let the wind take his next words. 'And would you want to work with him?'

Donald held out a hand, and James helped him aboard; a simple gesture that they did now, without thinking, almost every day. They stood face to face on deck.

'Things are different now,' Donald said slowly. 'Those children will starve if he's not working. What Jessie did last night, that was because of Mairhi. And the other thing, too; that happened because of her. The man's lost everything, and everyone saw. Even his own brothers have had enough of him. There's no coming back from all that, unless someone gives him a helping hand.'

James looked steadily at him. 'And you'd do that for Aly Bain?'

Donald took a deep breath. 'I would. But only if you're willing.'

'Well, now. We work well together, you and I; and that's no small thing, out there. I'd be sorry to lose that. But we do need another man.' James paused, thinking. 'I've a notion that working with his brothers doesn't bring out the best in him.'

Donald nodded. In his mind's eye, he saw the Bain brothers long ago on the strand, tossing a ball to and fro between them, and their father joining in. He'd throw the ball hard, and laugh when it hit one of them, or went high over their heads. The two elder boys tried to please him, braving it out when they hurt themselves, and mocking each other's mistakes. And all of them took it out on Aly, the youngest and smallest, until he broke down in tears and ran away, followed by their taunts. Donald, watching from a safe distance, had thought only of his own loss. He had no father to play with, no brothers or sisters to keep him company. And then Aly, stumbling up the path to the harbour, had come upon him.

At the time, after Aly had kicked over the sand he was building in and scattered the shells he'd gathered, it had just been one more blow from an unkind world. But now, he thought he understood.

'It's not good for a man to lose his pride like that. Maybe with us, he'd get a fresh chance.'

'I suppose we all deserve that. Even Aly Bain. Well, who am I to stand in the way?' James laughed. 'I never thought I'd see the day. And if we can get him out on the water, that'll be another thing worth seeing. But we'd better get a move on, or we won't get out at all today.'

'I'll go. Better just me.' And before he could change his mind, Donald was back on dry land and walking up the hill towards the harbour cottages. He could feel James' eyes on him, but he did not look back. The thing had to be done now, or not at all.

When he came to the Bains' cottage, the door was still closed. Donald raised his hand and knocked, perhaps more loudly than he had intended. The men might all be out on the water, but women and children were about, and some had already come out to watch. It could not be helped. There was no answer, so he knocked again, and finally he pushed the door open.

The wind whirled in, raising ash on the hearth. If Jessie's house-keeping had improved since he had last been in this house, there was no evidence of it now. The place smelled stale, musty. As he hesitated on the threshold, the bedroom door scraped open, and Aly stood in the doorway. He stared for a moment, as though not recognising who it was. Then Donald saw that he did know, that he remembered everything about the night before, and that *he* would have to be the one to speak first.

No turning back now. 'Aly,' he said.

Still the other man did not speak. Donald took a step or two into the room, closing the door behind him. The last thing Aly needed was more witnesses.

'It's a fine, fresh morning.' What could he possibly say? Aly made a small noise in his throat, and Donald took this for some kind of acknowledgment. 'Listen,' he said, and took another step forward; 'I've work for you, if you want it.'

Aly laughed then, and it was not a joyful sound. 'Get lost,' he said.

This, at least, was familiar territory. And as usual – as though anything could be usual about this moment – Donald ignored the words. 'We need another man on the boat today. Will you come?' His hands were curled into tight fists. Slowly, deliberately, he opened them. Another step, palms open. Everything in his body was crying out against it, but as he got to within a few feet, it came to him that he was the taller and stronger of the two. Perhaps he always had been.

Aly darted a sidelong look at him, like a lizard testing the air with its tongue. 'I can go on our own boat if I want. Why would I want to go with you?'

Donald shrugged, uncurled his hands again. 'Andrew's already out of harbour. You need to be working, to put food in the mouths of your children. Come out with us. The fish are still running, and there's more than we can handle.'

Aly looked away. 'I don't fish, now. I'll be away down the coast soon, find work there. Then you'll be rid of me.'

'Or you could stay and look after your own. Come out with us.'

Aly spat into the ashes. 'I don't fish,' he said again.

'You'll be fine with us,' said Donald. It was just words, just some-thing to say, but the effect on Aly was startling. His eyes widened.

'Will I so?' He stared, not at Donald but at some vision only he could see, and Donald felt the hairs on his neck rise. 'I'll be fine with you,' he repeated, sing-song. 'She looks after you, eh? Stay close to Macfarlane, you'll be fine with him.'

Now Donald was truly at a loss. For all he knew, it could even be true in some way – that Mairhi could keep him safe when he was at sea. He doubted it, though. Whatever it was she did, it worked on people very close to her, and no more than that. If anyone had ever found a way to charm the sea, he would have heard of it, surely. But what if Aly believed it? Would that be enough to get him back on board again?

'Maybe she does,' he said softly. 'I wouldn't know. But you'd be welcome to crew with us, if you'll come.' An idea came to him then, and he spoke without thinking. 'But only if you let Jessie be.'

Aly's head came up, and Donald almost stepped back from the other man's buffeting wind of rage and hatred. 'Get out,' he said, and somehow it was worse than a shout. 'You – here in my own house! What more do you want? Take it all, why don't you?'

Donald had expected stinging words, ready fists; he'd thought he could deal with that. But this was something else, something as familiar as his own heartbeat. He stooped, and picked up a piece of oat straw from the unswept floor.

'There's this much between you and me,' he said, holding it up. 'I've no right to be laying down the law for you; none at all. But if you hurt Jessie, or the children, Mairhi will know. Think on that.'

For a few more moments, neither man moved. Donald saw that Aly's pride would not allow him to give in while he stood there.

'We're leaving on the tide,' he said, and turned and went out, closing the door behind him. He had no word for the little group of children who waited outside, eager for more drama, but made his way straight back to the harbour.

49

'Almost ready,' said James as he reached the boat. 'Will he come?'

'I can't tell.' Donald took a deep breath and shuddered. 'Did I do right?'

James laughed. 'We'll see. Not the crew I'd have chosen, but we'll make the best of it.' He stopped, looking directly at Donald. 'You're a better man than he is, you know that? You did well.'

Donald looked down at the dry oat-stalk that he still held in his hand. He opened his fingers, and the wind snatched it away. James was watching him curiously.

'Just those baskets to load, now.'

They were almost done when James, looking back along the harbour, said, 'Ah, now we'll see.' He held out a hand to Aly, saying only, 'Watch your step.' A few minutes later, they were on their way out to sea.

∵

As Bridie had said, just over a year ago, nothing stayed secret for long. By the time they made harbour again that evening, everyone seemed to know about the changes aboard the Macfarlane boat. No-one remarked on it, not out there in the open; that was not the way. But as soon as they were out of earshot, making their slow way homeward, Bridie said, 'Well! You've given them all something to ponder tonight! So how was it, out on the water?'

Donald walked on a few paces before answering. He looked side-long at Mairhi and Jessie, trudging along with their burdens. 'Oh, I daresay we'll get used to each other,' was all he said eventually.

But later, when the babies were settled and Nancy had fallen asleep by the hearth, he got up to see to the beasts in the barn, and then stopped by the door. 'Jessie?' he said.

Jessie looked up at him, surprised. 'What's the matter?'

He came back into the room, and spoke softly, though there was no-one but his own family to overhear. 'When I asked Aly to come aboard, I told him…' Here his resolve almost failed him; he cleared his throat and tried again. 'I made a condition. He's not to hurt you and the bairns. He's not to touch you, unless you wish it. Do you see?'

Now all three women were staring at him. Nancy too, with her sure instinct for trouble, was awake, crouching by the fire like a wild creature, ready to flee. Then Jessie laughed. 'And why would he listen to you, do you think?'

The scorn in her eyes almost stung him into a sharp reply, but he only looked at her steadily until she dropped her gaze. Then he said, 'Why would he, indeed? Though he took orders from me well enough today.' He stopped, and cleared his throat again. 'Mairhi?'

From across the room where she was tending to the fire, she looked up at him.

Donald said, 'It's you he fears. He came out with me today because he thinks you protect the boat. And if he harms Jessie or the children, he thinks you'll be after him. And I let him think it.' He waited a heartbeat or two, but she made no answer. No-one spoke, or moved at all. 'Did I do the right thing?' he asked.

Nancy sprang up and ran, not to her mother, but to Mairhi. 'You will, won't you? If he hurts us, you'll punish him! But we don't want to go back. He can't make us! We'll stay here, with you.'

Throughout all of this, Bridie had not moved, but now she lifted her hands a little, and let them fall again. Donald had never seen her look so weary. For the first time that he could remember, he found himself speaking for her, rather than the other way round.

'You can't stay forever, Nancy. What about your brothers and sisters? And if your da makes a good crew member, he'll be able to keep the roof over your heads and food on the table.' But she only clutched at Mairhi, mutinous and utterly unconvinced. He could not blame her; he was far from convinced himself. Mairhi held her for a moment, gently stroking her hair, and then she let go and gave her a little push towards her mother.

Jessie stood rigid, not laughing now. 'You want us to go back, don't you?' Fists clenched, she turned on Bridie. 'You said if I had another child, it would be the death of me. And you spoke up for me in front of everybody. How can I go back now, even if I wanted to?'

Bridie raised her head. 'Jessie Bain,' she said, 'I've taken you in, you and your children. I stood up for you against your husband, and that's a thing I rarely do, at least not openly. There are ways to help women like you without tearing things apart, and God knows we've all tried. And you've thrown every one of them back at us, and so it's come to this. So now, for once in your life, use the sense you were born with.' She got up, pushing against the arms of the chair for support, and went over to Mairhi. Laying a hand on her shoulder, she went on. 'Don't you see? It doesn't matter what Mairhi can or can't do to protect you, or Donald, or anyone else, come to that. But it does matter that your miserable excuse for a husband thinks she can. And if that's the only thing that can make him behave as a man should, then so be it. Mairhi, my dear, I bless the day you came to us!'

Turning to Donald, she said, 'And if Aly Bain is so convinced that it gets him back out on the water, and taking orders from you – of all people! – then I'd say yes, you've done the right thing. You've done a good day's work, and not just for yourself and the boat. Now it's up to other people to do the same.' She paused, and Donald saw, to his astonishment, that she was holding back tears. After a long moment, she spoke again, more gently. 'I'm sorry to speak so plainly, Jessie. I know it's not an easy road. You're welcome here for as long as you need.'

Jessie had not moved at all, except to put an arm around Nancy. Then, into the silence, she said, 'We'll go home tomorrow.' And Nancy, for once, did not protest.

Bridie nodded. 'That's good, then. And now, I'm for bed. We've another early start in the morning.'

50

Those were long days, up before dawn and stumbling home after dark, as the hours of daylight shrank and the storms of winter gathered strength. Hugh recovered in a day or two, but when he saw how things were, he stayed ashore and left Donald in charge. There was no word of Rennie. Donald had grown used to the easy sharing of tasks between himself and James, especially since Rennie had taken himself off; but now he found himself giving orders, and watching to see that they were carried out. Aly Bain seemed to expect it; he worked well enough, but did nothing beyond what he was told to do. 'And he never looks you in the eye, but he notes everything you do; have you marked that?' James paused on the path up to the shieling, to set down his burdens and work the ache out of his arms.

'I have.' Donald stopped too and flexed his sore hands, grimacing as the cuts opened anew.

James, watching, said, 'Why do you never wear those gloves of yours ashore? They'd be a help, surely?'

Donald looked at his hands. The skin on the back of them was thickened and scaled, but the palms were always vulnerable, and they never quite healed. Even when he stayed ashore for a week or two at a time, there were tasks that had to be done.

He said, 'I'd be losing them all the time, leaving them in the wrong place. The boat's where I need them most, working the ropes.' He'd caught a sidelong look from Aly when he'd put them on that morning, and braced himself for some sneering comment; but times had changed, or so it seemed. Donald wondered what he might say to his brothers, back on dry land and out of earshot, but there was nothing to be done about that.

'You could keep another pair on shore, maybe.' There was no

mockery in James's voice, and Donald wondered now if there ever truly had been.

A good many people who used to despise him – or so he had thought – now seemed only too ready to give him the time of day. Just this morning, he'd passed by Hector's cottage while the old man was fetching water. He'd called out, 'Good morning!' as usual, expecting no response, but Hector had put down his bucket and come over to the garden wall to ask him, 'Do you think it'll rain later?' Which was no question at all, but just something to say. And he had learned that people use words like nets, to draw other people to them; except, of course, for Mairhi, who had her own ways.

'I could,' he said, seeing again the wild dance, the faces of Mairhi and Jessie in the firelight. 'But you know how Mairhi is about the seals. I wouldn't want to upset her.'

James laughed. 'She's a lucky woman!' He lowered his voice as Jeannie and Ailsa came running down the path to meet them. 'I hope I'll do half so well as you.'

Donald shot him a quick sideways glance. He could see nothing but warmth in James' eyes; warmth and admiration. If he only knew! The yearning to confide rose strong in him; to be understood, even to be forgiven – and not just by Mairhi herself. But the girls were almost upon them now, and the moment passed. And that was probably just as well.

51

As the year wore on and the winter storms grew ever stronger, Donald found himself closer to home, mending nets and weatherproofing house and barn for the winter. He had time to spend with little John, and sweet time alone with Mairhi, whenever they could. Jessie went back to her cottage, and it seemed that Aly, though he had never agreed in so many words, was letting her be. Donald neither knew nor cared what his motives were. He had his home to himself again, and a crewman who worked well enough, if sullenly.

Sometimes, when he and James were about their business, working with the easy familiarity he'd grown used to, he would be aware of Aly watching them. It was an odd look, almost puzzled. But that was fine, as long as he did what he was told. He made no move to rejoin his brothers on the Bain family boat, but that was fine too, with Rennie away and Hugh content to stay ashore.

What did concern Donald, now that he was often shorebound for days at a time, was the change in his mother. More and more now, when the summons came to attend a birth or help ease a death, it would be Mairhi who left her warm bed and went off, sometimes with Nancy Bain to help her. And at home, it would be Mairhi who hurried to lift water from the well or bedding for the cow. It seemed to him that this must have been going on for some time, but he had not seen it before.

One morning, coming back unexpectedly, he found Bridie alone. It was a blustery day, blowing sleet through the heather – too wet to settle. She was sitting on the bench by the front door, with the overturned bucket at her feet and the door swinging to and fro, her hand pressed to her side. Her face was the colour of ash.

By the time he had helped her indoors, made up the fire and put the kettle on, she was looking a little better. Her boots and the hem of her dress were soaked, and her feet like ice. He eased off her boots and took one foot in his hands to warm it, and then the other.

'You're not well.' Had they been hiding it from him, or had he simply not noticed? 'How long has this been going on?'

'A while.' Bridie's smile was rueful. 'For a time I hoped it would pass, but it's not to be, it seems.'

His hands were still. 'Mother? What are you saying?' He could not look at her; as though, if he could not see the signs, they might not be there.

'Donald.' Her voice was very gentle. 'I don't know how long it'll be. Maybe long enough to see my second grandchild into the world. I hope for that, at least.'

Now he looked up at her, seeing the lines of pain in her face, hearing the strain in her voice. It was so like her, to find something heartening to soften the blow. 'You're before me on that one. Again.'

'I know the signs. Who better?' she said, as she had said once before.

He looked away then, trying to hide his own pain. She laid a hand on his bent head. 'I've been more blessed than I ever could have hoped. Look at us now! A year ago, it was just you and me alone. And now we'll be needing to build on another bedroom for the children – and you'll have most of the village happy to help you do it.'

'It's not fair!' he said, childlike in his hurt and anger. 'You do so much for other people. You're always the strong one, and they take from you and never realise the cost.'

'Not nowadays,' she said, and there was nothing but love and pride in her voice. 'They turn to Mairhi more and more, and after Mairhi comes Nancy. She's learning fast, that lass, and she knows how to watch and wait, young as she is. She's seen too much pain already, but now she's finding a way to turn it to good account.'

'I don't care about Nancy! There's more to you than usefulness. You should have time to grow old with your grandchildren. Surely there's something we can do?' He stopped. 'Maybe Mairhi…'

She was shaking her head. 'She helps me every day. She seems to know when the pain comes, and she eases it. But she can't take away the cause of it. There are some things that can't be mended, Donald, and we have to make the best of it.' She leaned back, closing her eyes. 'It's better now. I'll be fine in a while.'

He knelt there a little longer, holding her feet until they grew warm under his hands, and her breathing came slow and regular. Then he got up, as quietly as he could, fetched a blanket to tuck around her, and went out to the barn.

52

It was almost dark by the time Mairhi came home, with John wrapped in her shawl and Nancy trailing at her side, all of them wet through. Exhausted by pain, Bridie had slept on while Donald made up the fire and set the stew to heat through for supper, and she only stirred when the door scraped open and the wind set the flames dancing. The look that passed between the two women had no need of words. Nancy set down her burdens, looked from one to the other and then, with a little cry like a wounded animal, flew to Bridie and burrowed into her arms.

'There now, hush now,' said Bridie, gently stroking the child's hair. 'I'm fine, see? What have you brought back today? That's a heavy basket for a wee one like you. You'd better have some hot stew before you go home.' Her eyes met Donald's, and he nodded, turning away to get an extra plate from the cupboard. He had never seen Nancy make any gesture of affection before, except to Mairhi; certainly never to her own family. Setting down the plates, he went to take the baby, unwinding him from the sodden shawl while Mairhi unpacked the baskets, holding things up for Bridie to see.

Bridie kept up a gentle flow of words, and Nancy's face stayed hidden against her breast. 'Well now, more carrots! As if we didn't have a garden full already. But you can never have too many, don't you think? And is that some honey there? That'll be the heather honey by now, from the MacDonalds, am I right? And a shirt for you, John!'

Hearing his name, the baby let out a sudden squeal, making them all laugh. Nancy's face emerged at last, red and tear-streaked, and Bridie gave her a little push.

'Off you go now and help put those things away. But keep some carrots to take home with you.'

When they sat down to eat, Bridie said, 'Now tell me what you've been up to behind my back. Who did you see, and what did you do for them?'

At a nod from Mairhi, Nancy began to pour out all the details. From time to time, she looked to Mairhi for approval, but it was clear that already she was forming her own ideas.

Bridie put in a word now and then, but at the end she said, 'Well done! It's plain to see that you two are getting on fine on your own. We'll need to make up some salve tomorrow, and take some medicine to John Rennie for his sore knees. To my mind, it's missing that boy of his that's the real problem, but we haven't a remedy for loneliness, more's the pity. Now if your mother can spare you, maybe you could come up tomorrow and help with that.'

Nancy's eyes were shining as she looked up from her stew. She was hardly the same child, Donald thought, as the pinched little creature who had hidden behind their garden wall. He remembered how he'd resented her intrusion, and realised that, in truth, he admired her. At her age, he'd turned his back on them all, but she had seen what she wanted and hung on with all her strength. He said, 'James brought down a pair of Ailsa's shoes today. She noticed yours were letting in the wet, and thought they might do for you. Will you try them on before you go?'

Nancy still would not look at him directly, but she came to him readily enough. Her shoelaces were damp and swollen, so he pushed back his chair, knelt down and helped her to undo them. Inside her boots, her stockings were wet too, but it could not be helped. Ailsa's boots were a little too big, but still sound. Nancy stood up to show them off, awkward, but glowing in the warmth of their approval.

Bridie said, 'Be sure to stuff them with rags when you get home, and set them by the fire. Take the smaller lantern, and mind yourself going down.'

'I'll see you safe home,' said Donald suddenly. But that was a step too far; the old hunted look came back.

Nancy said, 'I'll manage fine,' and was out of the door and away, without a thank you, leaving the lantern behind.

Donald got up to follow, but behind him Bridie said, 'Leave her be. She's not used to so much attention.' She leaned back in her chair, and he saw that all this time she had been keeping the weariness at bay, being cheerful for Nancy's sake. Now, she looked utterly spent. He, too, had been holding back, avoiding the place where the dreadful knowledge lay in wait. He put his hand over his eyes, as though he could somehow make it not be, and turned to the door to go out, away. But Mairhi stood in front of the door, with the baby in her arms.

He was used, now, to gleaning what she wanted to tell him from her eyes, her gestures, the way she held herself, but this look he could not interpret. The silence grew between them, until John set up a wailing. Still she did not move. The baby began to twist and struggle, but she did not try to soothe him. Donald felt himself flushing, trapped between the two women. Abruptly, he stepped forward and took the child. Mairhi held his gaze for a few moments longer, and then, with a fierce little nod, she moved away from the door and went to see to Bridie.

Donald bowed his head, resting his cheek against John's hair. He thought, now, that he understood, that here was one more thing from which there could be no turning away. John put up his hand to touch the tears on his face, and then tugged at him; look at me! And there it was.

'Are you hungry now?' he said, and John bounced up and down in his arms. 'Will I find you a crust to chew, maybe?' Nobody answered him, and that was an answer in itself.

53

Bridie seemed better for a while after that, as though, now that the word was out, she had no need to try so hard. For the first time that Donald could remember, she let herself be looked after. He began to hope that she might be wrong about what ailed her, though he dared not speak his hope aloud. But she had been right about one thing, at least. Some weeks later, as he and Mairhi lay curled together in the big bed, he felt her move suddenly as though something had startled her.

'What is it, love?' he murmured into her hair.

In the cradle beside them, John slept on. Under her breath, she laughed, and then took his hand and placed it on her belly. And after a moment, he felt it; a gentle touch, like a fish sliding away under his hand. And again, a ripple beneath the surface. Softly, he kissed the back of her neck. And in the darkness, she turned to face him.

::

Those were the months of growing. Every day, a few more minutes of light. Almost every day, it seemed, a new landmark: John's first steps, the first violets of spring, and a year since the wedding. John was beginning to try out words, too. While his mother used everything except human speech, it soon seemed that he would never stop talking. And news of the next baby was everywhere, all at once, spreading in that mysterious way that Donald had never understood and always dreaded. Now, he recognised and welcomed it like an old friend.

As soon as the weather permitted, work began on building a new room onto the croft, and people came whenever they could, bringing tools, building materials, food and drink, songs and gossip and laughter, the strength of their arms and the pleasure of their company. Donald watched with amazement as, over the next days and weeks, almost everyone who could walk made their way up the path to his door. That was the way of things, to be sure, and he had played his own part in these gatherings when it could not be avoided, but he had never thought that one day, in due course, his own turn would come. He said as much to Catriona, when she arrived with a group of women to stuff bedding and sew the new curtains.

She laughed at him. 'Did you think we'd just leave you to it on your own?'

'No, not that. But I never expected to find myself a married man with a growing family.'

'Well, I have to say, you've surprised more than yourself there! But don't deceive yourself, Donald. They're not doing it for you. There's hardly a man or woman within twenty miles who hasn't been grateful for Auntie Bridie's help, one way or another. And Mairhi's too, now, of course; but it's Bridie they're really coming for.' She paused, suddenly serious. 'Tell me the truth now, Donald. How do you think she is? It's no good my asking her outright. She just says she's fine. But she's not, is she?' Catriona stopped, watching him, trying to guess the answer before he could speak.

Donald looked away. To say it straight out gave it more weight than he could bear. 'No, she's not.'

'I knew it! Oh, you should be moving to the shieling with us, not staying on your own out here. It's not too late to change your minds. I'll have a word with father; she listens to him – at least sometimes.' She started away, but he caught her arm.

'Catriona.' That stopped her; Donald was usually trying to avoid her attention, not catch it. 'We'll manage. Mairhi helps her.'

'But the baby's on the way! She'll have her hands full, soon enough.'

'And so will you, by the look of you.' He could not help laughing at the look on her face. 'Mother told me – but I'd already guessed. James is not a man for keeping secrets.'

Catriona flushed scarlet. 'He promised not to say.'

'He's said nothing. He didn't have to.'

Catriona was defiant. 'It's only weeks now till we're wed. And who are you to be judging us?'

'I'm not judging you. It's a grand thing. They'll be of an age, won't they? Yours and ours?'

'Near enough.' She watched him. 'They'll be crewing the boat together some day. If they're both boys, of course.'

'Steady now. It's a long road between here and there. They might have their own ideas.'

'Yours might; you've always gone your own way, till now. Mine will do as he's told!' They both laughed, turning away about their business, and the matter of Bridie's illness was laid aside.

The next day was fair enough to go out fishing. Donald found James down by the boat, along with several other men, checking for storm damage. As soon as Donald was close enough for them not to be overheard, James said, 'You got me into hot water last night. Now tell me, what am I supposed to have said, or not said?'

'You never said a word. But you've not stopped smiling this past week or so. I made a guess, and Mother told me the rest. I'm happy for you.'

James grinned. 'That's the two of us happy, then. Who'd have thought it, this time a year ago?'

Donald considered it. This time a year ago, he'd been a newly married man, his path already opening up ahead. But for him it had taken longer than a year. Looking away, he said, 'Do you think, if something starts wrong, it can come right in the end?' And glanced up to see James staring at him.

'We wouldn't be the first not to wait for our wedding vows. What's so wrong about that?'

'Nothing at all. That's not what I meant.' But of course, he could not say what he was really thinking.

James was quiet a minute, and then, 'Oh! You mean because you and Mairhi weren't promised yet. Is that it?' And then, when Donald still avoided his eye, he said in a low voice, 'And maybe she wasn't ready. Or wasn't willing. That's it, isn't it?'

The silence went on and on, a vast gulf swallowing up the cries of gulls and the wind in the rigging. He heard Catriona saying, 'Who are you to be judging us?' He saw the eyes of Peggy Mackay upon him, and the mocking laughter of Euan Bain. With a few words, he could unmake it all; bring shame on the whole family. James and Catriona would never be married, his mother would be shunned, and he – he would take to the road and never set eyes on any of them again.

He had missed James' next few words: '… and it seems to me, even if it did start wrong, you've more than made up for it since. Donald, if I do half so well as you with my marriage, I'll be a proud man! Anyone can see how much you care for her – and she for you, never doubt it. Look at Aly Bain, now. He seems to be keeping his hands off Jessie for the moment, but it will never be right between them. It goes too deep. But you and Mairhi – for God's sake, man, she danced with you!'

Donald looked up at last. 'Aye, she did.' And could not bring himself to say the words, to spurn James' open-hearted generosity. But James was looking past him down the harbour.

'Speak of the devil. Aly's on his way. No more talk of babies now. Or women.' He stood up. 'Hoi! Ready to sail. What kept you?'

54

That year, as the days grew longer and Mairhi's time came closer, it seemed to Donald that the whole world was rejoicing with him. He went about his work in a kind of quiet ecstasy, even welcoming the longer fishing trips for their pleasures rather than their perils; the sounding whales out beyond the furthest islands, and the arrival of the arctic terns, bringing the white light of summer in their slender wings. Along with his catch of fish, he would bring back these treasures to share with Mairhi. Beyond doubt, he knew that she remembered her former life, and it would have been ungenerous to keep them from her. Especially now, when she seemed so securely landbound.

By April, the new room was finished. He had assumed that it would be Bridie's, but she would not hear of it. 'Why would I want to shut myself away in there? It's far too big for one, and I'd rather be here where I can keep an eye on you all.'

It was far too big and lonely for little John, too, but the time would come when he would share it with his new brother or sister. And Bridie seemed so much stronger these days that Donald had not the heart to argue. Most days, now, it would be Mairhi who set out with her basket of salves and medicines, and Bridie would stay behind to mind John. And if she was tired or in pain when Donald came home, she hid it well. He could not bring himself to ask about it, for fear of the answer.

On a bright, windy day in June, James and Catriona were married, and that was a noisy, joyful wedding. Mairhi was close to her time by then, and earned herself a telling-off from Mrs Mackay for dancing, but that had never stopped her before, and it did not stop her now. Nor did it seem to hurt the baby, who waited another three weeks before slipping quietly into the world, unattended by anyone this time except Bridie and Jessie Bain, and little Nancy, who would not be kept away. It was a girl-child, and they named her Sorcha.

∴

At summer's end, when the light was beginning to fade, there came a string of bright, still days, and a lull in the fishing before the rich harvests of autumn. They had been out since dawn and caught nothing, and so they came into harbour before midday. Unburdened for once, Donald decided to walk home along the shoreline and see what he could salvage.

He passed the place where he had seen Mairhi speaking to the seals, but there was none here today. They would come later, when it was their time to give birth and to breed; for now, the sun-warmed rocks were silent, waiting. By this time he had gathered an armload of driftwood, and so he began to climb the hill to rejoin the clifftop path, to save himself the longer walk around the headland. Reaching the top, he turned inland for home, and then paused.

There were sounds on the wind. Not seabirds, but the high piping voice of a child, and another voice answering, and then a great splashing of water. He could not be sure at this distance, but he thought it might be his own son, John. He went back towards the cliff edge on the further side of the headland, and looked down.

There were pools there, hollowed out of the rock and refilled at high tide. Now, after a morning's sunshine, they would be warm, and the shallows full of tiny crabs and anemones. But he could see no-one there. They must be out of sight under the headland, where the waves had undercut the cliff and made deeper pools. He would have to walk further along, until he could look back at the headland and see what was there.

He had gone maybe forty paces when another shout stopped him, and he turned. There, at the base of the cliff, was John, naked in the sunshine, standing on a rock by the dark water. He had spied his father and was waving; Donald could see his open mouth, and then the call came to his ears: 'Dadda!' And as he watched, the little boy flung up his arms and jumped into the pool.

55

Donald dropped the wood and began to run. Down over the cliff edge, sliding and scrambling, heedless of safety. He shouted, but the child would not hear him through his own splashing. And then, to his horror, John disappeared below the surface.

'Mairhi!' Dear God, where was she? As he got lower, more of the pool came into view, and at last he saw her. She was sitting calmly on the further side, her feet in the water and baby Sorcha between her knees. At his call, she looked up, but with no urgency, until she saw the terror in his face. Then she let go of the baby, and stood up.

'Mairhi!' He was splashing through the shallow pools now, but he could not cross the large pool to where she was. John's head reappeared at the far side, close to his mother; he shook the water from his eyes and held out his hands to Sorcha, who was moving across the pool towards him. Swimming like a fish. Like a seal.

Stepping in – up to his waist, and gasping for breath – Donald could go no further. He watched, unable to make sense of what he was seeing, as both children vanished again. He looked across at Mairhi, but she was making her way, with no hurry, around the edge. And then, quite close, the two little heads bobbed up. He held out his arms, and they came to him.

Sodden and shaking, Donald clasped his children to him, making his awkward way back onto dry land. From what he had just witnessed, they could have made their own way perfectly well, but he could not let them go. In his arms, Sorcha was just a tiny infant again, barely able to sit up; yet he had seen her paddling, diving, moving with ease and grace. And John! He wriggled now to be put down, slithered out of his father's grasp and ran to meet his mother.

She came to a stop a few yards away, frowning against the sunshine. Was she afraid of him? It was true that he had been angry. For a moment there, he had wanted to catch hold of her and … what? If the children had not been there … But then, if they had not been there, none of this would have happened.

He stood quite still, feeling his own heartbeat thundering in his chest, and laid his cheek against the baby's head. At that, Mairhi came forward.

'Oh, Mairhi.' What could he say? She came quietly into his arms, and John danced around them, shouting for joy.

After a time, Donald took a deep breath, and said, 'Show me.'

They went to sit on the warm rocks. Mairhi fed the baby while Donald held her, held them both, and wished he need never let them go. John, though, would not be still until he had shown his father how he could swim on his back and on his front, and dive under the water. Donald did his best, but he shuddered as he watched, and Mairhi set the baby down on her shawl, and took his hand from where it gripped her shoulder. She looked up at him, frowning a little. After a while, he began to feel the now-familiar magic. The slow, sensual rocking of the surf; the delicious slide of cool water over sun-warmed skin. How tempting, to slip open-eyed beneath the surface, to see for himself the secret underwater world…

He squeezed her hand. 'No, love,' he said. 'I need to find the way for myself. I can't go where they can go, but maybe I can learn to be easier with it, somehow.' He drew her to him, and she leaned her head against his shoulder. 'You've given me so much,' he murmured into her hair. 'Whatever I can do in return; just tell me.'

At that, she twisted round to look up at him. The urgency in her eyes brought him back from the sweet, drowsy state he had drifted into. 'What is it, Mairhi?'

She gestured towards the water, where John was still splashing. For a moment, he did not understand, and then he began to be afraid again.

'Oh, love.' Should he tell her, now, and bring grief into this precious place? He thought, *what would Mother do?* But the time was past when he could turn to Bridie for wisdom. He had just made a promise, though. Could he now say, *anything but that*?

'Sweetheart, it's gone,' he said. 'I don't know who took it. I searched and searched, but it was nowhere to be found. I'm sorry. Well, I'm not sorry for what it's brought us.' He looked around at the beach, the children, the warm water at their feet. 'But I am sorry for that. If I could give it back to you, I would.' And in that moment, he meant it with all his heart.

Mairhi stared at him, quite still. *All this time*, he thought. *All this time, she's been wondering, and hoping, and waiting for this moment.* The pity of it was almost too much for him, but he forced himself to meet her gaze. *I owe her that, at least. And if she wants to drown me now, then so be it.*

But he did not drown. It was Mairhi who looked away first. She shrugged her shoulders, and then turned to watch John, so that he could not see her face. Fair enough. Not so long ago, he'd have been off and away before anyone could see him so wounded, so naked. She, too, was about the business of learning to be human.

They sat there, close together but without words, until John had finally grown tired of swimming and wandered off to catch crabs, and Sorcha had fallen asleep, full of milk and sunshine. Then he turned again to Mairhi.

'I'm sorry if I scared you, love. When I saw them in the water, I thought … well, I don't know what I thought. It's what we all fear the most. You know that, don't you?'

She shook her head a little, watching his face. Of course she knew; she had seen for herself how a man might fear drowning. That was not what she meant.

'You see…' he paused, trying to think how to explain it in a way that would make sense to her. 'We fishermen, we don't swim. If you fall from a boat out at sea, you'll die. We can't stand the cold, not for more than a few minutes, not like … well, you know. So it's better to go quickly, and not to have false hope. D'you see?'

She made no move. 'Oh, sure, the children play in the water when they're little, but they don't swim. It's not our way. And if anyone saw them, they'd be scared, the way I was. They might start to think ill of you again. So…'

What on earth could he say? 'I don't know what's for the best,' he said, and that was nothing but the truth. 'I can't tell you not to do it, and even if you do keep it secret, the bairns themselves will give it away one day. Has anyone else seen you, besides me?'

She shook her head. She must have known, then, that other people would not understand. She had kept this even from Bridie, and from Donald himself. What had she thought they might do?

Donald sighed. 'There's no way around it, is there? If trouble comes, we must just weather it. But be careful, my dear. And…' He paused, then said, 'You can't swim yourself?'

Again, she shook her head, and tears glittered in her eyes.

'I'm sorry,' he said. 'For all of it. I'm so sorry.'

56

After the coming of the baby, Bridie had begun to fail, as though she had been hoarding her strength for that one task. Sometimes, in the middle of making up the fire or milking the cow, she would turn white suddenly and press her hand to her side. In the night, she would cry out in her sleep, and Mairhi would go to her and try to ease her pain. She was waking to tend to the baby now, too, and often both women would be sluggish and dull-eyed in the morning. Sometimes Jessie Bain would come, but there was always a straggle of children about her, and so she would sweep John up with her own brood, returning him hungry and dirty in the evening. Less often, now, Jeannie and Ailsa would come, but they were more demanding than helpful; and they would have their own baby nephew or niece to play with, soon enough.

Others would come too, bringing food and stopping to feed the hens or make up the fire, so that somehow or other, jobs got done. Donald stayed home whenever he could, but he had a responsibility to his crew too, and the fishing had to go on if they were to keep the roofs over their heads. For days together, though, his rowboat stayed drawn up on the strand, and his solitary life seemed a long-ago dream. In truth, he hardly thought about it at all.

Father Finian had begun to visit every few days. Often, he would simply sit by Bridie without speaking, and both of them seemed to gain some comfort from it. But, as autumn drew on, the pains grew more frequent, and even Mairhi's touch could not ease them alto-gether. One afternoon, when they had brought the boat into harbour before a rising storm, Donald met the priest coming down the hill from the cottage.

'Walk with me a while, Donald,' he said, and so Donald set down his baskets by the path, and turned back towards the village.

For a while, bent against the wind, they walked in silence. Donald thought he knew what the priest had to say, and was in no hurry to hear it; but after a time, the waiting seemed worse than the hearing.

'So, how did you find her today, Father?' he asked abruptly.

Father Finian stopped and straightened up, as though laying down a burden.

'Troubled. I found her troubled,' he said.

'The pains are coming hard now. I don't know what more we can do,' said Donald. He did not expect the priest to have an answer, but a bit of ready sympathy would be welcome.

'Aye. But it's not the pains I mean. Bridie is a brave soul, and she bears it better than most, that I can tell you. But there's something in her that won't let go. You know her time is coming?'

Donald could not speak, but he nodded.

'I have sat with the dying often enough to know that there is a shape to it. By now, she should be beginning to loosen her hold. She's made her confession, and so she should be free to be about it – heavens, Bridie knows the way it goes! But still she holds on, and so it goes hard for her. It's beyond me, Donald. I can't think what that good woman has done to trouble her conscience so. Whatever it is, she won't confess it to me.' He looked directly at Donald as he spoke, almost beseeching. 'It's a hard thing, to see someone you care for struggle so. Would you have any idea what it might be, hmm?'

Donald shook his head, but now it was not grief but dread that stopped his tongue. For a moment they stared at each other, in a kind of mutual horror. 'I'll talk to her,' he said at last, and looked away.

'Good man!' Father Finian gripped his arms with both hands. The wind gusted about them, and there came a sudden spatter of rain. The priest turned away. 'Now we'd both best be off home. I'll pray for you, Donald.' And he was gone, plodding away down the path, hunched against the weather.

Donald stood there for a while, hardly noticing the driving rain, until the thought of his baskets blowing about the hillside got him moving again. He faced uphill and let the wind take him home.

57

Up at the croft, he found Mairhi busy making an evening meal, with the baby under one arm and John under her feet. Bridie sat by the fire with the basket of mending on her lap; but her head had fallen back and she was dozing, despite all the racket about her, and even Donald opening the door and letting the storm blow in did not rouse her. He looked at her face in the firelight and could no longer deny that what Father Finian had said – and what she herself had said, almost a year ago – was true. She had always been so vigorous – younger-seeming than other women of her age; but now suffering, and perhaps the illness itself, had made an old woman of her.

He could not bear to disturb her. And, in any case, now was not the time for talking, not with the children and Mairhi about. Not yet, not yet. But even as he watched, she started awake, her eyes black with pain; she bit back a cry as her hand went to her side.

'Mother, what is it? What can I do?' She was struggling out of the chair and seemed hardly to notice him at first. Then she pushed at him with her hand, took a few steps and crumpled to the floor. John stopped pestering his mother, stared for a few seconds and began to cry.

Donald knelt by her side. 'Let me help you. Do you need the outhouse, is that it?'

She was gasping, almost sobbing, but her eyes were dry. 'I have to … I have to…'

'There's nothing you have to do now. Just tell me, and I'll do it, whatever it is.' He put his arms around her, tried to lift her up. She weighed almost nothing.

She looked at him and seemed to see him for the first time. 'Donald,' she said, and the pleading in her voice made him weep for the pity of it. 'I don't know…'

He lifted her and laid her on the bed, and this time she did not try to stop him. John was right there, pulling at her skirts and wailing.

'Here, now,' said Donald. 'Let's go to the barn and see if we can find an egg for Grandma's tea. She'd like that, don't you think?' He swung the little boy up into his arms, turning to block John's view of his grandmother as he did so.

Mairhi was standing by the table, quite still, with the baby on one arm and the stirring spoon in the other hand. It drooped, letting food fall onto the hearth, and still she did not move. Not since those early days had he seen her look so lost, and his heart went out to her.

'Ah, my dear,' he said. 'Some things can't be mended.' When had his mother said that to him? No matter now. 'You've done all you can. We'll weather this too. We will.'

She made a little motion of her shoulders, and that was all the answer he got.

'Now then,' he said to John. 'Let me wrap my coat around you, so. We'll need to make a run for it. Ready? Hold tight!'

They stayed in the barn as long as they could, hunting for eggs in the straw, finding a nest of late-born kittens and seeing to the cow and her calf. Donald took up a length of rope he had been mending; there were a couple that needed replacing on the boat, and he would not go to sea with frayed ropes. But John was hungry now and would not settle, and in the end they held hands and ran back to the house, leaning into the wind. There would be no going to sea for a few days, in any case.

There would also be no visiting, and no chance to speak to Bridie alone about what might be on her mind. No-one ventured out, except to the barn and the outhouse, and if anyone had fallen sick in the village or the hills, they knew better than to send for Mairhi at such a time. So Donald worked on his ropes, played with John and kept the fire stoked. There would be a time, but not yet.

58

By the third day the wind had almost blown itself out. The ropes were done, and it was high time to go fishing. Donald set off down to the harbour after breakfast, with the ropes coiled over his shoulder, breathing deeply as he walked, glad to be out of the house. He knew this feeling of old, knew that he was running away, even if other tasks were calling him. In his mind's eye he saw the path up into the hills; the bees would be busy in the heather now that the wind was down, and the streams running bright and lively after the rain. But that seemed a lifetime ago. John's lifetime, more or less. In a year or two he'd be old enough to make the climb himself, at least partway. Donald found that he was looking forward to it.

He had reached the row of cottages along the harbour. Some of the boats were tied up there, and men were aboard one or two, checking for damage. Then he stopped. His own boat was among them; there was Aly Bain on deck, and his two brothers alongside. Quietly, Donald moved closer, until he stood in the lee of the last house, about twenty yards away – near enough to hear, but not be seen unless they looked directly at him.

'Don't know why you're bothering. He won't thank you for it.' That was Euan, watching Aly busy about something. If Aly replied, it was too low to make out.

'He's soft in the head, that's why.' That was Andrew. 'He never took the trouble for us – not that you'd trust his handiwork. They must be daft to keep you on so long, little brother.'

Aly kept his head down. Donald could not make out what he was doing, with his brothers in the way. He took a step closer.

'And don't think you can come crawling back to us when they throw you overboard! What if young Rennie comes home, or Hugh Macfarlane has a mind to go back to sea? D'you think they'd keep a place for you then? Eh? Useless little coward.' Andrew turned away a little and spat into the water.

'Oh, but they've got him where they want him.' Euan spoke over his shoulder, still watching Aly. 'Haven't they? She's got you all under her spell, hasn't she, Aly? And now she's teaching Jessie all her tricks, and wee Nancy too. As long as you do as you're told, you'll be fine. But if you dare to touch your own wife … The sea has long fingers, eh?' Euan's own fingers reached out towards Aly, clawing at his throat.

Aly raised his head at last. 'Leave me alone!' he said, and both brothers laughed.

'Is that the best you can do?' Euan's voice took on a high, whining tone. 'Poor little Aly, always getting picked on. It's not fair.' It was the voice of Aly himself, as a child, and Donald thought again of that day on the beach, watching the Bains at play. Without making any conscious decision, he moved out from the shelter of the wall and walked straight towards them. His skin prickled, but he kept moving.

And they made way for him, a man boarding his own boat, so that he found himself on deck before he'd expected it. Aly sat crosslegged almost at his feet, with a pile of nets at his side.

'You can't have brought her in by yourself?' he said, low so that only Aly could hear. Aly shook his head, not looking up.

'I fetched James down. He'll be back soon.' Donald stared at him a moment, and then nodded. He went to look at the frayed ropes.

'It's done,' said Aly behind him.

And so it was; neatly done, too. There were many hours of careful work there.

'Good job!' Behind him, he heard Andrew's snort of derision. He went over to Aly, and squatted down at his side. 'You must have been out in all that weather, seeing to it. We'll get an extra day's fishing.'

Aly shrugged. 'I'm closest,' he said.

Donald put a hand on his shoulder, and felt the man flinch. Anger bloomed inside him, and he did not take his hand away. 'You've done a grand job,' he said loudly. 'We're a good crew, these days.'

He looked up, directly into the eyes of Andrew Bain. For a moment each held the other's gaze, and then Andrew turned away. Euan had already started down the harbour towards their own boat, whistling a little.

Donald stood up. 'James'll be back soon; we might catch the morning tide. Where shall we try first, d'you reckon?'

59

What with the fishing, and all the coming and going around Bridie, it was not easy to find some time alone with her, even if Donald had been eager to try. There was hardly a moment when one or other of the women was not about, or Hugh sitting quietly by, or Father Finian bringing news and good counsel. She seemed to rally again, for a time; the pain was easier, and some of her old spirit returned. But Father Finian was right. Something was troubling her, and Donald could not bring himself to dwell on what it might be. Time enough, yet.

Still, when Catriona's time came, it was not Bridie who went to help her, but Mairhi, and Donald's turn to keep company with James in the bar. All went well, as Mairhi told them when she returned late in the morning, but it was left to little John to announce that he had 'a new baby cousin, and his name is Hugh!'

In the following days, the house grew quiet. Mairhi was over with Catriona most days, and the children with her, and the tide of visitors turned that way too. Donald came up the path from the harbour one afternoon to find the place seemingly empty; but as he went across to the fire to warm his hands, he heard a sound from Bridie's bed. She was there, watching him from her pillow.

'Have you been sleeping, Mother?' She looked wide-eyed, far away. 'Will you take a cup of tea?'

She shook her head. 'Sit by me a while, Donald.' Her voice quavered, like Auntie Annie's when her joints were paining her.

Donald took his time, getting out of his wet coat and boots, fetching tea for himself; but at last he came to sit beside her. In the half-hour or so since he had come home, it had grown fully dark outside.

'I'd better light the lamp,' he said, and made to get up, but she caught at his hand.

'Don't go! The firelight's enough for now. I think they'll stay at the shieling tonight.'

He stayed, holding her hand, grown dry and thin like the claw of a bird. After a time she turned his own hand over, stroking the back of it.

'Your hands are better, these days,' she said. 'Still a little rough, but no cracks.'

It was true. He had hardly thought about them for weeks now; hardly needed to.

'Do you still wear those sealskin gloves?'

'Oh, yes. But not always.'

She nodded. 'They'll last you well, if you oil them.'

'I do.'

But her eyelids were drooping, and she dozed a little, he thought. Gently, he made to take his hand away, but she clutched at him with sudden strength and said, 'Donald! I can't do it any more. I've tried, and I can't—' Her voice caught, and to his horror she was weeping. In all the years, even those dark days after his father's death, she had been dry-eyed, but she was weeping now.

'Hush, Mother, hush. Oh, here now, here.' He went to lift her, to hold her against him, the way he had learned with John and the baby, but she pushed at him and fell back against the pillow.

'What can I do? Oh, Mother, let me help. Please, tell me what's the matter.'

There, it was out at last. And she fell blessedly quiet, watching him out of those shadowed eyes, the tears still running. He could not bear it.

'Whatever it is, just tell me,' he said.

She stared at him a few moments longer, and then made a little movement of her head, that might have been a nod. 'It was wrong, what we did,' she said in a low voice, as though someone might overhear.

Now, at last, he was on firm ground. 'What *I* did, you mean.' He took a deep breath. 'I did a terrible thing, and you did your best to put it right. You saw what had to be done, and look what's come out of it. The wrong was all mine, Mother, and I don't know if I shall ever make up for it, but I'll never stop trying.'

She was not listening. Her hands were working at the coverlet, and the tears were flowing again. 'It was wrong,' she repeated. 'She never had the choice, poor lass. All this, now; of course, it's everything a body could hope for. But she never had the choice.'

'But that's my fault, not yours. That's my load to carry. Please, don't torture yourself like this.'

'You don't understand!' She struggled to sit up, to get out of bed, but he held her as she wept. And then, muffled against his shoulder, she said, 'I hid it from you, Donald.'

'What?' He held her away from him, tried to look her in the eye. 'Hid what from me? What are you saying?'

'I knew you'd go back, and I was afraid of what you might do. While you were up in the hills, I went down to the boat, and I rowed across to the skerry, and I found it.'

'No. No, that can't be right.' He was shaking his head, trying to unmake her words.

'I found it, and I brought it back,' she said, calm now, watching his face. 'But I couldn't keep it here, in case ... well. So I took it and hid it, as safe as I could.'

Donald was staring at her. 'And that day, when Uncle Hugh brought the gloves...?'

She was nodding. 'Oh, that was a terrible thing! As soon as I could, I went up the hill. I had to see. And there it was, safe and sound.'

'Where is it?' Could it be that somehow he had always known this? Not some stranger, or someone who wished him ill, but his own mother? Why else would he be so terribly calm, now?

'I've kept it safe, Donald, and looked after it well. I've oiled it and wrapped it to keep the water out and the mice away.' She was speaking very fast, her eyes too bright, the words unsaid for so long now bubbling out of her. 'But I can't manage the hill any more. I've tried and I haven't the strength. Oh, Donald…' She was weeping again, grasping his hands as though she could somehow draw strength out of him.

'Where is it?' he asked again, very quiet.

'Up the hill a way, too far for me now. I thought it was for the best, or you'd have sent her back where she came from. But it's not right. I made my choices, for good or ill, and I lived by them. But she never had the chance. It's not right.'

'Mother. You've come this far. Now just tell me where it's hidden, or do I have to carry you up the hill on my back so you can show me yourself?'

She stared at him. 'But you can't go now! It's full dark, and a wild night besides.'

'Of course I can't go now. But as soon as I can, I'll find it, if you'll only tell me where to look.'

At last, she looked away, and her hands grew still. 'I've moved it, more than once. There's nowhere really safe. But you know the old shepherd's bothy up by the lochan over the hill? You used to go there sometimes, as a boy.'

He nodded. 'But that's just a pile of stones, these days.'

'There's a bit of the chimney still standing. I pushed it up inside, and built up the stones all around, to keep the beasts out. What else could I do? I always hoped the time would come when we could give it back; but then there were the babies, and the two of you so happy. Was it really so bad, when so much good came out of it?'

He shook his head now. 'Mother, I can't make it right for you. I can't make it right for myself. Maybe only the priest can do that, and we can never tell him. But he knows there's something.'

'I know.' And she smiled at the thought of him. 'He's a dear man, and I wouldn't burden him with it. I'll make my own peace with God, when the time comes. But there's not much time left, not for me. It's up to you, now.'

'I don't want this,' he said, very low. 'I wish it had been taken, or washed away, or … anything. But not this! I'm sure she cares for the children, and for you, and she's even come to care for me. But I know she hasn't forgotten, not any of it.'

'I know,' said Bridie, quietly now. 'Maybe she can't ever be whole in her heart. But at least she can choose.'

'But what if…' He could not bring himself to say it, to make it real.

'Donald. There are the babies; there's Nancy and Jessie and Catriona, and all the people she's helped. There's me, and there's you. She has her life here, now, and people look to her when they're in need. Surely, she'll make the right choice.'

He had no answer, nothing to say.

They sat in silence for a while, until the fire sank to a dim glow. He banked it for the night, and went to his own bed, but there was no rest to be had there.

60

Before first light, he got up as quietly as he could. The wind was still battering at the house, throwing hail at the windows, and if Bridie called out as he pulled the door shut behind him, her voice was lost in the storm. At least, he thought, he would not be missed at the harbour today. He went to the barn for a bottle of fish oil, and then set off up the hill. He could not see far in the driving rain, and there was no path to make the going easier, but he knew the way well enough, though it was a while since he had been to the bothy. As a child, he had made it a refuge, kindling a fire in the hearth and crouching under the half-ruined wall. What if someone else had been there too? Bridie was right; there was no safety.

It took him a good while, battling against the wind and rain, and he almost missed the way after all. It was slow going, stumbling over the heather and tussocks of marsh grass; a man could turn his ankle between them. Looking for the easier ways, he had veered too far to the north, and found himself in the peat-bogs in the next valley along. There was nothing for it but to climb the hill in the teeth of the wind, until he stood on the ridge looking down to where the lochan should be. The blowing mist obscured everything; but as he watched, it parted for a moment to reveal a glimpse of black water. That was his goal.

He made a careful descent, until he stood at the edge of the water – peat-brown, with hardly a ripple on it despite the wind. It was always still, here. The lochan drank up the rain and never changed, and folk said there was some uncanny spirit that lived there. Right now, Donald did not care, as long as it kept them away.

The bothy stood on a little rise some way around the shoreline. In fine weather, he remembered, you could see down the valley to a distant glimpse of sea. There was no chance of that today, and the bothy itself, as his mother had said, was nothing more now than a heap of stones. He wasted no time, going at them with both hands, throwing them aside to get at the hearth, or what was left of it. Rain-wet and jagged, the rocks tore at his skin, so that blood mingled with water as he worked, pooling in the mud under his feet. His sealskin gloves would be a blessing now, he thought, and smiled at the bitter joke.

When he had got the hearth clear, he knelt down and thrust an arm up into the chimney. His fingers touched something cold and unyielding; not stone, but he could not move it at all. His mother had piled rocks down on top of it inside the chimney, and he had to move these, too, until at last he could see the bundle, wrapped in oiled cloth. It was wedged fast. By the time he had finally got it free, most of the chimney itself was down, and after all, the knots that tied it were so swollen that he could not pry them loose.

Donald sat down, his back against what remained of the wall, and hugged the bundle to him with his numb and bloodied hands. He lifted his face, and the rain carried his tears away as he sobbed. The sounds that came out of him were animal, wordless. Not just for himself, but for the lost creature he cradled, stranded so far from home.

At last, he drew his arm across his face and set down his burden in the lee of the wall. Crouching over it to make a little shelter, he tried again to loosen the ropes that bound it. It was no use; only a knife would serve, and then how was he to secure it again? As he turned it about, looking for purchase, he could see little jagged holes in the cloth where mice, despite all Bridie's care, had tried to nibble through.

This would not do; and in any case, the thought of leaving it in this desolate place made him sick at heart. He gathered it again into his arms, got to his feet and turned his face for home.

More than once, on that long journey downhill in the face of the gale, he marvelled at his mother's determination, that she had managed all this time to keep the precious thing safe and hidden. All the while, as one blessing after another had come to him, this had been the price. It was an awkward thing to carry, and heavy, and he fell again and again; and somewhere along the way he let his anger slip away, and was left only with pity. When he stopped to rest, his arms shook so badly, he could hardly take up the burden again; but if she had borne it, then so could he. And so at last, step by stumbling step, he made his way down to his own back yard, where he unbarred the barn door, and went in.

61

Inside, it was still, and quiet, and dark, so that he felt as though he had lost all his senses at once. He set down the bundle, but it was some time before his arms would stop trembling enough that he could strike a spark for the lantern. And then, at last, he took out his knife and cut through the ropes, and spread out the sealskin on the clean straw.

Here it was. Donald ran his hand over the surface, as he had done once before, feeling the lie of the thick fur. It had been cared for, he could see that; but not recently. It should have been supple and glossy, but there were places that were beginning to dry out, and here and there, where mice had got in, little patches of bare skin. With hands that were still numb, he unstoppered the flask, and began to smooth oil into it, working with the grain. He stroked it tenderly, seeing the subtle play of colour in the fur, feeling down through the coarse guard hairs to the soft, fine layer beneath. The barn cats came to see what he was about, sniffing and then rolling on the fur in a kind of ecstasy. Mairhi loved the cats, and so he did not try to fend them off.

At first, as he worked, the blood from his wounded hands mingled with the oil and soaked into the dry skin. After a while, the bleeding stopped, and his hands grew warm and smooth. He began to sing under his breath, a cradle song without words, like the songs Mairhi herself sang to the babies. And when he had rubbed oil into every inch of it, he lay down, like the cats, and rubbed his face into the deep fur.

∷

The best of the day was gone. When he heard the lowing of the cow outside, ready for milking, Donald sighed and sat up. He ached in every limb, but there was warmth in his heart. Now, where would be a good hiding place? He thought about the caves down on the strand, or maybe a hollow tree, but it was too late to set out again now. In the end, he fetched a length of sailcloth and carefully rolled up the skin inside it. The summer's hay harvest was piled to the ceiling, and Donald climbed up to the top and wedged the bundle down behind the topmost bales, covering it with hay. One of the cats came with him, nosing about for nests of mice. 'Mind you do your job,' he said to her. For now, it would have to do.

He went to bring the cow in and shut up the hens for the night. There was a light in the house, so Mairhi and the children must have made their way home, despite the weather. He found himself eager to see them, to hear about Catriona's baby and find out what they had brought back from the shieling, to weave himself back into the fabric of an ordinary day. And yet … the sealskin under the eaves of the barn was a shining secret, the precious thing that made it all possible. He looked back once, and then took up the basket of eggs and the pail of milk, and went to greet his family.

They were at supper already, John shouting and banging his spoon on the table, and the baby wrapped in Mairhi's shawl in the fireside chair, clamouring to be taken up and fed. Bridie was sitting with them, but she had barely touched her food. She started up when Donald came in, but the look that passed between them told her all she needed to know, and she sank back into her chair, looking spent. If Mairhi noticed her tears, busy as she was with getting food into John, seeing to the baby and eating her own supper, she pretended she had seen nothing. It was Donald who helped his mother to the outhouse and then to bed, and sat holding her hand until she drifted into sleep.

62

Father Finian had been right. Almost overnight, Bridie seemed to shrink, becoming as little and light as a bird. The thing was done, and now at last she could be about the business of dying. There was always someone to sit with her, but more and more she would be travelling her own road, sometimes talking to people no-one else could see.

At midwinter, Donald set the lantern in the window just as she had always done, and turned to see her watching him from her bed. In the last few days she had seemed further and further away, but now her eyes were clear.

'He won't come now,' she murmured.

Donald went over to the bed. 'What's that?'

'Your father. You've a look of him these days, did you know that? But he's far out to sea. He won't be back tonight.'

'Well. We'll set the lantern there, in any case.'

'Will you light the way for me, when I'm gone?'

He turned his face away. When he could speak again, he said, 'Of course I will. But you'll be down by the church, and we'll come there to see you and talk to you all the time. You won't need a lantern to guide you home.'

She closed her eyes for a moment, and felt for his hand. 'That's a comfort,' she murmured. Her breathing grew regular, and Donald thought that she had fallen asleep, but when he went to take his hand away, her grip tightened. 'And you'll make it right with Mairhi? Promise me, Donald, you'll make it right?'

'I promise, Mother. In the spring, when the better weather comes. I'll do it then.'

She nodded, once. Under his fingers, the pulse in her wrist slowed, paused for a moment, and started again, but so weak, he could barely feel it. He stayed there, holding her hand, until he could feel it no longer.

∴

There were folk at the funeral whom Donald had never set eyes on before, come down from the hills or along the coast to pay their last respects to Bridie Macfarlane. And afterwards, at the wake, he heard tales that showed him, again and again, how she had spent herself for other people's benefit, all without him knowing. They also showed him how good she had been at keeping her own counsel. But none of it came close, somehow, to telling the story of his own mother. Who had been so strong, and wise, and had known what to do, always. And who was no longer there.

That night, they went home at last to a quiet, empty house. They settled the children and went to bed, but it was not long before John woke up, crying for his grandmother, and then Sorcha roused for her night-time feed, and so they spent that night all in the big bed together. There was not much sleep to be had for any of them, but the living warmth of skin on skin answered a stronger need.

It was now deep winter, a time for keeping close to home, and Donald was grateful for it. His family had never seemed so precious, or so fragile, and he rejoiced with Mairhi over every new word that John discovered. Sorcha learned to roll over and began to crawl; very early for an ordinary child, but then she was not quite that. There was no more chance for swimming, though. He had seen the joy it gave to Mairhi and the children, but he could not help but be glad. Next year would have to look after itself.

For now, he mended nets and tended the house and garden, and slipped away to the barn by himself whenever he could, to oil and care for the sealskin. It could not stay there forever, he knew that, but there was no sense in moving it yet, when the weather was so bad. And the day would come when he would give it back to her. He would explain, and ask her forgiveness once more, and surely,

surely she would make the right choice. But not now, not when the sea was wild and dark, and ice lay on the pools where they had swum. Not yet.

63

Slowly, by just a few minutes each day, light began to come back to the world. Out at sea, it was the birds who brought change, some moving north as the retreating ice opened up new places, and others arriving from the unimaginable south. But on land, the signs were everywhere – in the new green shoots, the urgency of birdsong and the rush of meltwater down from the hills. There was a restlessness, an itch in the blood.

On fine days, Donald would take the cow out further afield to find fresh grass, and to eke out the dwindling supply of hay in the barn. Sometimes, he would take John with him, and show him this and that along the way; a spray of blackthorn blossom, or a bird's nest in a may tree. He was too small, yet, to go on the boat, and so, when the time was right for fishing, the children would stay behind with their mother.

Mairhi still went out and about to care for the sick, and often Nancy went with her. When she could, she left the children with Jessie or Auntie Annie in the village, and so they managed, one way and another. But the new room was unused for now, and Bridie's bed, too, lay empty.

Returning to the house one blustery morning, he was surprised to find Mairhi there alone. As usual at the tail-end of winter, there was an outbreak of coughs and fevers, and she had set out early to do her rounds. Jessie was sick and her children with her, so Auntie Annie had the care of John and Sorcha.

'What's the matter, love?' he said as he strained the milk into the tall jug. 'I didn't think to see you until evening, the way things are with folks just now. You're not sick yourself, are you?'

Mairhi shook her head. She was sorting through her supplies of herbs, and now she made a noise in her throat, of impatience or exasperation maybe, and pushed away the bundle she'd been holding. Donald came over to look.

'That's thyme, isn't it?' He said. 'Or should be. Looks as though the damp has got into it; see the mildew there. Folks won't thank you for giving that to them! Isn't there any more?'

She shook her head again, then leaned against him. After a moment, he realised that she was weeping.

'Oh, here now.' He turned her about and took her in his arms.

She was sobbing now, open-mouthed; not the terrible, silent tears of those early days, but wailing, loud and unashamed, like the children. He held her, as he held the children, and rocked her gently. All through the time of Bridie's illness, neither of them had wept. Always, there were people about, someone else to be strong for; but now at last they were alone. His own tears fell, and there was a strange kind of joy in giving way at last.

Time passed; he could not have said how long. At length, they drew apart a little, and looked at one another. He kissed her wet face, tasting the sea.

'Oh, love. You ease me even when you don't mean to.'

She gave him a watery smile, then looked again at the bundles of herbs on the table, and frowned.

Donald sighed. 'There's not much left now, is there? Mother wasn't up to it last autumn. But there should be some fresh thyme coming, if we're lucky.'

She stared at him, hopeless, and suddenly he understood.

'You don't know where it grows! That's it, isn't it? But I do. I used to help her all the time when I wasn't doing what I should have been. Going to school, going out on the boat, all that. There's a place where it always comes a bit earlier than anywhere else. Come on, I'll show you.'

Walking out along the path, away from the village, he felt his heart lift. He took Mairhi's hand – for once not encumbered with children – and she swung it high, catching his mood. 'It's a while since we've done this, eh, lass?'

For answer, she took off across the hillside, pulling him with her, and they ran together into the teeth of the wind. But the hills were full of new streams, leaping down to the sea with their cargo of fresh water, and they had to slow down soon enough to pick their way across.

'Careful now, the rocks are slippery here.'

They must have crossed a dozen or more of these newborn waterways before they came to the one he was looking for; old enough to have worn its own little valley, crowded with stunted birches and rowans all combed one way by the wind. He turned upstream, and they followed its course until, a few miles inland, the valley widened out and the river spread itself through a tumble of boulders and bogs. Here, at last, the air was still, and the sunlight slanting through bare branches fell gently warm, like a blessing, on their heads. Mairhi looked around her and smiled.

'See here?' said Donald. 'Over here on the dry ground. Here's the fireplace I made – oh, twelve years ago, maybe. It was me found this place first, roaming around by myself, and I don't think anyone else has been here since … well, since Mother. She'd have made the last fire here.'

Mairhi crouched to look at the blackened stones. She ran her finger through the wet soot, and beckoned him to come closer. When he sat down beside her, she marked him, cheeks and forehead, and took his hand to the fire so that he could mark her in turn. A strange thing, he thought, for her to learn. It was only the older folk who did that now at funerals, but she must have seen it and remembered. A mark of respect for the dead.

They sat there a while in silence. The wind was muted here, and even the stream had lost its voice among the boulders. After a time, there came the song of a robin from somewhere near by, and when Mairhi whistled back to him, he came to perch a few feet away, waiting to see what they were about.

'We'll bring the children when they're old enough,' said Donald then. 'But for now, I'm thankful it's just you and me.' He touched the mark on her cheek. 'And I'm thankful to Mother, too, for giving us this day.'

Mairhi smiled, and rubbed her face against his hand, like the cats in the barn. He thought of them, and the secret they kept for him. Should he tell her now? Times like this were precious few; who knew when there would be another? But still, there was frost on the ground in the morning, and the water in the stream was icy cold. And to speak now might undo all the sweetness between them. And yet, it was his mother who had led them here, and he heard again her last words to him. 'Promise me, Donald, you'll make it right.'

Mairhi was watching him, puzzled. He took her hand.

'Sweetheart, you've given me so much,' he said. 'Places like this used to be my refuge from it all; all the things I was scared of. But because of you, I have friends now. I have the family, and our children. And I have the sea. I used to hate the sea; did you know that? It took my father from us, and gave nothing but grief and hardship in return. But then, it gave me you.'

He paused, choosing his words. 'Because of you, because of you and me, it all knits together. The land and the sea and all the creatures, your kind and mine. And I've given you this – ' he looked around, at the rocks and trees and the new green grass at their roots ' – and I hope it's made you happy, too. I hope I've made you happy. Are you happy, Mairhi?'

She sprang at him, tumbling him backwards into the damp moss, finding the ticklish places with her searching fingers, growling and worrying at his neck and face, licking his eyelids. It was a game she played with little John, rolling him over and over until they were both screaming with laughter, and so he played it with her now, giving as good as he got, saying with teeth and tongue and hands what could not be said in words. And in time the biting turned to kissing, and the tickling to caressing. They gave themselves to each other, and as far as he could tell, she held nothing back. That was his answer.

It was the patter of rain that roused them at last, falling through the still-leafless branches of the rowan tree above their heads. 'We'd better gather some thyme,' he said, helping her to her feet, 'or we'll lose the daylight going home.'

Up on the hillside he found it, where the early sunshine had warmed the rocks. 'And there should be mint down by the water, too.' They filled their bags and set off for home, walking close together, holding hands whenever they could. *She's right not to speak*, he thought, looking down at her as she walked by his side. *This happiness, this joy between us, is too big for words.*

Soon, I will tell her.

64

After the long days and nights ashore, the fishermen needed to go to sea again whenever they could. There came a fresh spring day when the catch was good, and they stayed out casting the nets again and again, until the boats were full and riding low in the water. Donald and his crew waited their turn outside the harbour, as one by one the boats slipped in, to tie up at the harbour wall and unload their catch.

James was the first to notice. 'There's a lot of folks waiting there,' he said.

'The word's spread already,' said Donald. 'More hands to help.'

Aly lifted his head, shading his eyes against the dazzle from the sea. 'Something's not right,' he said. He still spoke little beyond what was necessary, but there was a kind of ease between them all these days, borne of shared work and the gentle, unspoken growth of trust. 'They're just standing, watching.'

Donald looked. At this distance, he could not make out faces, but there was something about the way they were standing, all looking out to sea. Too still. 'Something's happened,' he said. No use to wonder, now, as they went about the task of bringing the boat safely in; but he kept glancing over to the harbour, and that waiting crowd. They all did.

Gradually, as they came closer, he began to recognise people. Most of the village seemed to be there, and a good many folk from the hills too. There was Hugh, standing with his arms around Jeannie and Ailsa, and Catriona holding her baby. Donald waved to them, but they did not wave back. The Bains' boat had come in ahead of them and was tying up, but Shona and Jessie stood together, with a crowd of children about them, still watching. And then – surely that was his own boy, John? Jessie had him by the hand, and a baby on her arm. Not her own child; it was too small for that. And there was one person, search the crowd as he might, whom he could not see anywhere.

James and Aly exchanged glances, but no-one spoke. Slowly, so slowly, they drew in alongside the harbour wall, and Hugh came forward to catch the ropes and make them fast. Still he said nothing, and now Donald was afraid to ask. Seeing his father, John began to try to break free of Jessie's hand, but she held him fast. Shona took the baby from her, and he knew beyond doubt that it was his own daughter, Sorcha. Everything seemed to slow down, but he could not make it stop. Moving as if through water, he got down off the deck, and faced his uncle at last.

'Where is she?' he said. And Hugh said simply, 'She's gone.'

Donald stood still, absorbing the blow. And then a second blow, as John came running across the harbour and burrowed into his arms. He was howling, a wordless cry of loss and terror. Donald picked him up, and John wrapped his arms and legs about his father as though he might grow there, like ivy. For a long moment, they stood still, shutting out the world. Into the child's hair, speaking low, Donald said, 'Show me.'

Hugh stood back, and the crowd moved aside to let them pass. People spoke to him, and one or two touched him as he went by, but he never paused, carrying John all the way along the path, not down to the shore but away from the sea, up the hill, towards their home. Some of the children followed at first, but at the last house of the village, he stopped and turned.

'Go home,' he said, and at the sight of his face, they scattered without a word.

65

The door to the cottage was closed. Inside, all was in order, the fire banked and the kettle laid aside, as it should be. Donald set down his son and stood a moment, breathing in the scent of the turves drying on the hearth. He'd need to get more in, later. John tugged at his arm.

'In the barn,' he said, looking up at his father. And Donald said, 'I know.'

He let himself be pulled along by the child, around the house, where the hens came running. In through the open barn door, swinging on its hinges, to and fro. In where the last of the hay was piled against the walls, and the egg-basket lay on its side, spilling the morning's gathering. The hens were starting to lay again now, as the days got longer. Some of the eggs had cracked in their fall, and the cats were licking them, but at the sight of Donald they scattered like the village children.

And there, spread out in the hay, the ropes cut through where she had taken her knife to them in her haste, the oiled sailcloth, open, empty.

'Was it you that found it?' he said, speaking low. 'Were you playing in the barn today?'

John shook his head. He had few words as yet, but plenty of other ways to tell a story. After all, he had had the best of teachers. He showed his father how he had climbed the haystack after a stray kitten – he made the sound, 'Mew! Mew!' just as his mother would have done – and had scrambled all the way to the top.

Not so very far, thought Donald. Most of the hay was gone; an easy climb, even for a little one.

'And you found – this?'

John nodded, watching his father's face.

'And you showed it to your ma,' he said, very gentle. 'And what did she do?'

John stared at him. 'The eggs broke,' he said. He opened his mouth and began to wail.

'Oh, dear God!' Donald held out his arms, and the child came into them. 'There now, whisht now. It's not your fault, you weren't to know. You weren't to know.'

A time went by. The cats crept back, and the hens came about them, questing for grain, then wandered off again. The light changed, a little.

And at last Donald lifted his cheek from the child's hair and said, 'So you went down the path, then? You and your ma and the baby?' *Because I have to see this through, step by step, all the way.*

And so, step by step, hand in hand, they went down the path together. John showed him where he had fallen and grazed his knee, and Mairhi had set down the baby and her precious bundle, and come to kiss him and set him to rights. The path was in shadow now, the air growing cold, though the sun still caught the rocks on the skerry. She had not gone there, though. The boat still lay safe on the shore, pulled far up in case of storms. Maybe she had thought of the children, left alone on the beach. Maybe, full of anger at him, she had thought only of getting away. Maybe, full of joy, she had thought of nothing at all.

At last they came to the place – to the flat rocks where the seals basked sometimes on sunny days. There was none there now. Nothing at all. Just her boots, her faded green dress and her shawl, dropped where she had let them fall. The incoming tide was curling around them now, and John ran to gather them up out of the wet. There might have been footprints in the sand, but the sea had already taken them.

'So here.' It felt wrong to speak, to say out loud what must have happened, as though by saying it he would be making it real. Donald cleared his throat, tried again. 'You came down here, to the water's edge. And then?'

John shook his head. He pointed to the rocks some twenty yards out, now an island in the rising water. And as the child, prompted by his father's questions, began to show him what had happened, Donald saw with his mind's eye. Saw all too clearly the fierce, wild joy in her face, which had frightened John so he began to cry, until she hugged him and held him close. Saw how she had fed Sorcha, sitting there on the rocks, and then walked up the beach to find a safe place to leave her, out of the rain and wind and beyond the reach of the tide. And then, how she had told John to mind his sister and wait there, and held him again, and laughed, and wept. And then at last, as he sat obediently by the sleeping baby, how she had taken off her clothes, walked down to the rocks again through the first waves of the turning tide, back to where she had laid out the sealskin.

And for the rest, he had no words.

::

'Come here. Come sit by me.' Donald patted the flat stone beside him. He held his son close against him, and they both gazed out to sea. No seals moved in the restless water. Only the gulls called, endlessly, on the everlasting wind.

'It's too cold,' said John, twisting round to look up at his father.

For a long moment, Donald could not speak. He lowered his head, to rest his chin on the boy's head, the way Mairhi often did of an evening. 'No, lad,' he said. 'She won't feel it.'

'Where's she gone?'

'Home.' The word was out before he thought. 'No, John. Not our home. Before she came to us, she had another home. That's where she is, now.'

Donald would have done with words, then. She'd never found a use for them, and he had left it too late to speak the words that mattered, that might have made a difference. But the child was restless, needing answers.

'Sorcha got hungry. She cried,' he said.

'Oh, my dear. She never meant to leave you,' Donald said, and hoped to God that it was true. 'But we can't go where she's gone.'

'Come back!' John was on his feet now, shouting at the sea. 'I called and called and she didn't come!'

'John, look at me.' Donald knelt down on the sand and turned the child around to face him. 'What did she do, before she went?' But John only stared up at him, not understanding. Trying to read his face, to see what he wanted to hear.

'I stayed here. It got cold,' he said at last.

'She told you to wait for her?'

John nodded, still watching him intently.

She thought she was coming back! The secret joy of it flooded him so that he could not speak. *Of course, she would never leave the children. She made her choice, and she chose us.* Then he remembered John. 'You did well,' he said, and his voice shook only a little. 'You looked after your sister.'

John stared at him. 'She cried,' he said again.

How long had it been? Time enough, Donald thought, for the tide to have gone out and come in again; time enough for a small child to grow frightened and hungry. Once again, he took his son into his arms, picked him up and held him close.

'So who was it found you here?' And even as he spoke, there came the sound of boots on the shingle. It was a long moment before he turned, cherishing the brief, bright flare of hope, though he knew that if she came, she would be barefoot. It was Hugh, trudging along the strand, and for a mercy he was alone.

He stopped a few steps away, looking not at Donald, but at the little pile of clothes.

'Who found them here?' Donald's voice sounded too loud above the wind. John huddled into him.

'Sam Bain was out salvaging,' said Hugh, coming close. 'He went for his mother. And Jessie came back with him and found them, so. And the baby crying, but she's fine, no harm done.'

Donald nodded. *No harm done.* But then Hugh spoke again.

'Donald, why would she do such a thing?' His voice was raw. 'She'd everything to live for. Did someone hurt her? And with the bairns watching!'

He doesn't know about the sealskin. He thinks... Donald raised his head. 'Uncle Hugh, she's coming back. It's not what you're thinking.' *Don't say those words, not with John listening. Don't make it so.*

But Hugh was too upset to hear him. 'For God's sake, why would she go into the water? A body can't bear it, not at this time of year. She'd know that, wouldn't she? What on earth would make her do it?'

There was nothing he could say that Hugh would understand. Not unless he told the whole story. And then, when she came back...

'Don't say about the skin. It's Ma's secret,' he whispered into John's hair. And to Hugh, he said, 'I don't know. But she'll manage, in the water. She's a good swimmer. I know, I know; but she learned when she was too young to know better.' *And maybe she's not far off, even now. Watching us, waiting for Hugh to be gone.* He rose to his feet. 'We should go home, get the fire lit for when she comes back. Would you ask Jessie to mind the baby for now?'

Hugh stared at him. 'Donald, it was hours ago! She was hungry, so Catriona fed her with her own wean. She can bide with us, for now. You should come back with us too.'

Donald shook his head. 'Will we go home now?' he said to John. 'The cow will want milking, and your ma will be cold and hungry when she comes back. Let's put her dress over here, so, where it's dry. She'll want it later.' And to Hugh, 'That's fine, then. We'll go up to the house. Will you come with us?'

There was a long, long silence, filled only by the surf breaking on the rocks offshore. Nothing moved there.

Hugh let his hands drop. 'I'll be off home,' he said. 'I'll come by in the morning.'

He turned and began to trudge away down the strand, back towards the village. And Donald, holding John close against his heart, began the slow climb up the cliff path. More than once, he stopped to look back, but the light was fading now, and still, there was nothing to see.

Up at the cottage, he found the door open and the ashes scattered by the wind. The barn door was still swinging to and fro, to and fro, and the cow already waiting inside. He saw the sailcloth cast aside in the hay, but could not stop himself from looking again, anyway, in the place where he had stowed the sealskin. Nothing. Of course, nothing.

Back in the house, he fetched food for them both, talking all the while of everyday things. There should have been fresh fish today, but it could not be helped. John sat quietly at the table to eat his supper, and watched as Donald cleared it all away – 'She won't be pleased if we make a mess, now, will she?'

When Donald went to pick him up and take him to bed, he saw that the little boy had something in his hand.

'What have you got there?'

John made a move as if to hide it, and Donald's heart began to beat fast.

'Show me,' he said.

John held out his hand, but when Donald went to take it, he pulled it back, just as Mairhi had once done. So long ago, now! His knuckles were white around the carved wooden seal.

Donald made his voice gentle. 'Did you take it?'

John shook his head. 'She gave it to me,' he said.

66

In the small hours before dawn, when John was sleeping soundly, Donald eased himself out of bed. The lantern he had left burning in the window was dark now, the tallow all used up. He had lain awake, listening for the scrape of the front door, but there had been no sound. Quietly, he relit the lantern and went out.

The wind had died down, and there was only the sigh of the sea as he made his way down to the shore. There were her clothes, just where he had left them. Setting the lantern down on the rocks, Donald took off his own clothes. He stood up and walked to the water's edge, to where the little waves broke over his bare feet. There had been footprints earlier, where he and Hugh had walked, but the tide had come and gone and there was no trace now.

'Mairhi,' he said, raising his voice to be heard above the sound of the sea. 'You've no use for words, but there are things I need to say. Things you don't understand. When I told you it was gone, that was the truth.' He took a few steps further, and stopped to listen. 'But then I found it. It was hidden from me, all this time. Hidden from us.' Again, he stopped, but there was only the quiet water, surging and hissing all around him. He was up to his waist now, bracing himself against the cold. 'And I've looked after it for you. I was going to give it to you! Because you have to be free to choose. I was only waiting for the finer weather, I swear it.'

He stepped forward, barely keeping his balance now. Salt on his lips, and the shingle dragging from under his feet. 'You've a right to be angry.' He spoke more loudly now, though the crash of the surf was behind him. 'But I know you're coming back. If not for me, then for them, for the bairns. Only don't be too long.' One more step. 'Mairhi!' Water pushing at his chest, splashing up into his eyes. 'I can't bear it,' he said, very quiet. One more, and his feet went from under him and he cried out, beyond words, as the sea took him.

Had he hoped that she would come, then? Or had he truly thought that he might drown? Afterwards, he could not remember what had been in his mind. The intense cold locked his muscles, shocked the breath from his body, and there was only salt water to take its place. But instinct took over then, and he fought to keep his head above the waves, choking and gasping as they rolled him over and over. He was not so very far from shore. It seemed an endless time, but when he finally crawled out onto the rocks, bruised and numb, it was still night, and she had still not come.

He lay there, his skin flushed fiery red with returning blood. Great racking sobs tore through him. He lay there, and the salt drying on his skin made him itch all over, and nothing changed. In the end, the cold drove him to his feet again, and back to the shelter of the cliff where his clothes lay. He dressed, and pressed her shawl to his face for a long moment, breathing in the everyday human scent of her. Then he folded it, and laid it down, and went on his way.

::

The next day, torn between hope and despair, Donald could not be still. He set the house to rights and then swung John up onto his shoulders and set off for the shieling. Hugh was right; it would be better for the little ones to bide there for a while, where there were folks to care for them and the girls to play with. He took a path through the hills, to avoid meeting anyone in the village, and so came almost into the yard before the dogs scented him and set up a racket. Jeannie came running out, and John clamoured to be set down. And after Jeannie came Catriona.

'Oh, Donald, oh, I'm so sorry!' She took both his hands, and her eyes were full of tears. 'We always knew she was a little touched, but to do such a thing! You must stay with us now. And don't worry, I'll look after Sorcha as if she were my own. She's no trouble at all, and the girls are helping too. We'll manage fine, so we will. But you've brought nothing with you! Never mind, I'm sure Father can lend you a shirt. John, don't chase the hens now! They're just starting to lay again. Come in, come in.'

Hugh had been digging in the kailyard behind the house, but he came now to stand a little behind her, watching Donald carefully.

'I won't stay,' said Donald. 'I just came to bring John for the moment, while Mairhi's away. I can't leave him on his own when we take the boat out.' Inside the house, he heard the wail of a hungry infant, and his heart turned over, but he would not go in to see his daughter. It was better so.

Catriona was staring at him. 'While she's … whatever do you mean, while she's away?'

Behind her, Hugh said, 'Enough, now.'

But she rushed on. 'Donald, she wouldn't last two minutes in the water! Even if she can swim, which I don't believe for one moment' – she glanced aside at her father – 'she'd been gone for hours by the time we found the bairns; poor little Sorcha crying her eyes out and John not knowing what to do for the best. Well, what are we supposed to think? It's as well Sam Bain was dodging school again, or who knows what might have happened? At least he's done some good for once in his life, even if it was by accident.'

'Catriona, that's enough!' said Hugh. 'Donald, come in and take some tea. You look done in.'

'I won't bide,' he said again. 'I don't want her coming home to an empty house.'

Neither of them seemed able to meet his eyes. Catriona started to speak again, but Hugh laid a hand on her arm.

'Let him be,' he said. 'He'll have to come to it in his own time.'

And they watched, quite still, as he turned and went down the path that led to the harbour.

Now he could not avoid the village any longer. He thought again of all those faces turned towards the boat – yesterday, was it only yesterday? – and shuddered. At least the older children were in school today, so there was none out and about to give warning of his coming. But there, seated on the wall in the spring sunshine, were Mrs Mackay and his aunt Annie. They got to their feet when they saw him coming. He quickened his stride, but then checked himself. Sooner or later, it would have to be faced.

'Donald Macfarlane, I'm sorry for your loss,' said Mrs Mackay formally. Waiting for her next words, he discovered suddenly that he was not afraid, any more, of her judgments and condemnations. It made no difference what anyone thought; none of them knew how it really was. When she said, 'But I can't say I'm surprised,' he almost laughed aloud. Was that all? He made no reply, only stared at her, hard and fierce. No-one stood up to Peggy Mackay, but then on this day of all days, nothing was as it should be. She dropped her gaze, and he walked on by. His aunt had not moved at all.

Down at the harbour, he found that James and Aly were getting ready to go out, with Sam Bain helping after a fashion.

'The weather's changing,' he said as he got close. 'We might have better luck today.'

James made no move to help him aboard. 'Go home, Donald,' he said, looking down at the deck. 'We'll manage. You need your feet on dry land the day.'

'I'll be fine,' he said, though in truth he was yearning to go back to the beach again. What if Mairhi had returned while he was away? He had banked the fire, but she would need hot food, dry clothes. Gentle holding. His arms tingled.

James, he saw, was at a loss. Good friend that he was, he did not know what to do with misfortune like this. In his life, he had known only fair weather.

It was Aly who said, 'We'll take Sam out with us; it's time he started to learn. Go home, man.' And when Donald made no move, he said, 'Her kind don't bide for long. Go home. Look after your children, or you'll lose them too. I should know.'

Donald stared. 'What do you mean, her kind?'

Aly shrugged. 'She's a special one, isn't she? They don't stay, not with the likes of us. But maybe she'll watch out for us still, d'you think?' He looked away, then, with a quick sidelong glance, said, 'I'll still come out with you. If you'll have me.'

Donald shivered, though the wind was mild. 'I need to go,' he said. He walked away down the harbour, fighting the urge to run, until he rounded the corner of the last house.

He had meant to walk back along the strand, just in case, but as he left the houses behind, he saw that on the cliff there stood a woman, small and upright, shawled against the light rain that had begun to fall. Through the drizzle, he could make out only that her face was turned towards him.

67

Now he did run, as fast as he dared over the rough ground, looking up as often as he could to make sure that she had not vanished. But she stood quite still, waiting. Joy surged through him; he wanted to shout, 'You're wrong, all of you!' But his breath was coming hard and his heart was pounding as though it would burst from his chest and take to the air. He got closer, and she made no move. And then his steps slowed, came almost to a stop. It was his aunt Annie.

She held out her hand, then. 'Walk with me a way, Donald,' she said.

Almost, in his bitter disappointment, he turned his back on her. But this was his aunt, who had always been kind to him. She waited while he got his breath back, and then, slowly, they began to walk along the cliff together.

Neither of them spoke for some time. Donald scanned the rocks below as he walked, always searching. They passed the first headland, and his eyes went at once to the place where the seals liked to bask. Was there some movement there? His aunt had stopped beside him, looking where he looked.

'Donald,' she said, 'she's not coming back.' And when he made no answer, she said, 'I mind the day I saw them here, and you watching.'

He swung round to stare at her. 'That was you on the clifftop, that day?'

'Aye. It was.'

'You followed us from the village! Why would you do that?'

She sighed. 'I had begun to wonder, a while back, even before what happened with Aly Bain. The way she was, the pictures she put into your mind …'

'And what were you wondering?'

She looked up at him, and he saw that her eyes were misted with age. 'I don't see so well now, but my eyes were keener then. I could make out the seals, down there on the warm rocks. And Mairhi, when she came along the beach and saw them. She went right up close, and they never moved. That was when I knew for certain.'

'But you never said a word! Not to us, nor anybody. Did you?'

She shook her head. 'Only to the lassie herself. She used to come and sit with me sometimes, when you were out at sea, and Bridie away over the hills. Did you know that?'

'I didn't know. So many things I didn't know, and she couldn't say.'

Auntie Annie gazed down at the shoreline that she could no longer see. 'I was angry with you, Donald.'

He was quiet for a minute, and then said, speaking low, 'You had the right.'

'I had the right. True enough. But then I saw how set you were on making the best of it, and how much you cared for her. And I thought, "Her skin must be lost. She can't go back." Was that the way of it?'

'It was. But she cares for me too. And the children! We've made a good life together. Surely you can see that?'

'Of course. You've made a fine job of your marriage, Donald, never doubt it. No man could have done more.'

'But then, why do you say she's not coming back? She meant to, I'm sure of it. She never would have left the children alone like that, and no-one else near by!'

'I think you're right, at that. But how did this happen, Donald? How did she come to find it after so long?'

He walked away a few paces, trying to master himself. It felt so strange, after keeping silent all this time, to be speaking these things aloud. Even with his mother, as her illness grew worse, he had not talked. His mother, who had always been so strong, so certain. She would have known what to do. That loss, obscured until now by relief that her suffering was at an end, and then by his own dilemma over the sealskin – came home to him with devastating force. Tears sprang to his eyes.

'It was mother,' he said, and now he let the tears fall unheeded. 'She took it and hid it away; and cared for it all the while. I never knew until her last illness. She told me then. It wasn't right, she said. Mairhi should be able to choose. And I meant to talk with her, when the weather was better, and tell her what had happened, and ... and give it back to her. I was going to give it back!' He drew a deep, ragged breath. 'It was John who came upon it and showed his mother. And she'll be thinking I had it all the time, that I kept it from her! She has to come back, d'you see? I have to tell her!'

His aunt had not moved. 'So it was Bridie,' she said softly. 'I should have guessed that. And once she'd decided on a thing, nothing on earth would move her.'

'I think she always meant to give it back one day,' said Donald. 'Or why would she have cared for it all that time? Why not just get rid of it?'

'There's that, at least,' said his aunt. 'But it would have been a hard secret to keep. A thing like that, it eats at you. For all the good that came of it.'

'How can you say that?'

She smiled. 'When you're old, you see things differently. Maybe you'll understand one day.' She watched him for a few moments, and then turned away. 'Well, I'm away home now. It's cold up here in the wind.'

'Wait!' He caught hold of her hand. 'We've a good marriage; she's a good mother, you said so yourself. So why would you think she's not coming back? Has something happened to her? For God's sake, tell me!'

'Oh, Donald. I'm sure she meant to, even if she was angry with you. But she can't.'

'Why would you say that?' There was a dreadful certainty in her voice, but still he could not let go.

'Think about the old stories, Donald. In all the tales you've ever heard, does it ever happen more than once? They change, the selkies, they change once in a lifetime. Then they go back to the sea, and there's an end of it.'

He was shaking his head. 'That can't be right. If she'd known that, she never would have done it.'

'But I don't think she did know. Or in that moment, she wouldn't have thought. Could you stand back, if someone offered you the birthright you thought you'd lost for ever, and not take it?'

'Oh, dear God. There must be a way! You're wrong; you can't know that for certain. How could you?'

'Donald,' she said, suddenly fierce. 'Do you think you're the only fisherman to go out on a moonlit night and catch more than he bargained for?'

He hardly took in her words at first. Too full of his own thoughts, his own growing terror. What was to be done? He was pacing again, unable to be still. And then the sense of it came to him, and he stopped and stared at her.

'Auntie,' he said, but now she would not look at him. 'You were married, weren't you?'

She lifted her shoulders. 'He was lost at sea, long before you were born. If he had a secret, it died with him.'

'And you had no children. All that time alone … How could you bear it?'

She smiled at that. 'You'd be surprised what you can bear, Donald. When you have to.'

'And I do have to. That's what you're telling me, isn't it?'

She said nothing. Then, as if it had only just come to her, 'But you won't be alone. People come together at times like this. It's what we do.'

After a long moment, she turned again to leave. She had taken a few slow steps along the cliff path when he called out to her. 'Auntie!'

She stopped. 'Donald?'

'Just tell me this. If such a thing happened to you; if you had the chance to … go back, now, would you take it?'

'Even now, after all these years?'

'Even now.'

He waited. And after a long moment, in a voice full of pity, she answered.

'In a heartbeat.'

∴

He comes down to the shore when he can, and he tells her the small details of his life. He brings her offerings: the shell of a robin's egg, the flowers of the rowan tree, a curl of their daughter's hair. Sometimes the children come with him, and sometimes they talk to her. More often, now, they wander off to play and gather treasures on the beach. Perhaps, one day, they will bring their own children here. Or perhaps, in time, they will forget.

He does not forget.

THE LEGEND

There are many stories told about the selkies along the northern coasts of Scotland, but this is the one I have chosen to work with.

Once, there was a fisherman who spent many nights fishing alone. One night at full moon, he witnessed a marvel: nine seals came ashore, put off their skins and became beautiful young women, dancing on the beach. The fisherman hid himself, and as he watched, he began to fall in love with one of them. Secretly, he hid her seal-skin, so that when the others returned to the sea, she was left behind.

The fisherman took her home to be his wife, and he hid the skin at the bottom of a chest. They lived together for some years, and she bore him children. She seemed to be happy, but from time to time she would look out to sea and weep.

One day while he was out at sea, one of the children found the skin and showed it to his mother. When the fisherman returned at the end of the day, she was gone, and he never saw her again.

ACKNOWLEDGMENTS

First of all, enormous thanks to the inimitable Karen Sullivan of Orenda Books and to her team, especially West Camel, for championing and helping to shape this book.

To Broo Doherty of DHH Literary Agency, for awarding me the first Exeter Novel Prize and later for becoming my agent.

To the many friends and fellow writers who have listened, commented and given their time and support: especially Cathie Hartigan, Martin Wright, Dan Knibb, Margaret James and Jim Howell.

Thanks to the Creative Writing Matters team, who run the Exeter Novel Prize and other writing competitions; to the Write-Group, and to Exeter Writers.

Thanks always to Martin, Tom, Rosie, Paul and Orelie: my lovely family.

And finally, to all those storytellers who have shaped this legend, in all its many versions. We'll never know your names, but we hear your voices still.

If you enjoyed *Sealskin*, you'll love Amanda Jennings' *In Her Wake*

'Hauntingly beautiful' CLARE MACKINTOSH

'Thoughtful, atmospheric and deeply immersive, it wields an almost mesmeric power over the reader' HANNAH BECKERMAN

in her wake

A perfect life ... until she discovered it wasn't her own

Amanda Jennings